After Julie

Linda Ferrer

Published by New Generation Publishing in 2022

Copyright © Linda Ferrer 2022

First Edition

The author asserts the moral right under the Copyright, Designs and Patents Act 1988 to be identified as the author of this work.

All Rights reserved. No part of this publication may be reproduced, stored in a retrieval system or transmitted, in any form or by any means without the prior consent of the author, nor be otherwise circulated in any form of binding or cover other than that which it is published and without a similar condition being imposed on the subsequent purchaser.

ISBN
        Paperback   978-1-80031-035-3
        Ebook   978-1-80031-034-6

www.newgeneration-publishing.com

 New Generation Publishing

A story of two families across the generations spanning the 20th century.

Forever a Stranger is Julie's story

After Julie is Sarah's story

The books can be read and enjoyed independently.

Julie confides in a friend,

'I could walk past my daughter in the street and

we would remain forever strangers.'

This is a work of fiction. The characters and their experiences are the product of my imagination.

Also by Linda Ferrer

Forever a Stranger

This book is dedicated to my two wonderful

grandchildren

Lyla Faye and Eli Robert

&

to my ever-patient husband Alan

for his continued support throughout this project.

I also wish to posthumously thank my parents

Fay & John Deckers

for just being there for me.

Family Tree for *After Julie & Forever a Stranger*

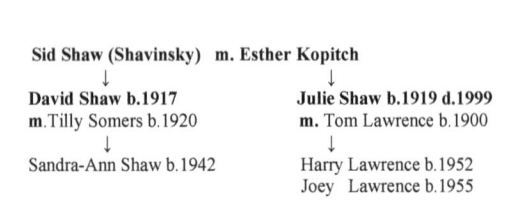

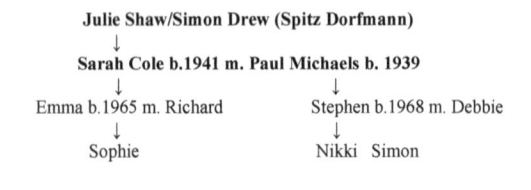

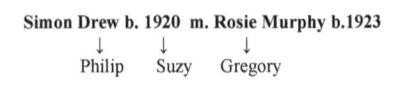

Jacob Shavinsky b.1865	Samuel Kopitch b.1870
m.Sadie	m.Miriam
↓	↓
Sid b.1892 + 3 siblings	Esther b.1893 + 6 siblings

Sid Shaw (Shavinsky)   m. Esther Kopitch
  ↓   ↓
David Shaw b.1917   **Julie Shaw b.1919 d.1999**
m.Tilly Somers b.1920   **m.** Tom Lawrence b.1900
         ↓   ↓
Sandra-Ann Shaw b.1942   Harry Lawrence b.1952
                                               Joey Lawrence b.1955

Tom Lawrence b. 1900 m. Sophie b.1905 d.1940
↓
Sam b. 1935

Julie Shaw/Simon Drew (Spitz Dorfmann)
↓
Sarah Cole b.1941 m. Paul Michaels b. 1939
        ↓   ↓
Emma b.1965 m. Richard   Stephen b.1968 m. Debbie
        ↓   ↓
    Sophie   Nikki   Simon

Woolfe Dorfmann m. Dora	**Frederick Dorfmann m.Eva**
↓	↓
Annie b.1918 +5 siblings	**Spitz**

Simon Drew b. 1920 m. Rosie Murphy b.1923
      ↓   ↓   ↓
   Philip   Suzy   Gregory

Chapter 1

Birth: 15th September 1941
Denby Hall Mother & Baby Home, Norfolk, England

In spite of the mild September sunshine pouring through the window, the room remained bleak and cold. It was sparsely furnished with only a bed, washbasin and infant weighing scales. A young woman in the late stage of painful labour crawled on all-fours on the flagstone floor.

Forty-eight hours earlier Julie's waters broke. Now her pain increased with every contraction and still the baby refused to be born. She fantasised her unborn child was mindful of its uncertain future and now fought against the inevitable of being born into a world at war.

'Don't make me leave you. I'm so cosy and warm. Please let me stay. I've ruined my mother's life. My father's run away. My grandma won't stop crying and my grandfather denies my very existence. Please let me stay inside your warm body.'

'I can understand why my child doesn't want to be born into a world of war and destruction to face an unknown future,' thought Julie.

Sheila Dunstan, the manager of Denby Hall Mother & Baby Home, explained the process of birth to every young woman in her care. But Julie wasn't prepared for her body to be so utterly racked with pain.

Her abdominal contractions were crushing. Unbearable waves of pain shot through her lower back and swollen abdomen. Julie could neither comfortably lie down nor stand up. For a modicum of relief, she crawled on all-fours.

***

The Luftwaffe was busy that night, back in December 1940. Bombs fell and exploded creating a night sky awash with fires. While London burned Julie and Simon, the family lodger, huddled together under the Morrison shelter. She was alarmed by a new sensation. Emotions ran high and Julie yearned for words of comfort from Simon they weren't going to die that night. Moreover, she was fearful and alarmed just how much she wanted him. She didn't want to die without being loved. Her home could be hit in an instant and they could be jettisoned skyward and disappear into oblivion to metamorphose into tiny sand-coloured granules of floating dust. Julie imaged the grief and devastation her parents would feel if they returned from the air-raid shelter to find she was missing and their home destroyed.

After discovering she was pregnant, Simon proposed marriage. But a week before the wedding he disappeared.

The pregnancy was a dreadful shock. However, over the following months Julie grew to love the precious embryonic baby moving and growing inside her. But now she was overwhelmed with the reality of caring for this new little person alone.

Her urge to push was intense.

"This baby doesn't want to come out," moaned Julie.

"Don't push … let me check first," said the midwife.

She bent down. "Don't push. You're not ready."

'Must be some pretty smart baby who knows its own future,' thought Julie.

Fifteen minutes passed. Julie was desperate. The baby was restless. Arms and legs grown to full-term inside her womb pushed and wrestled to be released. She felt her stomach was about to explode.

Julie cried out, "I can't wait any longer."

"One more check. Okay, you're fully dilated. Push, push," the midwife yelled. "Come on, come on. I can see the baby's head. You're doing well."

Alone, with no husband, Julie wasn't ready to have a baby. At that very moment she just wanted to die.

"One more push."

The baby's head forced its way into the world and Julie's infant was safely born. The midwife slapped the baby on the bottom and she opened her lungs and screamed.

"You have a perfect baby girl."

Julie watched while the midwife washed and weighed the tiny scrap of humanity, then wrapped the baby in a blanket and handed her back.

"Do you have a name?"

"I shall call her Sarah. My beautiful Sarah," Julie replied groggily.

Sarah was born on 15th September 1941 a perfect autumn day. Butterflies, wasps, and bees drowsily enjoying the warm, balmy sunshine, before perishing in the cool nights.

"God bless my beautiful Sarah. I hope we can stay together forever," Julie whispered before slipping into a pain-free sleep.

Chapter 2

Stepney, East End of London, England - 1942

Sarah was a year old when Sandra and John Cole adopted her in the middle of a world war. Whilst John fought overseas for six years, Sandra had the full responsibility for caring for a small baby. It was a huge challenge. But they both agreed it was the best decision they had ever made.

John was thirty-five years old when he returned from France in 1945. He came home with no particular skill. He left school at fourteen with little education and worked as a warehouseman for a large London department store. After returning to civilian life he took a similar routine job in a large engineering company.

However, after six gruelling years in the army, John was ambitious to give his family a better life. He enrolled in night school classes to improve his job prospects and passed the Generation Certificate of Educations exams in Maths and English then studied accountancy.

Sandra worked in the local hairdressing salon at the weekends, while John studied and looked after Sarah. They saved hard and moved from their over-crowded tenement building, near the docks in Stepney, to the leafy suburb of Harrow in north London where the air was cleaner and a healthier environment to bring up a family.

1947

One sunny afternoon Sandra and Sarah were travelling home by bus when, at the top of her voice, Sarah asked,

"What's adopted?"

"It means you're special."

"Maureen at school said I was adopted. What's adopted?"

"Wait until we get home."

***

"Adopted means you're special because you weren't born to Mummy and Daddy. We chose you," said Sandra.

This was a difficult concept for six-year-old Sarah to understand. But she didn't question her mother's reply. After all, they were her mummy and daddy, she loved them, and that's all that mattered.

***

"I want a baby brother or sister," wailed Sarah. "Everyone in my class, except Wendy's got a brother or sister. Why can't I have a brother or sister?"

"Things don't always happen when you want them to," was Sandra's troubled reply.

"How do you get babies?"

"When mummies and daddies love each other, they can make a baby."

Sarah looked thoughtful,

"Is that how you got me?"

***

"We know how much you want a baby brother or sister. Well, we've got some good news, you're going to have a new baby brother or sister for Christmas," Sandra smiled.

Sarah had never seen her mummy and daddy look so happy. She remembered her mummy saying 'only mummies and daddies who love each other can have babies'. So this was proof they loved each other very much.

"We're all going out to celebrate," her father smiled.

"Wow, I'm going to be a big sister!" Sarah danced around the room ecstatic.

"Can my friend Pamela come?"

"Of course, the more the merrier."

Pamela recently had a baby sister. She grumbled the baby woke her up at night. Sarah didn't care about being woken by a crying baby. Now she would be like everyone else at school and have someone to play with. She was lonely after school, especially when Sandra worked and she was sent to a neighbour or friend's house. Now her mother was expecting a baby she would have to be at home to look after her new brother or sister.

***

Sandra had a difficult pregnancy and spent months in bed. Sarah convinced herself her mother's sickness was all her fault. Every afternoon, after school, Sarah sat on Sandra's bed drinking milk and munching on biscuits.

"Mummy, I don't want a brother or sister if it's making you ill."

"Don't worry. When the baby's born everything will be fine," Sandra reassured.

But everything wasn't fine. After a long and painful labour, Brian was born. Sandra needed several blood transfusions and stayed in hospital for a further three weeks to recover.

"Mummy, why were you in the hospital so long? I missed you. Mummy, mummy, why do Brian's eyes look so funny?"

Brian was born with multiple health problems. He didn't look like other babies, but Sarah was just happy to have a baby brother, and she adored him. A warm equanimity surrounded her by day just knowing Mummy was at home with baby Brian whilst she was at school.

Every afternoon Sarah ran home from school anxious to help mummy feed and bathe her precious little brother. But even seven-year-old Sarah could see there was something radically wrong.

In the early days, following Brian's birth, Sandra was in denial. Sarah overheard her on the phone telling a friend,

"It's because he was a difficult birth."

The truth was catastrophic. Brian was born with spina bifida, hydrocephalus (water on the brain) and impaired sight. It was never clear how much vision he actually had. Sarah treated him like one of her precious dolls. She loved her baby brother unconditionally, and on good days he responded to her with weak smiles.

***

As Brian's first birthday approached, it was clear, even to Sarah, her little brother wasn't developing as a healthy baby should.

"What's the matter with Brian?" Sarah asked time and time again.

"He's special."

"You said I'm special."

"You are special. But Brian is extra special because he was born sick."

"Will he get better?"

"Brian will always need our attention and love."

Sarah never understood her parents' explanations. She just knew she loved Brian and he needed her care. He was sick. By the age of one, his back still needed supporting. Her mother warned Sarah to be prepared that Brian may never sit up unaided and never walk.

***

One morning Sarah went into her baby brother's bedroom and found his cot empty. Brian was gone. He was two years old.

"Where's Brian?" She screamed, then ran into her parents' bedroom crying inconsolably.

"He's gone," replied her father.

"Where?" she wailed.

"Last night someone came and took him to a safe place," he replied.

"I want to see him ... has he died and gone to God?" Sarah's friend Celia had an uncle who recently died in a car crash. After it happened, Celia and Sarah were told, "God has called him back home." They thought this was a strange explanation when he already had a home down their street.

"Brian's fine. It's just he's grown too big for us to look after, so we've found him another home in the country where nurses can look after him," her mother replied with some compassion.

"I said we should have told her," Sandra protested later that evening.

"She's too young to understand," John replied.

"No, she's not. I shouldn't have listened to you. You forget she's eight and very smart. We should have talked to her before he went. She'll remember this for the rest of her life. You know how much she loves him."

"She'll get over it. She can come along when we visit. If she wants, I'll buy her a dog."

But this one incident planted the seeds for a stormy relationship.

Chapter 3

It was flaming July. The scorching sun reached over 90 degrees Fahrenheit. Sarah began the journey stretched out on the back seat of John's new two-tone, blue and cream, Ford Anglia car. Inside, the car was stiflingly hot and filled with wafting smoke and fumes from Sandra's cigarettes. She refused to open a window, complaining the breeze would blow out the curls of her permed hairstyle. Sarah complained of feeling sick from the motion of the car and cigarette smoke. At the grand old age of eight years, she still used her old potty for emergency stops.

This was the family's first trip to visit Brian. He was living in a home for disabled children and adolescents in Oxford. A trip of this distance, from their home in north London, would normally take a matter of two hours, but with multi-sickie and comfort stops, a normal ride of two hours took much longer.

"I want to do a wee," Sarah moaned, jumping up and down on the back seat.

"Stop that. You're ruining my new car!" yelled John.

She stopped jumping and rested her hands on the back of the passenger seat, accidentally pulling on Sandra's curls.

"Sit down. If I have to stop sharply, you'll go flying through the windscreen," shouted John.

"This is the second time in an hour. Can't you hold it until we can stop somewhere safe?" added Sandra.

"I wanna be sick."

"You're gonna have to wait until I find a safe grass verge," mumbled John.

Ten minutes passed.

"I want to do a wee. When are we going to be there?"

"We would have been there and halfway back by now if we hadn't made all those stops," growled John.

"I was told not to get there during the younger children's lunchtime," said Sandra.

"When's that?"

"Between twelve and one … Why don't we have our picnic by the river to kill time?" Sandra suggested.

"That sounds fun," Sarah replied.

"I was hoping to get there by eleven, but it's clearly not going to happen. So take it easy, John, and let's just enjoy the ride."

They had a leisurely picnic, on the banks of the river Isis and sheltered from the midday sun under the trees, then freshened up in a waterside hotel. They reached Brian's new home, Foresham Manor, at twelve forty-five.

***

The Manor was built on ten acres of lush Oxfordshire countryside. A huge vegetable garden was created during the war and the children still enjoyed the benefits of a healthy diet of fresh vegetables.

John drove past a cricket pitch. The older children had just finished a match. Several were clearing up, whilst others were being marshalled by a carer towards the house for their lunch.

John parked the car.

"Stay here," he said to Sarah. "Mummy and I will go in first to see if it's convenient to see Brian. We don't want to disturb him if he's having lunch."

Sarah waited in the car for a few minutes. The temperature inside rose very quickly. She opened the door for some fresh air then decided to go and help the children carry their equipment.

She had almost reached a group of boys when a young woman hurried towards her. She had a soft voice and a kindly face.

"You're not one of ours. Are you visiting?"

"Yes, I've come to see my little brother."

"What's his name?"

"Brian Cole."

"Where are your mummy and daddy?"

"They've gone in first to see if it's okay for me to see him." Sarah pointed towards the building.

The woman was concerned Sarah had been allowed to run loose and could be disturbed to see the disabled children.

"You shouldn't be here. You should be with your parents. Our children are ill and have many problems."

It was too late. The boys had formed a circle around Sarah. They weren't ill in the way she had imagined. But their malformed bodies frightened her. And she was scared of their strange, staring faces. She turned and ran as fast as her legs would carry her back to the car. The woman sprinted after Sarah with words of comfort.

She called out, "Let me take you to find your mummy and daddy."

But Sarah didn't hear her. The boys stood confused watching Sarah disappear towards the car park. She jumped into the back seat of the car and curled herself up into a tight ball on the floor. She pressed her hands tightly over her eyes hoping no one had followed her or discovered her hiding place. But two boys had followed Sarah to the car and stared through the window.

"Stop it! Go away!" she screamed. They tapped on the window. She looked up into their staring faces.

"Stop it! Stop it! Go away!"

Two women gently eased the boys away from the car. A young woman, in nurse's uniform, called to Sarah through the back window of the car. She was crying.

"There's nothing to be frightened about." The woman had a calm voice. Sarah cautiously opened the car door.

"Where are your mummy and daddy?" she asked. Sarah pointed to the house.

"What's your name?"

"Sarah Cole. I've come to see my brother Brian," she sniffled.

"You shouldn't be outside in this heat. Come with me and we'll find your mummy and daddy. Have you had lunch?"

Sarah nodded, sobbing, tears rolling down her face. The woman took out her handkerchief and wiped Sarah's tears and grubby face.

"My name is Mrs Sanders. Would you like some ice-cream?"

Sarah nodded.

"What's your favourite?"

"Chocolate," replied Sarah between snuffles.

"We'll go and get you some chocolate ice-cream and then we'll find your mummy and daddy."

***

Brian and Sarah had a happy reunion. Immediately she entered his room he gave her a warm smile of recognition. He was fully dressed and sitting in his wheelchair supported by a neck brace. She bent down to kiss him on the cheek.

A young woman called Cynthia sat at the end of Brian's bed. She told Sarah she was his best friend. Cynthia was about twenty and had lived in the home for five years. She suffered with downs syndrome. She clearly cared for Brian and he responded positively to her. Even young Sarah could see how Brian was stimulated by Cynthia. He also showed pleasure when his young friends came into his room to see him.

Brian still couldn't sit up unsupported, and he never would, but Sandra was pleased to see an improvement in his demeanour and reactions. Brian clearly enjoyed being amongst people. He was aware of his surroundings and could now express pleasure.

"I think Brian would like some ice-cream like Sarah's," said Cynthia.

"Can he eat ice-cream?" Sandra looked surprised.

"Of course he can. Brian's favourite flavour is strawberry."

Cynthia beckoned to Sarah. "Come with me."

She followed Cynthia to the cafeteria.

After clearing up Brian's messy ice-cream, John said it was time to leave.

"We've all had enough excitement for one day. It's time to go."

"Brian seems much better. I feel happier leaving him there," said Sandra on their drive home. "I'm surprised he can eat ice-cream."

"He's doing well," John agreed. "And that Cynthia seems good for him."

"Do you think we could have done more for him?" asked Sandra.

"Don't beat yourself up. Cynthia's got all the time in the world to play with him. And they've got all those nurses on hand," replied John.

"I suppose you're right."

Then quietly, not wanting Sarah to hear, he murmured, "Too depressing; not a place to take Sarah again."

***

The next, and last, time Sarah saw Brian was one year later. Cynthia welcomed Sarah with a huge sisterly hug, as if they'd been best friends for years. Cynthia told them she came to see Brian every day. But now he lay unresponsive and motionless in his cot.

"What's the point of it all? He just lies there. They say he feels no pain." Sandra was daily tormented she had given birth to such a sick child.

Throughout her entire life Sarah mourned the tragedy of Brian. No one would ever take his place, nor compensate for her loss. After he died, Sandra and John never spoke about Brian's tragic short life and Sarah was too traumatised and sensitive of their feelings to talk about him. And the relationship became further strained.

Chapter 4

The all-important letter arrived this morning telling Sarah she had failed. It was so unexpected. She rushed upstairs to her bedroom to try to make sense of the word *failed*, then crushed the letter into a tight ball and stuffed it into her pocket.

"I've failed my junior *11-plus* exam," she yelled out to the four walls, before flopping on to the bed and bursting into tears. Sandra Cole watched her daughter with compassion through the crack of the semi-open door. Sarah pulled the scrunched letter from her pocket, flattened it with her hands, and read it for the umpteenth time. Then, in a fit of despair, she tore it into tiny pieces and tossed the fragments over her head. They fell like confetti on to the cold linoleum bedroom floor.

"What's the matter?" her mother called.

"What am I going to do now?" Sarah wailed.

"You'll be okay, a bright girl like you. It's not the end of the world."

But it was the end of the world for Sarah. Failing the most important exam of her young life was a major crisis and Sandra felt impotent to show her true feelings. Later she would regret her harsh reply.

"Hurry up. Clear this mess and come downstairs."

"It's the end of my world. I thought I was going to Harrow County Grammar School. Now I'll have to go to that awful secondary modern school Greenborough. My life is ruined. I'm a failure at eleven!" Sarah replied sulkily.

"Greenborough isn't an awful school. I know the headmistress, Mrs Doyle. I'm sure she'll put you in the top stream."

"You don't understand. Everyone will think I'm thick. You know my friend Judy didn't pass her *11-plus* last year and she's going to that little private school. She has a lovely uniform. It's green and purple, and the girls have smart green berets with purple tassels. You've seen them. Aren't they smart? Please, please can I go there?"

"You know your father can't afford to pay private fees. Anyhow, you don't need an academic education. When you're married you won't need to work at all."

"That's not fair."

"Life's not fair. Come on tidy up your room and come downstairs."

***

Sarah was born in September 1941. A World War Two baby. At the tender age of eleven she proclaimed herself a failure to the whole world. All because (in her opinion) she had failed the all-important entry examination to a grammar school. Now her dreams of achieving a university degree, she believed to be the crucial pathway to a meaningful career, were ruined. She was destined to complete her education in a mediocre secondary modern school, where the leaving age was fifteen, with no prospects to move on to higher education.

Chapter 5

As it happened, Greenborough Secondary Modern School suited Sarah very well. Throughout her years at the school she remained fiercely competitive and determined to continue her education beyond the legal school leaving age of fifteen to study for a worthwhile career. Something that eluded most young women in the 1950s.

But by the age of fifteen Sarah had no idea how to plan her new status of *working woman* and had no one to advise her. There were no long-term career opportunities for a fifteen-year-old girl with no qualifications. She could be a shop girl. A friend now worked in one of the new smart fashion stores in Chelsea. She could become an office filing clerk or a hairdresser. Sarah rejected all of them.

Then she discovered an alternative. If Mrs Doyle, the head teacher, agreed Sarah could stay at Greenborough for an extra year to study shorthand, typing and bookkeeping. This would also allow her to take the school's leaving certificate exams. But she was disappointed when her form teacher reported to Sandra and John that Sarah's spelling and grammar hadn't reached the required standard to work in an office.

As the school year was coming to a close, Mrs Doyle had second thoughts. She agreed Sarah could stay at school for one more year. Not to study office skills, as she had previously hoped. But would Sarah consider joining her friend Jennifer in the fifth form pre-nursing class? A place had become vacant after a student decided not to accept the offer. Sarah was thrilled. She had never considered a career in nursing. Rather immaturely she fondly remembered the nurse's uniform she was given on her fifth birthday, and how she enjoyed playing doctors and nurses with her little friends. Even now, as a young woman, she still fancied herself in one of those cute caps and a smart blue starched nurse's uniform.

Sarah took full advantage of the extra year and gained the required academic qualifications to enable her to apply to a top teaching hospital in London. The following September Sarah and Jennifer became proud probationary nurses. Sarah also proved her form teacher wrong. In her final year of school, she matured from young girl to young woman and her spelling and grammar improved by leaps and bounds.

***

However, any romantic notion of becoming a nurse, and wearing the uniform, very soon dissipated. The work was tough and the days long. The girls worked forty-eight hours a week. During the first year, all probationary nurses were forced to live in the nurses' home. The living accommodation was abysmal, cold and smelling of damp. Hot water was a luxury and the girls had no privacy and discipline was strict. Sarah had never lived away from home and was initially excited at the prospect of being independent, but she never imaged the hardship and restrictions of living in a dormitory, where doors were locked and lights out at ten-thirty, and no men friends!

Jennifer and Sarah shared a dormitory with Suzy, Lorraine, Carole, and Rona. The girls came from very different backgrounds, but all were eager to succeed in nursing.

Suzy always dreamed of becoming a nurse. She came from the Welsh valleys, north of Cardiff. Her father and five brothers were all miners.

Lorraine's family were wealthy landowners. They farmed a huge estate deep in the countryside of Yorkshire. Her father enjoyed weekend fox hunting and her mother was chairwoman of the annual hunt ball committee. The proceeds went to *the needy* of the parish.

Carole came from the lace capital of Nottingham, in the Midlands, where her father managed a manufacturing company. Her parents were unhappy when she told them she was moving to London. But they were also indulgent and only wanted Carole to be happy.

Rona was a vivacious, fun-loving girl with a broad cockney accent and a lively sense of humour. Her home was adjacent to *Spitalfields Market* in the East End of London. Her mother was a war widow and, as revealed by Rona on many occasions, "When I was little, there were always new uncles coming and going." The men often gave Rona cinema money to disappear and leave them alone. Sadly, Rona was eventually forced to leave home at sixteen.

It didn't take long before the girls discovered Rona had men friends of her own coming and going. During her year of nursing, she had many skirmishes with staff in the nurses' home, when, by the skin of her teeth, she just managed to slip her way through the smallest opening in the building after lights out. She may have become a good nurse, but unfortunately she was never sufficiently tested. At year-end Staff Nurse Walters suggested Rona might find herself a more suitable place to work elsewhere.

Jennifer was Sarah's long-time school friend. She was tall and slender, with big blue eyes and long blond hair. John, Sarah's father, teased Jennifer and called her *Twiggy*. She was a double of the famous British 1960s model.

"Why do you want to become a nurse?" John would say, "When you can make so much money modelling."

Appreciating his flattery, Jennifer spent a fortune on portfolios of photographs and sent them to modelling agencies all over London. She was disappointed when agencies failed to reply, or return her precious photographs.

Even as a young girl, Sarah was ambitious. Now she was maturing into a self-assured young woman. She was slim, of average height with stunning hazel eyes. Her crowning glory was the mass of tightly curled auburn hair that rested on her shapely shoulders. At one time she used straightening tongs, but decided it was a waste of time when her curls only sprung back. Her hair was as strong-willed as Sarah herself. For special occasions Sandra rolled Sarah's hair in rags, to create ringlets in the style of the child star Shirley Temple.

From a young age Sarah was curious to find out about her birth parents. On days when she was feeling low she would wonder what they were like, and what they were doing now. Then, she rationalised, if her birth mother was a good woman, why had she given her away for adoption? But these thoughts were fleeting and she quickly got on with her life.

But Sarah never forgot *Topsy*. As a young girl Sarah had a fascination with the book *Uncle Tom's Cabin*, with special interest in the little black African-American girl, *Topsy*. When she's asked where she came from, *Topsy* replies,

'I suspect I just grow'd. Don't think nobody never made me.'

As a young woman, there were days when Sarah had irrational thoughts of growing from nowhere, just like *Topsy*. However, during her student years she was too busy to research into her birth, and even more apprehensive to learn the truth. She was mindful the knowledge could cause unnecessary pain. She decided the past should remain in the past, where it belonged. And there was also the question of loyalty to her adoptive parents.

***

In spite of being secular Jews, Sandra and John decided to adopt a Jewish child. They were never active in the Jewish community, nor were they members of a synagogue, but after living through the horrors of World War Two they had a strong desire to love, raise and cherish a needy Jewish child. Sarah was a year old when Sandra and John Cole adopted her. At the time, the adoption society had little information about Sarah's birth parents. Only they were both Jewish, and never married.

John Cole's parents were Orthodox Jews when they escaped the persecution and pogroms in Eastern Europe in the early 1900s, with thousands of their fellow Jews. However, after the family settled in London, they made a firm commitment to their new country to integrate into the British culture and changed their name from Cohen to Cole.

Chapter 6

Hierarchy in the hospital was strict, and discipline inflexible. The first-year student nurses worked long hours and were under intense pressure. They spent six months in the classroom and six months on the wards. By year-end they were exhausted. Some were homesick, living away from home for the first time. Sarah quickly learned hospital routine and the duties of a student nurse. To the point that when Staff Nurse Walters was off duty, and time allowed, she sat with her patients and their families. They enjoyed her cheerful chatter.

***

Regularly at nine o'clock every Tuesday morning Professor Stein consulted on the ward attended by his student doctors. Ten minutes before his due arrival, Staff Nurse Walters lined up her student nurses for their personal hygiene inspection.

"Quickly girls, line up, hurry, hurry, no time to waste. Professor Stein will be here in ten minutes. Quickly, hands, nails. Get that cap tidy, adjust your apron."

The Professor stood beside Mr Jones' bed with a semi-circle of serious-looking young doctors standing around him, watching and listening to his every word. With one exception; junior doctor Paul Michaels. He was dreaming of Sarah, as he did each week. Every Tuesday, during the Professor's weekly rounds, Paul's eyes searched for Sarah. As soon as he spotted her, he was captivated. Although he didn't know her name, he couldn't stop thinking about her. Paul had even told his flatmate David,

"I've never seen a girl like her. How can I attract her attention?" That was until this Tuesday.

"Nurse Cole, get some fresh dressings from the storeroom for Mr Jones," called Staff Nurse Walters.

Sarah walked smartly to the store cupboard and returned with a handful of dressings. She carefully made her way back towards Staff Nurse Walters and, to Paul's amazement, forced her way between him and another junior doctor. Paul couldn't believe his luck. He quickly bent down to the floor, pretending he had dropped something, and pushed a note into Sarah's hand. She panicked and dropped the dressings on to the floor. Sarah turned the colour of beetroot and crawled on all-fours to pick up the fallen dressings, and stuffed the note in her pocket.

"Sorry, I'm so sorry," she looked up into the face of an astonished Staff Nurse Walters.

"What on earth do you think you're doing, nurse? We can't afford to throw away good dressings. Throw those away and get me some more. We can't keep the Professor waiting." Staff Nurse Walters was clearly very angry. "And when Professor Stein is finished on the ward come to my office," she added.

"Yes, Staff Nurse."

Before reporting back to Staff Nurse Walters, Sarah slipped into the ladies' toilets and read the note.

Dear Nurse
I see you every week and I would like to invite you out for coffee. This is not a joke. If you don't want to, just tear up this letter and I apologise for any embarrassment. Otherwise, can we meet at Gigi's Coffee House on Earl's Court Road next Saturday at seven o'clock? If you can't come because you're on duty, you can ring me on Earl's Court 3470. If you feel safer you can always bring a friend. I hope you say yes. Looking forward to seeing you.
Paul Michaels.

"Will you go?" Jennifer asked.

"After all the trouble he caused," Sarah replied.

"I'm sure he was embarrassed too."

"I was the one who got told off. Staff Nurse was furious," replied Sarah.

"I wish he'd asked me," said Jennifer with a wry smile. "He's very good looking. I don't suppose you'd like a chaperone?" she joked.

'Don't be silly. Gigi's always busy. I can always say I'm meeting someone later if I don't like him."

"Lucky old you!"

"I'll keep you posted."

Chapter 7

Sarah arrived at Gigi's Coffee House five minutes early. She peered through the plate glass window. Paul was already seated in a booth close to the door. His fingers chipped away at the cold hard wax on the side of an old chianti bottle, previously used as a candle holder. She watched him carefully place the waxy chards onto a napkin so as not to make a mess. An indication he was also nervous.

Sarah took three deep breaths, and with her head held high she pushed open the heavy glass door. Paul immediately jumped up to greet her with a peck on the cheek and Sarah slid gracefully into the seat opposite.

"I've been looking forward to tonight all week," greeted Paul.

"Hello," she smiled.

"I'm glad you came. Did you have a good week?"

"Apart from Staff Nurse Walters lecturing me. She said I'll never be a good nurse if I can't even carry out such a simple task. She was very angry."

"Don't worry about her. She's a good egg. I still don't know your name."

"Sarah Cole."

"Pleased to meet you, Sarah Cole." He smiled and offered his hand across the table to greet her formally.

"I hope you're hungry, Sarah?" He handed her the menu.

"I'm famished. It was a rush. I didn't finish my shift until six o'clock." Her face was flushed with embarrassment.

"Good, I'm hungry too. I should have said in my letter, don't eat. Have you been here before?"

She shook her head.

"The food's good. I always think Gigi sounds French, of course after the film, but the restaurant's Italian. The lasagne's good. Would you like a glass of wine?"

"Yes please."

Sarah studied the menu.

"I won't have lasagne. Can I have spaghetti and meatballs please?"

"Of course. That's good too. Do you like red or white wine?"

"I'm not sure."

The waiter took their order for meatballs and lasagne and Paul also ordered a bottle of merlot.

"I think you'll like it," he said.

Sarah didn't know her reds from her white wines. She just smiled and nodded.

"How do you like nursing?" he asked.

"I like it. But I never thought it would be so hard."

"The first year's always the hardest. Once you can move out of the nurses' home it gets easier."

"I'm sure you're right. I hate the dormitories. We don't have any home comforts. You know they think hot water's a luxury."

"I know," Paul laughed. "It'll all be different when you get your own flat."

"I can't wait. How long did you have that letter in your pocket?"

"You probably think I'm a sad nerd. I've written you a new letter every Monday evening for the last six weeks hoping somehow I could get your attention."

"You're not a sad nerd … I'm very flattered."

***

"Well, what's he like?" Jennifer was anxious for a report.

"He's really nice. We got on well. Yes, I like him. He said he'll call for another date."

"So, no chance for me then," replied Jennifer, smiling.

"I'll fight you for him first," Sarah joked. "He asked me to choose a wine. You know I'm clueless when it comes to wine. He ordered merlot. It was good. And he didn't try to persuade me to drink more than one glass."

"He sounds like a nice man. You're a lucky girl."

Sarah smiled and nodded.

***

A week passed with no call from Paul. Sarah was disappointed. She wondered whether she'd misread his body language.

"He said he'd call me. He talked about seeing me again."

"Men can be fickle," replied Jennifer.

But for Paul it was love at first sight and he just decided to play it cool.

***

On the tenth day Jennifer answered the telephone in the nurses' home lobby.

"Is Sarah there? It's Paul."

She returned to the common room and gesticulated to Sarah, "It's him."

"How are you?" he asked.

"Fine."

"I enjoyed our evening at Gigi's."

"So did I."

"I'm sorry I left it so long. I'm studying hard for my end-of-year exams and been lumbered with two extra shifts," he explained.

"No problem. I've been busy," she replied, trying her best to sound laidback. It was just as well he couldn't see her flushed face and hear her heart beating ten times faster than it should.

"I've got two tickets to see *The Pirates of Penzance* on Saturday? Would you like to come? It's at the Haymarket Theatre."

"I'd love to. Remember, I'm living in the nurses' home so I can't get back late," Sarah replied.

"There's always a way."

"My friend Rona always seems to manage. It's ridiculous how we're locked in so early."

"You're young women of the world. Valuable to the hospital. They shouldn't treat you like children."

"You tell them that. Next year we'll get our own flat."

"This is 1961, *and times they are a changing*," he chanted in a light-hearted banter.

"The girls will see I'm okay. Where shall we meet?"

"Can you be outside the Haymarket theatre at seven-thirty?"

Chapter 8

Immediately Sarah came into view he waved enthusiastically and welcomed her with a fulsome kiss on the mouth.

"I missed you. I'm sorry I didn't ring sooner. I've got important exams coming up and the hospital increased my shifts," he greeted her apologetically.

He looked more handsome than ever, in his smart navy suit, and he was very polite.

"I didn't know whether you preferred milk or dark chocolate." He handed her a huge box of luxury Thornton's plain dark chocolates, extravagantly wrapped with a large red satin bow which partly covered a picture of snow-covered mountains.

"I like plain chocolates best. Thank you ever so much. It's just if I have too many they go straight to my hips," she joked.

Sarah was reluctant to tell Paul she didn't know anything about opera. She always thought of performers singing in foreign languages and not making much sense. Seated next to him she enjoyed the singing and humour of the show. At this euphoric time, she would have enjoyed any show with Paul holding her hand.

"This is my first time at an opera," Sarah opened the conversation as they were leaving the theatre. It was ten-fifteen.

"They call Gilbert & Sullivan's works operettas. I think they're fun. Light and amusing, not the heavy stuff."

"Did you know W. S. Gilbert lived in a large country house with a lake near my parents' home in Harrow?"

"Your parents must be rich," he replied with a smile.

"No way!" she laughed. "Harrow's a big town. We have a very small house. My parents took me to his home once when I was little. I remember a large old house with ivy growing up the walls and beautiful gardens beside a lake with lots of greenhouses full of exotic fruit and vegetables I'd never seen before. Remember it wasn't that long after the war."

"I've done my research too. Did you know W. S. Gilbert drowned in that lake?"

"No way!"

"The story goes he was giving swimming lessons to two young girls, when one of them got into trouble and called for help. Gilbert dived in to help her, but he died from heart failure in the middle of the lake and drowned."

"What a tragedy. Did the girl drown?"

"I don't know. Did you know the house is being converted into a hotel?"

"No. I'd like to see what it looks like after all these years."

"Maybe you can take me there sometime. Do you have time for a coffee?" he asked.

She looked at her watch. It was gone ten-thirty, already lock up time.

"I'm already late. I suppose half an hour's not going to make that much difference."

***

It was eleven-thirty by the time Paul walked Sarah to the door of the nurses' home.

"This sounds theatrical and corny. But the girls said to throw a stone up at that window and they will let me in around the side."

"Let's do it."

Paul was a good aim, but even after six attempts he still couldn't attract the girls' attention. Sarah was worried a stone might crack a window. The building was dark and looked deserted. She expected to see a light, and a wave from a window, some indication they were letting her inside the building. But no one came, and the house remained silent and shrouded in darkness.

She began to shiver. Paul put his coat around her shoulders.

"What am I going to do?"

He threw more stones at the window. The girls always stayed up late at the weekends. Sarah remembered Jennifer had a date, and Rona and Lorraine were on duty. But Carole and Suzy said they were staying in. And where were the other girls who lived in the building?

Sarah began to panic. "I don't understand. They said someone would let me in."

"You can't stay out here all night. If you can't get in, you'll have to come back with me. I'll bring you back first thing."

"I can't do that."

He ignored her comment.

"When do they unlock the building?" he asked.

"Five o'clock."

"No worries. I'll get you back by then. What do you say?"

"There must be some explanation. I feel such a fool," she replied.

"Things happen. Don't worry. I share a flat with my friend David. We'll keep you safe."

"I shouldn't be doing this."

"You'll be fine, I promise. I wouldn't do anything to spoil this evening. We've had a good time. Trust me, I'll take good care of you."

"I've got no choice."

But as they travelled back to Paul's south Kensington flat, Paul suddenly remembered David was away.

"I must apologise for what I'm going to say. It's because I've enjoyed this evening so much, I completely forgot David's gone home for the weekend. It's just you and me tonight. I'm very sorry. Can you forgive me?"

Sarah looked aghast. How could Paul forget his flatmate was away? The evening had been fun. Had he deliberately deceived her? He seemed genuine. Paul guided Sarah through the revolving doors of a luxury mansion block. A smartly uniformed concierge sat behind an ornate desk.

"Good evening, Dr Michaels."

"Evening, Jack, this lady's my cousin Sarah. She'll be staying with me tonight."

Jack nodded in their direction.

"Good night, Dr Michaels, miss."

"Good night, Jack."

Paul called for the lift and they travelled to the third floor.

'Has he taken me for a fool? How many other girls has he brought up here?' Sarah wondered.

"You've tricked me," were her first words.

"No I haven't. I'm sorry. I genuinely forgot about David. He stays away a lot. I promise it'll never happen again."

The flat was big and spacious and expensively furnished. She wondered how a young doctor could afford to live here. He must have read her thoughts.

"This is David's flat. He's a banker. He recently divorced and asked me to keep him company."

"The concierge knows I'm not your cousin."

"Of course he doesn't. Anyway, it's none of his business. Go into the living room and make yourself comfortable."

Paul busied himself in the kitchen.

"Tea or coffee?" he called.

"Coffee please."

He placed a tray of coffee and biscuits on the table.

"You can have my bed. I'll sleep on the sofa … I have some pyjamas you can wear."

"I can't stay here. I should have checked into a hotel."

"You can't stay in a strange hotel all alone."

It was nearly midnight. South Kensington was an assortment of apartment buildings, hotels, and large Victorian homes, many converted into bedsits. It wasn't unusual to see prostitutes trawling the streets and certain hotels vying for clients. Suddenly, alarm bells began to ring. Surely Paul didn't think she was one of those girls who would sleep with him tonight?

They sat in silence drinking coffee and nibbling on chocolate digestive biscuits.

"This is a big mistake. I shouldn't be here. I've got to go."

"I had no idea you'd be locked out. I promise I won't let it happen next time."

"There won't be a next time."

"You said you enjoyed the evening?"

"Yes, I did … the show was great. It's just … I feel stuck. I can't sleep in your bed. If I stay, I'll sleep on the sofa. Just don't let me oversleep. I've got to get back by five-fifteen."

"Trust me. I'll get you back in time. No one will know."

***

By one-thirty Sarah was lying on Paul's sofa but still very much wide awake. She was embarrassed to be in this situation. If the hospital treated nurses like responsible young women this would never happen. With lock up at ten-thirty, girls often stayed out all night. Rona did regularly. This wasn't Sarah's intention. She'd been unlucky.

With Paul only a few steps away, she was shocked by thoughts of lying by his side. She was even tempted to slip into his bed. Paul, on the other hand, had proved himself to be a true gentleman. So this hadn't been a ruse to have his way with her after all.

She eventually drifted into a fitful sleep, dreaming of falling asleep with his arms wrapped around her. Then she remembered her mother's salutary words, "A respectable young man won't take a good girl seriously if she doesn't respect her own body …"

She didn't want to lose his respect.

Chapter 9

There was trauma and tears during the first year. The tough work regime proved too much for some young nurses who dropped out before year end. Rona accepted, with good grace, that nursing had been a poor career choice and quickly found a job in a London department store. Sarah, Jennifer, Suzy, Carole, and Lorraine all passed their end-of-year exams. Now they could move out of the nurses' home and into a flat of their very own.

Over the past year Sarah had matured into an independent young woman. She never intended to become a nurse. Not until Mrs Doyle, her head teacher, offered her a place in the pre-nursing class after a student had dropped out. It had been a gamble, but Sarah was pleased with her choice of career and proud of her past year's achievements.

***

The girls couldn't wait to leave the inflexibility of the nurses' home and were eager to find a flat to share where they could come and go as they pleased. They began their search close to the hospital in south Kensington, but the rents were more than they could afford.

During the 1960s, investors were quick to buy up large, often derelict, properties in Kensington and bordering areas to convert into multi-occupied bedsits. The tenants were mainly young and transient, and landlords could demand high rents. The areas were within easy reach of the West End of London and popular with students and young people from all over the world.

250 Grosvenor Gardens, Earl's Court, London

The girls moved into a self-contained semi-basement flat in a three storey, late 19th-century terraced house in Earl's

Court, on the poorer side of Kensington. All the rooms above the basement were bedsits. The house never slept. Day and night the noises were nonstop with young people endlessly running up and down the wooden staircase. A continuous cacophony of music boomed out from almost every room, twenty-four hours a day. And the girls loved it!

The flat hadn't seen a splash of paint for years. The threadbare carpet and heavy walnut furniture had probably been in place since the early 1930s. The semi-basement had little natural light and an unpleasant aroma of damp. But this was the smell of freedom for the girls who clearly envisioned a new life of independence and a yearning to become part of the *swinging sixties*. No more overbearing and intrusive parents. No more lockouts at ten-thirty.

"After all, this is *swinging London*, the centre of the world, and we're young," they cheered.

"I think we should have a party. Invite the whole house and let them bring friends. How cool would that be?"

"I know a guy who's a guitarist who's trying to break into the pop scene," said Suzy.

"Ask them all," said Carole with excitement.

There was a knock on the door. A pleasant looking woman, in her early forties, stood on the threshold holding a chocolate cake.

"I'm Patricia White and I live on the second floor. This is to welcome you to the house." She handed the cake to Carole.

"How kind. Come in and meet the girls."

"I saw you move in. I hope you don't think I'm being nosey," said Patricia.

"No, of course not. Nice to meet you," said Carole. "This cake looks scrumptious. You must help us eat it. Would you like some tea?"

"That would be very nice if you've got time. I don't want to keep you if you're busy."

"We want to meet everyone living in the house," said Sarah.

Carole put on the kettle.

"I'm really pleased you've moved in. I was the only woman living here. There were some young men living in this flat before you and they were very noisy."

"Dirty as well," added Carole. "I don't think they ever did any cleaning."

Patricia looked around the room and replied, "Well, in the short time you've been here the flat's beginning to look lovely. You can't beat a woman's touch."

"It's taken a lot of elbow-grease," said Carole. "How long have you lived here?"

"Five years. I've seen a lot of comings and goings in that time. It should be time for me to move on, but rents are so high."

"We can only afford this flat because there are five of us."

"Yours is at least self-contained. I have to share a bathroom with hordes of long-haired hippies."

"I wouldn't like that," replied Sarah, trying to supress a giggle.

"Not when you see them running around in their underwear each morning. They laugh at me, but it's a daily grumble of mine. Needs must ..." Patricia sighed. "Every day it's me with my box of Ajax bathroom cleaner."

"Sounds like a Whitehall farce. Anyone hot?"

"I couldn't tell you. At six o'clock in the morning I'm in my hair rollers and they're in their underpants and we're all making an undignified dash for the bathroom. I keep my head down."

Sarah couldn't contain a giggle any longer.

"I can see how lucky we are down here," said Lorraine.

"That's why I'm so pleased you moved in. I hope we can be friends."

Carole placed the tea tray on the coffee table.

"Sorry I laughed, but my imagination ran riot," said Sarah. "Come on, let's have some tea. Your cake looks yummy."

"That's okay. You're right. We wouldn't look out of place in a Whitehall farce. But it's not all bad, if I get up early enough the bathroom's empty and I have the best of the hot water."

"At least you can see the funny side," said Carole.

Patricia smiled. "I'm glad you like my cake. I nearly became a professional baker but I had to earn enough money to keep myself after leaving school. That's why I went to work in an office. What do you girls do?"

"We're nurses," replied Suzy.

"That's interesting. I've always wanted to do something important like that."

"Where do you work?" asked Suzy.

"In the city. I work for stockbrokers."

"That's interesting."

"Not really. I suppose it's not too late to do something more than just being a secretary."

"All work's important," chipped in Sarah.

"What's that phrase – *the world's your oyster*, so go for it," Suzy smiled.

"You're right. The trouble is I'm on a good salary and to change now would mean I have to re-train and I can't afford to do that. Of course, there are night classes, I suppose ..." Patricia's voice drifted off in contemplation.

There was a short pause in the conversation while the girls devoured their chocolate cake and Patricia decided how best to caution the girls about an electrical problem in their new home without creating fear.

"This cake is very good," piped up Carole. "You said you wanted to be a professional baker. You could make a business out of this. This is so much better than shop bought cake."

"Thank you. But it's a case of making enough money to pay my bills."

"I'm sure lots of shops would take your cakes and once you've got a good client base, with luck, you could do it full-time. Please forgive me if I'm being too pushy," added Sarah.

"No, I appreciate your honesty. I don't have many girlfriends and it's refreshing talking to you," replied Patricia.

"If you need us, we're here," added Sarah.

"Look, there's one important thing you need to know about this house … I don't want to alarm you … but I need to warn you the house is prone to power cuts," Patricia began.

"That sounds serious," replied Sarah.

"Not really. These are very fine houses, but they do need some work on re-wiring. I've been on to the landlord ever since I moved in, but it's like talking to a brick wall. Be aware of power cuts, especially in the evenings when everyone's using electricity after work. And the hot water, that sometimes runs out."

The girls grimaced, remembering the cold water in the nurses' home.

"Are you okay?"

"We had a problem with cold water in the nurses' home. But thanks for the tip," replied Carole.

"Also, just one last thing, try not to overload the electric plug sockets. I was stupid recently. I was going out and needed to quickly iron my dress and dry my hair at the same time, so I plugged the iron and hairdryer into the same socket. Would you believe it? The socket blew and caused a small fire? Silly really."

"Were you hurt?"

"No."

"You make this sound a pretty dangerous place to live."

"No more than many old houses around here. They're all probably just as bad. You'll be fine. Just be aware."

"Thanks for the tip," said Sarah.

Patricia stood up to leave.

"Thanks for the tea. I'm really pleased to have some female company."

"Perhaps we could go out for a drink sometime. We know the pubs are good around here," said Carole.

"The best, and so are the restaurants and coffee bars. We're very cosmopolitan."

"Can you recommend some?" asked Suzy.

"Why don't we all go out for dinner?" suggested Carole.

"Brilliant idea," replied Sarah.

"How about next Wednesday?" said Patricia. She was excited to make new girlfriends and hoped they would like her favourite clubs and restaurants.

The girls checked their diaries. None of them were on duty that night.

"Would you like to try Spanish, Indian, Chinese, Italian, Turkish, or Persian …? We've got restaurants from all around the world here."

The girls agreed to try Chinese.

"Okay then, I'll take you to my favourite Chinese, the Beijing Dumpling House on Earl's Court Road. They have a wonderful speciality of spicy pork dumplings. They're to die for. Next Wednesday it is. Seven o'clock okay?"

"We look forward to it," said Carole.

"I hope I haven't made you feel anxious. I wouldn't have stayed here for so long if I thought the house was dangerous. This is a fun house, with fun people. I'm sure you'll enjoy living here. Let me know if there's anything I can do."

"Oh, yes," said Sarah jumping up. "There is one thing. Can you introduce us to your hordes of long-haired hippies? We're gonna have a party."

"That sounds fun."

As Patricia was leaving, Suzy called out, "Thanks for the cake."

Chapter 10

The flat was rocking. Even Patricia White rocked.

"I thought, in the end, she wouldn't come," said Carole. "She must be at least forty."

"Did you know she baked six beautiful cakes? I said again she should leave her office job and take up cake baking as a career," said Sarah.

"I said she should go to evening school to learn cake decoration. She could make a fortune making wedding cakes," Suzy replied.

"Do we need all those cakes? I thought this was going to be a cheese and wine party," interjected Carole.

"Of course we do. Everybody loves cake," replied Suzy.

It seemed to the girls that 250 Grosvenor Gardens, Earl's Court, London was home to young people from all over the world. There was Rory, from America, who studied at the Royal Academy of Music and practised his double bass in his attic room. Two young Australian men, Guy and Jonathan. A South African called Kurt, Miguel from Brazil, Alfonse from Spain and Ari from Israel. And, of course, Patricia White from Yorkshire.

The party began peacefully. Everyone circulated and chatted.

"I've seen you so many times in the hallway. It's so good to meet properly."

Paul dimmed the lights. *The Stones* and *The Who* boomed over the *Dansette* record player. The dining table groaned with sandwiches, dips, and cubes of cheese and pineapple on sticks, and, of course, Patricia White's delicious cakes; chocolate, honey, coffee and walnut. All food for the soul. Guests brought the booze. It took no time before the voices grew louder and the volume on the turntable was turned up to maximum.

Patricia was twenty years older than most of the crowd and Sarah wondered whether she would even come to the party. When she arrived, it was clear she was already a little bit tipsy, and remained in the party spirit with regular shots of alcohol. The girls appreciated her deprecating and feisty sense of humour.

"I should have moved away from here years ago. I'm still a poor secretary and still searching for my elusive knight in shining armour," she lamented.

Patricia and Miguel from Brazil sat together on the floor propped up against a wall drinking like fish. Initially laughing and joking until they passed out, blind drunk.

The air was stagnant. Sarah's eyes began to sting from the pungent aromas of cigarette smoke wafting above and around her and the smell of alcohol, cheap perfume, and body odour that penetrated the nooks and crannies of the overheated room. She pushed her way towards the windows to open two small fanlights in the semi-basement living room. Ravers were still pushing into the room. With no room to dance, couples clung together swaying to the music.

Sarah had a premonition something unpleasant was about to happen. She began to panic. She was appalled at what she now witnessed. Unintentionally, the girls had let their home be hijacked by strangers. Where were her friends when she needed them? The only two familiar faces she could see were Patricia and Miguel, and they were inebriated and no longer approachable. The party grew wilder and the music louder. Where was Paul when she needed him? She pushed her way out of the living room, past Patricia and Miguel who were now curled up together in a drunken stupor, then squeezed herself into a corner of the hallway and watched powerless while a young woman in the kitchen screamed out she could fly.

"Look, I can fly!" She lurched on a high window ledge, with her arms held high over her head swaying back and forth in a flying motion before plummeting head first to the floor and gashing her head as she fell. Blood spewed from the wound. Suzy's friend Sam was in the kitchen. She removed her headband to make a temporary bandage and asked a young man to run to the corner telephone kiosk to ring for an ambulance.

The bedroom door was almost off its hinges. The mob inside resembled a lunatic asylum. Paul forced his way towards Sarah.

"What the hell's going on?" she yelled.

"Get out. It's not safe in there. Go and wait for me in the coffee bar across the road. Someone's dealing drugs in there."

"Oh, my God. We've got to get the police."

"I will. Before I do, I need to speak to that Australian fellow, Guy. I think he's dealing drugs. They're literally climbing the walls in there."

***

An hour later Paul joined Sarah in the *Mellow Brew* coffee bar. Noise from the party reverberated all the way down the street. Sarah was surprised the neighbours hadn't called the police.

"Sorry I've been so long. I phoned the police and the duty manager said they're very busy tonight and we'll have to wait our turn," said Paul.

"I never thought for one minute it would end up like this," replied Sarah.

"Once drugs are involved it's a recipe for disaster."

"What are they taking?" asked Sarah.

"Purple hearts; also smoking cannabis. Couldn't you smell it?"

"How do the drugs affect them?"

"They're powerful hallucinogens. You're on top of the world one minute, then you feel awful. Things can look distorted and you can see things that aren't there."

"Is that the psychedelic pill, or the happy pill?"

"More the misery pill. A girl in there thinks your dressing table's a big furry monster that's trying to jump on top of her. Another one's screaming the walls are falling in on her. Some see psychedelic lights and shapes. One girl in your bedroom thinks I'm a dog. She hates dogs. So she won't let me near her."

"I'm scared. They all look like zombies. I just want to get my home back! I've seen girls behaving strangely in dance clubs. I would never be tempted to smoke cannabis. I'm scared of losing control."

"I hope you never do. The pills contain a very powerful stimulant and a strong sedative all rolled up into one. The amphetamine gives you a psychic lift and the barbiturate produces a woozy, calming effect."

"It's horrible to see girls losing control. They could end up in anyone's bed and get pregnant."

"It was lucky Suzy's friend Sam was around when that stupid girl jumped off the window ledge," said Paul.

"How is she?"

"She'll be okay. Sam and I managed to stop the bleeding and she went with the girl in the ambulance. Stupid girl could have knocked herself out and died."

"Lucky you were both there. What's Sam like?"

"She seems very nice. Suzy came out and waited with us for the ambulance. You missed all the fun."

"I saw the ambulance arrive, but couldn't see what was going on. What's Sam like?"

"I said she's very nice," Paul replied.

There was a long silence.

"Are you sure you're talking about Suzy's Sam? Suzy's Sam's a man."

"This Sam is definitely a girl. Why do you look so puzzled?"

"I suppose Sam must be short for Samantha."

"I suppose you're right. Does it change anything?" asked Paul.

"You mean Suzy is going out with a woman. Does that mean she's homosexual?" Sarah asked coyly.

"I've no idea. She could be bisexual. Either way, if what you say is true, Suzy and Sam will need our support. Don't look so serious. Nobody's going to die," replied Paul.

"I never thought ..."

"She's still the same old Suzy."

"You're right. This is the 1960s and things are changing. Everything's now open for discussion."

"Don't you think that's a good thing? No more sweeping things under the carpet and pretending."

"Yes. I've got a lot of growing up to do. My parents were very secretive and never discussed sex. All they wanted was for me to get married. But I wanted a career."

Paul laughed.

"Sadly, most of our parents still live like puritanical Victorians. But we all know Victorian men had mistresses and were highly sexed."

"You are funny," Sarah replied.

"It's true. The aristocrats had nothing else to do all day. They slept around with both men and women. They didn't care. Seriously though, there were openly homosexual guys at university and others, we knew were homosexual, who tried to hide it. Us heteros made their lives a misery, poking fun, calling them names. I'm ashamed now. When all they wanted was to be left alone."

"That's horrible."

"One guy deliberately crashed his car. The tragedy is he didn't die immediately but ended up in an induced coma for a year before he died. I'll never forget meeting his family and watching him die."

"Why do you think Suzy's kept Sam a secret?" asked Sarah.

"I thought you girls were so close."

"We are, but some things are difficult to discuss."

"You've answered your own question. Because people still don't understand and it's swept under the carpet."

"Do you know why some people are attracted to their own sex?"

"I've read several research papers. There are various conclusions. An imbalance of genes and chromosomes: exposure to toxic chemicals: nature versus nurture: nutrition and poverty. Or none of the above. I'd put my bet on imbalance of genes and chromosomes."

"I've led a very sheltered life in Harrow," Sarah pondered.

"Don't worry about it. Most people don't have an opinion one way or another, unless they know someone, and it's causing distress. The tragedy is when men try going *straight* and it doesn't work. Another fellow at university was so anxious about his sexuality he thought getting married would cure it. The marriage only lasted a couple of months. The average man-in-the-street doesn't understand the misery they go through trying to hide their sexuality."

"I don't think I've ever met a homosexual or lesbian."

"You must have."

"I think people who prefer their own sex should be allowed to live as they want," said Sarah.

"I agree. It's pushed underground because it's illegal. But there could be a change in the law soon. If so, we'll never need to discuss it again," replied Paul.

"I hope so too," replied Sarah.

Mr Jones, proprietor of the *Mellow Brew* coffee bar, was delighted to keep his shop open into the early hours serving coffee and cakes to locals, partygoers and voyeurs.

***

The police arrived on the street at twelve-fifteen. The screech of brakes and sirens rivalled the pulsating, booming sounds coming from the flat. Ravers had congregated outside on the pavement. As soon as they heard the sounds of approaching police sirens they began to disperse. However, a few, high on drugs, became aggressive and a scuffle broke out when the arrests began. Police stormed the basement flat and brought out the remaining ravers in various states of inebriation. Rona was carried out semi-conscious. That night was her first experiment with cannabis. She remained semi-conscious in a police cell overnight. Rona was one of the lucky ones and was released without charge the following morning.

It was gone two o'clock in the morning before the police finally left. The girls were told to find somewhere else to stay for the night. The flat was now a crime scene and the drugs team would be there to make their investigations first thing in the morning.

The girls were distraught to see their trashed home. They collected a few personal belongings and stayed two nights in a hotel. Andrew and Dominic, gate-crashers and strangers, turned out to be their saviours. Paul was embarrassed when he later discovered the boys had paid the girls' hotel bill and, after the police had released the flat back, rallied round to clean up.

***

Several days later Constable Brady informed Paul that Guy Saunders was a major player in a London drugs ring. On the night of the party, 8th May, 1962, he was arrested and taken into custody to await trial for possession and dealing illegal drugs.

Chapter 11

The *swinging sixties* wasn't the decade of liberation for women. In 1960 only seven percent of girls went to university. Contraception was unreliable and the *pill,* as a general rule, was only dispensed to married women. Illegitimate babies were still being forcibly removed from their unmarried mothers. Women needed male guarantors to acquire mortgages, and their husband's consent for certain medical procedures. Additionally, it was still customary for young girls to live at home with their families until they married.

But after the gloom of the post-war 1950s, the 1960s began full of hope. Modern innovative companies joined the fashion market and produced contemporary styled clothes, using state of the art fabrics, in fresh vibrant colours.

With a strong economy and full employment, the young generation spent their money on fashion and pleasure. Fashion-conscious young women no longer imitated their mothers. They experimented with the new fabrics and up-to-the-minute styles. Skirt lengths gradually rose from below the knee to high thigh.

The eccentric nonconformist young men, the trailblazers of the 1950s, grew their hair to shoulder length and wore clothing, more reminiscent of the first decade of the 20th century, the period of the Edwardians and King Edward VII. They were nick-named *teddy boys*. The less bold also grew their hair long and confounded their formal dark suited and hatted fathers. They wore more conventional, but cutting-edge styles, and chose bright colours.

A new pop scene exploded, cultivated by the young post-war generation. It was an extraordinary time for exporting British rock bands. And an extraordinary time to be British and to be young!

Chapter 12

Paul rudely pushed Andrew aside and marched into the flat.
"Hey dude, where ya going?" challenged Andrew.
Sarah stood in the hall.
"Where the hell have you been?" she shouted.
"Who's that?" Paul pointed an angry finger at Andrew.
"Why haven't you called?"
"I have, but no one's been here."
"We've been in the hotel whilst the police checked out the flat."
"I forgot. I'm sorry."
"So you should be. Andrew and Dominic are helping us clean up."
Paul turned to leave.
"I'll phone you,"
"Don't bother," Sarah replied and slammed the door in his face.

***

Paul returned to the flat a week later.
"What the hell's been going on. Where have you been all this time?" Sarah was angry.
"I'm sorry I didn't help. I've been tied up with work."
"Just when I needed you."
"I said I'm sorry," he yelled.
"Andrew and Dominic helped us clean up and insisted on paying our hotel bill."
Paul ignored her reply. "I said I'm sorry … I apologise. Things have got on top of me at work and I've been giving us a lot of thought."
Sarah shook her head. "I don't want to know. You really let me down."
"Please hear me out."
"Why?"

"Because I have something important to say. I've been thinking … how would you feel moving out?"

"No!"

"This is a rough area."

"You said it's very cosmopolitan and want to move around here."

"It's rougher than I thought."

"You're embarrassed because you didn't keep those gate-crashers out and you let those long-haired idiots upstairs destroy our home. Guy ruined our party dealing drugs. I hope he gets a long prison sentence," said Sarah.

"You know I tried to stop them coming in. I could smell cannabis and pushed myself into the bedroom and saw what was going on. We've learnt our lesson."

"We certainly have. We were stupid telling the boys upstairs to bring friends," replied Sarah.

"I didn't know there are so many crazy people living around here."

"A lot of good ones too. Andrew and Dominic were amazing."

"I never thought to warn you about drugs. You sometimes get gate-crashers, but that was way over the top. I thought you could move in with me until we find somewhere safer."

"I'm not moving anywhere. I like it here." she screamed. "You're jealous of Andrew, aren't you? You think he made a pass at me when you saw him here with Dominic cleaning up? You think he fancies me, don't you? Well, he does and I went out with him. You're jealous," she yelled. "And he wants to see me again."

"Are you going out with him again?"

"I might."

"Sarah, listen, this has got nothing to do with Andrew. I'm only thinking of your safety."

"Rubbish. You saw Andrew and flipped. You don't own me."

"You clearly can't discuss this rationally."

"No, I don't think I can. You're really annoying me. I think it's time you went!"

***

The following evening Suzy again answered the door to Paul.

"Do you want to see him?" she asked.

Sarah was watching television. He bent down to kiss her on the cheek.

"I was bang out of order yesterday. Will you forgive me?" He attempted to put an arm around her shoulder. She moved out of his reach.

"Will you forgive me?" he repeated in a little voice. "I behaved badly."

"You let me down. Why did you disappear for a whole week?" she remonstrated.

"I was overwhelmed by the party. I made mistakes and I'm sorry. I'll never let you down again. I was awake all night thinking about you."

"The boys just helped us clean up." She began to cry. "There's nothing between Andrew and me. We went out once, but I'm not seeing him again."

"Sit down, I've got something to ask you."

Sarah wiped her face with a handkerchief and reluctantly sat down in the nearest chair. Paul took hold of her limp hand.

"I admit I was jealous. I want to protect you. I love you and I want to spend the rest of my life with you."

"I don't need protecting and I don't want to move. This is the best time of my life living with the girls."

His face dropped. "But you won't need to share when we get married."

"Stop it ... I don't want to get married until I'm twenty-five. I want to go travelling first."

"I thought you felt the same as me. Don't you love me just a teeny-weeny bit?"

"I did," she replied almost reluctantly. "Until last week. How do I know I can trust you again?"

"What about a long engagement? We can travel around Europe together and see my cousin in Australia then get married."

"You're such a dreamer. When will you grow up?"

"I'm not a dreamer. You're the best thing that's happened to me. We're young, we've got time on our side."

"Things have become too intense. We need a break," said Sarah.

"Why?" he replied.

"You still don't know much about me."

"I know enough to want to marry you."

"I don't think so," she replied.

"Come on, now you're being ridiculous."

"You said your family's Catholic."

"I'm a lapsed Catholic, what of it?"

"I'm different."

"You're different 'cause you're talking crazy."

"It's not that simple."

"Why? Have you come from outer space?"

"It's not like that … I'm Jewish."

"Okay, so you're Jewish."

"I thought you wouldn't want to go out with me if you knew I'm Jewish."

Paul took hold of her hand. "I promise it makes no difference."

"You must have heard those anti-Jewish comments in the hospital."

"Yes, and if I was more senior, I would tell them all to button up. Have you noticed it's usually the older staff? Those who went through the war, and should know better. With everything the Jewish people suffered."

"I'm glad you feel like that. I thought it would be a problem."

"It doesn't make any difference to me. My parents are Catholic. They say they're practising, but they're not really, and I'm agnostic."

"I left home to become a nurse because I wasn't getting on with my parents. And I was adopted."

"So? What of it?" He took her in his arms. "Why are you so sensitive?" he asked.

"I suppose it's because I was the only Jewish girl in my school and was always left out."

"You're with friends now. And as for being adopted, well … do you know anything about your birth parents?"

"No. Only that they were both Jewish."

"How interesting. Stop making excuses. You'll have to teach me about Judaism."

"I can't," Sarah smiled. "My adoptive family are secular Jews. So I've never had a Jewish education."

"As for family … I'm very different from my parents. We always argue. You know, we can't always love the people we call mother and father. Don't feel guilty. We all have hang-ups of one kind or another," replied Paul.

He couldn't have been clearer. He said he loved her, wanted to marry her and accepted her Jewish birth unconditionally.

Chapter 13

Sarah couldn't sleep that night. She tossed and turned in bed thinking of Paul. She had left home to become a nurse, not to fall in love and get married. Her mind was full of questions. What if I make a decision I may later regret? A life-time is a long time. Am I too young to know true love? Am I in love with the idea of being in love? Am I over-analysing?

Paul is my first boyfriend and I certainly have intense feelings for him and want to be with him. On our very first date I had a strong heady sexual desire to be loved by him. He said he loved me. I have no reason to doubt that. Am I looking for problems where none exist? I LOVE HIM! Phew.

Paul was a new post-war man who clearly respected equal rights for women in education and careers. Not like her father who believed women should be married with children by the age of twenty. He once said he distrusted educated women.

When Sarah left school her father declared, "Now it's time for you to prepare for marriage." Sarah never understood what he meant by the word *prepare* and never bothered to ask.

"A young woman needs a man to marry. And a young man needs a woman to look after him," he had said.

"A bad marriage is worse than a death sentence. Being married to the wrong man, day in, day out would be like hell on earth," Sarah replied.

"Balderdash," her father replied. "A woman needs a man, and a man needs a woman to care for him. It's been the same throughout millennia. Nothing will change that now."

Paul convinced her he was different, and she didn't want to risk losing him.

***

"The doctor will see you now."

Sarah entered the surgery and was pleased to see Dr Porter was a woman.

"My name is Sarah Cole. I'm a new patient. I've read about the contraception pill in the papers and wondered if you would prescribe it?"

The doctor stood to shake Sarah's hand.

"Pleased to meet you, Mrs Cole."

Sarah was taken off-guard. It hadn't occurred to her the doctor would question her marital status.

"No ... I'm ... I'm not married."

There was a hesitation, before Dr Porter replied sharply.

"That's impossible. The contraceptive pill is only available to married women. Anyway, it's still being tested under supervision and I'm not yet convinced of its efficacy and safety. I won't be prescribing it to any of my patients for the foreseeable future, and certainly not to unmarried girls. Is there anything else I can do for you?"

Sarah was taken aback by the doctor's insensitivity. She turned and made a quick exit.

"No thank you, doctor."

***

"I asked the doctor about going on the pill," said Sarah.

"So you've decided to stay with Paul," Jennifer replied.

"Not exactly."

"Has he pressured you to sleep with him?"

"No. He wants us to get engaged."

"Oh my God. Lucky you. Why didn't you say?"

"It's too soon. But I also don't want to risk losing him. Am I being selfish?"

"You must be honest with him. You can't keep him hanging on indefinitely."

"That's what Carole said. I've got myself into such a mess ... I've had sleepless nights thinking what to do," Sarah cried.

"Have you discussed the pill with him?" asked Jennifer.

"No. It's so new."

"He's a doctor, he must have an opinion."

"I went on a foursome with Dominic, Carole and Andrew," Sarah continued.

"I know. Carole told me you and Andrew got on well and he wants to see you again."

"He asked me out again, but I put him off."

"Why have you changed the subject? We're talking about Paul not Andrew."

"Because if I hadn't met Paul, I would definitely go out with Andrew. But Paul's special," sighed Sarah. "I think I fell in love with him on our very first date." She smiled, recalling Paul's jealousy when he saw Andrew in their flat.

"So you've made up your mind?"

"I met Paul too soon."

"You're exasperating. I wish I had someone like Paul."

"I was confused when I went to the doctor for advice about the pill, and to make matters worse, she called me Mrs Cole. When I said I wasn't married, she read me the riot act and said they don't give unmarried girls the pill. She spoke to me, like I was a prostitute."

"I did read they're only giving it to married women," Jennifer replied.

"She could have been a bit nicer."

"Why don't you try the *Marie Stopes Clinic*? I know from girls at work the clinic is more relaxed about contraception. Wear a fake wedding ring and pretend you're married. They won't know the difference," Jennifer suggested. "I'll come with you if you want. You shouldn't be embarrassed. Can't you see you're just struggling to supress your natural sexual urges all women have? Years ago, girls were married at fourteen!"

Sarah laughed. "You are funny. You're right. I'm a grown woman and it's about time I grew up!"

"It certainly is," replied Jennifer.

***

(Marie Stopes opened her first controversial family planning clinic in London in the early 1920s, initially licensed for married women only. Unmarried women had to wait until the mid-1960s before they could use the clinics.)

Chapter 14

Sarah gazed enviously at Rona's clothes as she made her way towards her table in the restaurant.

"You look fabulous. I love your dress," said Sarah.

The girls were meeting for lunch in the Mirabelle Coffee House in Camden.

Rona was wearing a black and red wool geometric patterned shift dress. The soft material flared gently away from under her bust and finished halfway up her thighs. The look was completed with high black patent boots that reached to her knees. Her hair was styled in a perfect bob that flicked up just below her ears.

"Thanks," Rona replied breathlessly. "I love your blue suit. It's been a long time. How are you?"

"Fine."

But, looking at Rona's face more closely, Sarah was shocked to see she looked haggard and pale.

"What's kept you away so long?" asked Sarah.

"This and that. It's been a bad six months. How are the girls?"

"Fine. We tried getting in touch, but you don't answer your phone and never reply to letters. We thought you might have moved. It was pure luck Lorraine bumped into you at Oxford Street Station."

"No, I still live in Windsor Way but I'm looking for something cheaper. Forgive me for not replying." She flicked her hair then attempted to pull her extremely short mini-skirt closer to her knees.

"We were worried when we didn't hear. What's been going on? How's Bob?" Sarah asked.

"We broke up. I feel like I'm only just emerging from a long dark tunnel." She gave a huge sigh, forced a smile, then deliberately changed the subject,

"I do have some good news. I've got an exciting new job which has helped get me through all the rubbish that's been thrown at me. It's in an ultra-modern fashion store in Knightsbridge. You know how much I love fashion."

Rona was avoiding the subject of Bob.

"What's happened with you and Bob?" Sarah asked.

"We're finished. I got pregnant and he didn't like it. He left me high and dry and I had an abortion."

"I'm so sorry. Why didn't you tell us?"

"I was in a very bad way. The only person who knew was my mum. She helped me get an abortion. She knows this gynaecologist who has a clinic off Harley Street. He took a risk and did it illegally. He told his nurses I was having a spontaneous miscarriage."

"I'm so sorry. When was this?"

"Three months ago. I'd just started my new job and told my boss I had to go to Scotland for my grandmother's funeral just so I could have some time off."

"How are you now?"

"I never realised I could get so depressed. I still can't stop crying when I think what I've done, and how my baby would be due in three months."

"Could you have kept the baby?"

"How can I look after a baby? After the abortion, Mum said she would have looked after it. But she's getting on a bit. She told me to get some anti-depressants, but how could I tell the doctor why I was so depressed? I couldn't tell her I'd had an abortion."

"You could have stayed with us."

"Thanks. We went through so much together that year of nursing and living in the nurses' home. You're my best friends. I know you would never be judgmental."

"You shouldn't suffer in silence."

"Mum was amazing. You're the first friend who knows. Bob was so nasty about the baby. He just didn't want to know."

"How far gone were you?" Sarah asked.

"About thirteen weeks. You can't imagine how much love you can feel for your unborn baby in three months. It was just the worst thing I've ever done."

"I wish you had come to us."

"I panicked and thought there was no other way but an abortion. My mum's too old to look after a baby. Now I wonder if I should have had the baby adopted."

Rona had unwittingly struck a raw nerve. This could have been Sarah's birth mother's story.

"For heaven's sake, don't ever get pregnant without a ring on your finger. I'm still feeling like hell. Believe me, this baby, and the abortion will live with me for the rest of my life."

Both girls' eyes stung with tears. Sarah reached over to give Rona an affectionate hug. Sarah cleared her throat.

"Now tell me about your new job," she asked, swiftly changing the subject.

"Have you heard of Mary Quant?"

Sarah shook her head, "Should I?"

"Not really. It was pure luck I got this amazing new job working in her new boutique. She has the most ultra-modern new fashion store you can imagine in Knightsbridge and she designs all the clothes. She's amazing. She said I have a good eye for design and suggested that I sign up for a course in fashion design, so I enrolled for night classes at Chelsea Art College. It's great. I've made friends and when I'm busy it takes my mind off other things."

"That's good. Is your dress one of hers, whatever her name is?" Sarah asked.

"Mary Quant. Yes." Rona stood up and gave a twirl. "You must come into the boutique. You'll love it."

"I will."

"Are you still with Paul?"

"Yes, only recently things have got intense between us. He's talking about marriage and it feels too soon for me. I wanted to do so much, like go travelling. But I don't want to lose him. I don't know what to do."

"You shouldn't mess him about. Have a break for six months. There are plenty more fish in the sea."

"That's what the girls said. I don't want a marriage like my parents, and it's scary to think we could be together for fifty years."

"Only fools believe marriage is forever. But I envied you and Paul. You make a good couple. Are you sleeping with him?" asked Rona.

"Not really."

"You either are, or you're not. I hope you're being careful. You don't want to end up like me."

"I've just gone on the pill."

"I was on it for a few months, but I felt bloated and tired so I stopped taking it. I always liked Paul. I'm not sure you should get bogged down taking pills until you know your relationship is permanent. Let Paul take charge."

"What did you use after you stopped taking the pill?"

"Don't do what I did. We stopped taking precautions and I got pregnant.

Chapter 15

The winter of 1962/63 was the coldest on record for two hundred years. The River Thames was an ice-skating rink from bridges Tower to Kew. On New Year's Day 1963 twelve inches of snow fell and froze. Water pipes refused to thaw and burst. Shoppers and commuters desperate to reach the safety of their homes, slid and fell on ice packed pavements. Buses and cars skidded and crashed on treacherous black ice.

Meanwhile, Sarah and Paul were contentedly curled up on his sofa covered in a warm blanket with the lights dimmed and the coal fire burning. Her cheeks burned from the warmth of the fire, a good meal and several glasses of mateus rosé. Tonight, they had the flat to themselves. David was staying with family over the New Year and planned to return the following week.

Traumas of a normal hospital day ebbed away. Paul wasn't on call that night and Sarah could finally relax.

He eased himself off the sofa and pulled his jacket off the back of a chair.

"Oh, one minute, I'd almost forgot," he said casually. "I bought you this."

He handed her a small box. She opened the lid. A beautiful diamond ring twinkled inside.

He pulled her towards him. "Marry me."

Paul hadn't mentioned marriage for months.

"I can't wait to see what it looks like on your finger."

Sarah was stunned and confused. Her mind raced, do I accept? She was tongue-tied. He looked so excited and she didn't want to spoil the evening.

"What's the matter? Why the hesitation?"

"You didn't warn me."

"I don't believe this. Did you expect me to warn you last week that this week I would propose?" he joked. "Don't you want my engagement ring?" Paul's face dropped.

"Of course I do."

"Why the hesitation? I've been planning this for months," he said.

She held out her hand and he slipped it on her finger.

"It's beautiful," she exclaimed. "And a perfect fit!"

He bent down on one knee and reached out for her hands.

"Well, Miss Cole you haven't answered my question. I want to make you Mrs Michaels. Will you marry me?"

The flames in the fire reflected onto her face. Sarah flung her arms around his neck and kissed him gently on the lips.

"Yes. I'm sorry, it's just … I felt overwhelmed."

"You know you make me so happy," he said, "We're so right for each other. We go together like … strawberries and cream."

Sarah laughed, "Which one am I?"

"The cream of course. I love to lick the cream."

The ring sat perfectly on her finger. The flames from the fire caught the fire in the diamond. She hadn't planned to stay the whole night with Paul. But his marriage proposal, the engagement ring, and the appalling winter weather, had changed everything.

Her body tingled with anticipation. Tonight, he proved he meant what he said all those months ago. He loved her. She had fallen in love with Paul during the early weeks of their relationship but was apprehensive to show her true feelings. Now he was her friend, her soul mate, her lover and soon to be her husband.

He held her tightly in his arms. Adrenalin pumped around her body, her breathing became heavy and erratic. With the intensity of the moment, stirred an erotic sensation from the tips of her fingernails to the soles of her feet. She lay limp and submissive. Paul continued kissing her deeply on the lips, whilst his hand searched inside her brassiere. Every part of her body burned with anticipation.

"Have you got protection? I don't trust the pill," she asked timidly.

"Of course," he whispered.

Paul began to nibble on her ear and lick the back of her neck, whilst his hands hungrily roamed her small crevasses and explored the shape of her body. This time she didn't push him away in fear. She yearned for intimacy, relaxed and enjoyed the moment.

Chapter 16

Suzy cried down the phone.

"Can we meet for lunch tomorrow in Regent's Park?"

"You sound awful. What's the matter?"

"I need to talk to you and I don't want the girls around."

"Does it have to be so far away? You know it's below zero out there," Sarah replied.

"I don't want to run into anyone I know. The café in the park does a wonderful goulash. It's good and nourishing on a freezing day, and the restaurant's full of students."

"Okay. Can we meet outside Baker Street Underground Station at one o'clock?"

The melting snow from two days ago had frozen and become icy slush. They shuffled towards the outer ring road of Regent's Park then turned right towards the café in the park.

"You could have suggested somewhere a little closer to home," grumbled Sarah sarcastically as she shed her hat and gloves. "I'm surprised the café's open in the winter."

Sarah self-consciously avoided displaying her treasured new diamond engagement ring. But it had a life of its own and resplendently twinkled on the third finger of her left hand.

"For heaven's sake, why are you hiding your beautiful ring? Why didn't you tell me you got engaged?" Suzy looked astonished.

"It happened so fast. I'll tell you about it later. First, tell me what's so important you had to bring me out here on such a freezing day."

"Let me see your ring first," pressed Suzy.

Sarah splayed out her hand. "It's beautiful," she replied. "Why didn't you tell me?"

"Because you sounded so upset; I thought something awful had happened," Sarah replied.

"It's true we have a crisis, but no one's died. It's just ... Sam's pregnant."

"Oh my God, how did that happen? I mean, who's the father?" Sarah leaned over to give Suzy a reassuring hug.

"She had a few dates with a man called James. They got on well as friends and he agreed to have sex just to get her pregnant. I've always known she wanted a baby."

"I never imagined ... Is that legal?"

"It's not illegal to have a baby."

"Congratulations. If you need any help ..."

"Thanks. We know we can trust you and Paul. You know, Sam's been confused about her sexuality for years. She had counselling with a psychotherapist in her teens but I think it left her more confused."

"Sam having a baby. That's the last thing I expected to hear. When's she due?"

"June."

"And James was simply a means to get her pregnant?" Sarah reiterated.

"Yes."

"He's okay with that?"

"Seems so."

"The baby is going to affect your life as much as hers."

"Between you and me, I don't think Sam's given the baby enough thought. I'm still struggling to get my head around it. We haven't told anyone except you. I think the girls will be shocked."

"I'm sure that's not true. We'll rally round. Do you think James will want to play father?"

"We've agreed he can see the child. Sam doesn't want a relationship with him. She loves me and I want to be there to support her. It was simply a means to have a baby."

"You'll need somewhere to live together."

"That's the idea. At the moment she's got a small room in this elderly couple's house, but she'll have to move before she starts showing ... and who's going to rent a flat to two lesbian women and a baby?"

"Wow, you're going too fast."

"Am I being too sensitive?" Suzy asked.

"Of course you are."

"There's something else. We'll need to find some cheap accommodation until she can get back to work."

"That will be tough."

Sarah looked thoughtful,

"Although ... you might be in luck. I was talking to Rory from upstairs only this week. He's graduating from the Royal Academy of Music and going back to America soon. Maybe you could move into his bedsit until you get sorted. The rent can't be much, the room's so small. It could work at least until Sam goes back to work and you can afford something bigger. And we'll be around to babysit."

"That's a good idea. As long as the long-haired dudes don't mind a screaming baby," replied Suzy.

"They make so much noise no one will notice. Unfortunately, it's an attic room and you'll have to share a bathroom, but it could be a solution for a few months."

"You'll need to find a girl to replace me," said Suzy.

"That's no problem. Obviously, Sam needs to move as soon as possible. Why don't you speak to Rory? Find out the rent, and when he's planning to leave. I'll also try and catch him."

"I know Sam would like to live in our house. I'm going to pluck up courage and tell the girls about the baby tonight. I hope they won't be too shocked. It's only fair you have plenty of time to find a replacement for me when I leave," replied Suzy.

"They'll still be four of us paying the rent, so money's not an issue."

Suzy stood up from the table and gave Sarah a hug.

"Phew, thanks for understanding. I hope the landlord hasn't found someone new."

"A problem aired is a problem shared. Right?" Sarah smiled.

"Sam and I are so lucky to have you and Paul."

"You can always rely on us. We've been through so much together. These last two years I've learnt so much about the world and myself. I led a very sheltered life before nursing," replied Sarah.

Suzy looked more relaxed.

"Now let me see your beautiful engagement ring."

Sarah looked bashful.

"It's gorgeous. When did he propose?"

"Two nights ago."

"So you'll also be leaving the flat soon."

"Not for a long time. I want a long engagement."

"You're a dark horse. Congratulations. You're a lucky girl. You and Paul are a perfect match."

Sarah smiled. "You were right about the goulash. It is as good as you said, and because it's so cold out there, how about we really indulge ourselves with bread and butter pudding and custard?"

"And a coffee?" smiled Suzy.

***

Two months later, Rory returned to America and Suzy and Sam moved into his room on the top floor of 250 Grosvenor Gardens, to await the birth of their son Stuart.

Chapter 17

Paul was very fond of his grandfather Cyril, who secretively regarded Paul his favourite grandchild. When Cyril was first diagnosed with prostate cancer Paul arranged for him to have the best medical treatment. He visited him regularly at home, and then daily when he was in the hospital. Paul was heartbroken when Cyril passed away only two months after announcing his engagement to Sarah.

Cyril Michaels' major asset was his home. The day Paul took Sarah to meet him in hospital, and introduced her as his fiancée, Cyril decided to leave his home to his favourite grandson. The following day he instructed his lawyer, Mr Bentwood, to change his will. He wanted Paul and Sarah to modernise his home and bring it back to life. He didn't want his son Albert to sell it to strangers. Cyril was property rich and cash poor, so there wasn't much money to leave. Just a beautiful large Victorian four-bedroom house.

Cyril's death caused a family feud which never healed. In fact, the sore festered beyond Paul's father Albert's death decades later. All because Grandfather Cyril changed his will and bequeathed his home, in Edmonton north London, to Paul and Sarah two weeks before he died.

Four weeks after Cyril's death, Paul received the following letter from Mr Bentwood, his grandfather's lawyer.

Bentwood & Adams
Lawyers
8th April 1963 *2 Regents Street*
London, W.1

Dear Dr Michaels
My condolences for the loss of your grandfather. You need to be aware there has been a recent change to his will. I believe it will be in your interest for you attend the reading of the will in my office next Wednesday, 16th April at 2.30pm.

Please telephone our offices on Mayfair 2651 to confirm you will be attending,

Yours faithfully
M Bentwood.

Edith and Albert Michaels, attended the lawyer's office, together with Sarah and Paul at two-thirty on 16th April, to hear Mr Bentwood formally read Grandfather Cyril's will. Paul's parents always assumed they would be the sole beneficiaries and were curious when Mr Bentwood handed a letter to Paul to read, hand-written by Grandfather Cyril, prior to the formal reading of the will. The contents of the letter left his parents shocked and angry.

24 Magnolia Gardens,
Edmonton, north London

24th February 1963

My dearest Paul & Sarah
First of all, don't let my family persuade you I'm not of sound mind. My mind is clear, sadly my body is rapidly failing. Note, my doctor, Dr Sheldon, and my lawyer, Mr Bentwood have both witnessed this letter and agree I still have clarity of mind.
I want to congratulate you on your forthcoming marriage. I fear I won't be there to celebrate with you. Because you are both beautiful and caring young people, I have decided to pass on my home in its entirety to you. I don't want Edith and Albert to have it because I know they would only sell it. My home has been lived in by my family for five generations and I want you to bring it back to life and fill it with many children.
Farewell, my dears and enjoy married life. Your ever-loving grandfather.

Cyril Michaels.

Albert Michaels' face began to crumple as he listened to Mr Bentwood reading the letter out loud and angry red blotches began to appear all over his face and neck. Paul was worried the shock could trigger a heart attack. After Mr Bentwood had finished, Albert barked, "F..k the letter. F..k the lies. That's not what the will says."

"Language, Albert," said Edith.

"F..k you, woman. That letter's a fake. I'll prove it's fake." Albert turned to Mr Bentwood.

"How could you let this happen? Everything was sorted."

"Calm down. You can't blame Mr Bentwood," said Paul.

"I can blame him. Why didn't he tell me? How come he's left everything to you?"

"I'm as shocked as you. He didn't tell me," replied Paul.

"Father always knew I was planning to use the house to invest in our pension. He must have lost all sense of reality."

"No, he had all his faculties right 'till the end. He even complained he never saw you."

"That's not true," shouted Edith.

"I promise you, he knew exactly what he was doing. As he said in the letter, his body was failing not his mind," Paul added.

"Stop the arguing. It's all very undignified in front of Mr Bentwood," shouted Edith.

"You're the one shouting," said Paul.

"We'll revoke the bloody will. It's ridiculous," added Albert.

"I promise I didn't know anything about the will. He just said he was happy I was getting married."

"To a Jewess! How can you marry a Jewess? Did Grandfather know she's Jewish?"

"He didn't ask, and I didn't tell him," Paul shouted back.

"Stop it," screamed Edith.

Sarah burst into tears and ran from the room.

Paul had to think quickly. He had to stop the bickering. If he ran after Sarah now, his parents could leave and he might never see them again. Acutely embarrassed by his father's offensive outburst of venom, he pushed them out of the lawyer's office and into an ante-room.

"What you just said was unforgivable. I expect you to calm down and apologise to Sarah and Mr Bentwood," Paul admonished.

"This isn't her fault," added Edith honestly.

"She knows she's making a good marriage marrying a doctor," Albert grumbled.

"Stop it. You've said too much. You've upset everyone. Go home and calm down. I'll come over on Saturday and we can talk."

Paul returned to Mr Bentwood's office.

"Thank you for everything." The men shook hands. "My grandfather spoke very highly of you. I must apologise for my father. This was a terrible shock for my parents. They planned to use the money from the house for their retirement."

"Think nothing of it. Sadly, this kind of thing is not uncommon," Mr Bentwood replied.

Edith and Albert were waiting in reception.

"What did you say to Mr Bentwood?"

"I said you were sorry. How could you embarrass yourselves like that?"

Turning to the receptionist Paul asked, "My fiancée had to leave our meeting early. Did she say where she was going?"

"She's waiting for you in the coffee bar downstairs."

"Thanks."

"We'll talk again on Saturday afternoon," he called after his parents, watching them move as fast as they could out of the reception hall.

***

"Are you okay? I'm so sorry. I thought it would be a routine meeting. It never occurred to me it could end up like this," said Paul apologetically.

"I shouldn't have come," cried Sarah.

"I had no idea my grandfather was going to give us his house."

"How can I ever have a proper relationship with your parents after all that?"

"I'm proud of you, Sarah. I wanted you to meet them, but it was the wrong time."

"He doesn't like me because I'm Jewish."

"He's angry about losing the house. He'll apologise. You're going to be my wife and be part of the family. I never thought for one minute it would end up like this. It's all my fault. I bet you he'll be on the phone tomorrow full of apologies."

***

But Albert didn't apologise to Sarah the next day, and clearly, he had no intention to apologise the following weekend when Paul visited his parents. In fact, Albert was angrier than ever.

"You've made a lot of people unhappy. Please think again and apologise to Sarah," Paul pleaded.

"She seems a nice enough girl," Edith added. "Can't we put all the bad feelings behind us and start again."

"Sarah will never forget Dad's nasty, racist comments. Just say sorry and we can move on," replied Paul.

"She knows doctors make a lot of money," said Albert.

"Come on Dad, you're crazy. I've known Sarah for two years. She's a nurse in the hospital. She's a good girl and a hard worker."

"If you must marry that girl, then do it in church," Albert added sharply.

"That girl has a name – her name is Sarah," replied Paul.

"With all the lovely Catholic girls in London, how come you've fallen for a Jewish one? Is she pregnant?"

"You're disgusting!" Paul could hardly believe his ears.

"Marry in a Catholic Church, or you're no longer a son of mine!"

Paul had hoped his visit would clear the air. Clearly, it wasn't going to happen.

"I can't take any more of your rubbish and racism. Well done!" Paul shouted. He slammed the front door behind him with such vigour a pane of glass fell out and smashed on to the front step.

"Edith, what am I going to tell the golf club? I'm responsible for enrolment. It's me who tells the bloody Jews they can't join."

"Don't swear … Don't you think I'd also like him to marry a nice Catholic girl? We've got nothing in common with her people. But can't you see you're not doing any good? We'll lose him if you don't say sorry. We either accept them or lose them," said Edith.

Paul hadn't grasped the depth of his father's racism. Edith phoned him later that day to apologise on behalf of Albert. But Paul was adamant. Dad must make his own apologies to Sarah.

Chapter 18

Sandra had to get something off her chest and chose her words carefully.

"I'm disappointed you haven't considered getting married in a synagogue," she began.

Sarah was prepared for her mother's question.

"Why? You're not religious. You never go to synagogue, and now you expect me to have a religious wedding. Don't you think you're being hypocritical?" Sarah was clearly annoyed.

"I'm not looking for a row. It's just ... on special occasions, like births, weddings and funerals I feel a special bond with my religion. I'll never be an Orthodox Jew, but deep down in my bones I'll always be a Jew."

"I never thought you cared about religion."

"I've surprised myself. Only now you're getting married I've been thinking about our family and our roots."

"As long as it's got nothing to do with Paul being Catholic."

"It's not about Paul. It's all about me, and growing up between the wars and what Hitler did to the Jews. We didn't know the full truth until after the war. But we did know Jews were disappearing in Europe. We were scared. He nearly reached England but fortunately, he didn't cross the Channel."

Sarah calmed down. "I'm sorry. I've been insensitive."

"We love you and I don't want to interfere with your wedding plans. I suppose now you're getting married Dad and I are feeling sentimental about the family he never knew back in Poland. All his uncles, aunts and cousins perished. They lived in a small village called Lodz and only Granny and Grandpa Cole managed to escape. They told us how soldiers rounded up Jews and set fire to their homes and places of work. Even after they moved here, they still had nightmares about being in Poland and waiting for the expected knock on the door."

"I will never forget Grandpa telling us how soldiers set fire to the community hall during their wedding party. I don't think I could have been more than five, but it made a huge impression on me."

"That's why when you were growing up we tried to shelter you from bigots and anti-Semites walking the streets."

"You shouldn't have wrapped me up in cotton wool."

"We know that now. You were so precious. The daughter we waited so long for."

"Do you remember when I told you I wanted to be Christian because some of the children didn't want to be my friend because I'm Jewish? You said ignore it. Sometimes I thought you didn't care."

"Of course we cared. I complained to your head teacher."

"That was unkind of me. I'm sorry, I remember. It got better after that," Sarah agreed.

"It hurt us, when you were unhappy."

"I know. Why don't you ever go to synagogue services?" Sarah asked.

"I don't want to go alone and Dad won't go."

"I'll come with you if you want."

"I'd like that," replied Sandra.

"I wish we could have had grown up conversations like this when I was still living at home."

"I'm sorry too. I've often thought we should have sent you to Hebrew school and given you a Jewish education."

"You had more pressing things to keep you busy."

"Yes, we did," replied Sandra with a sigh, remembering Brian's short life. Then changing the subject, she added, "You know, Dad and I are very proud you decided to become a nurse."

"Thanks."

"Also, and he won't tell you this himself, but I think he's slowly becoming a 20th century man and beginning to understand why women want equal rights in education and job opportunities."

"About time! It should have happened years ago." Sarah gave her mother a warm hug. "How about this compromise?" she suggested. "We can't marry in a synagogue or a church. So, how about we marry in a hotel and ask a rabbi and a priest to give us their blessings?"

"I think that's a very good idea. Paul's a lovely man and he'll make you a good husband," replied a relieved Sandra.

"I think so too. Let me know when you want to go to a synagogue service. I'm sure Paul will join us."

Chapter 19

When John Cole learned the full truth about Albert and Edith's opposition to Sarah's marriage to Paul, he was so incensed he decided to splash out with money he could ill-afford to pay for a big wedding. He was a man of modest means. Sandra showed little interest in their financial position. So, without discussing the funding for the wedding with her, he met with his bank manager who agreed to advance him an additional £3,000 to the mortgage on their home.

"I'll show 'em," he told Sandra. "I've got some money saved," he lied.

"Have you thought where we can we have the wedding?" Sandra asked.

"I've already booked the Regent Palace Hotel in Piccadilly. I'll show those snobs I'm every bit as good as them."

"It sounds very expensive. Are you sure we can afford it?"

"No problem, I've got plenty of money in the bank. I've been saving up for Sarah's wedding for years," he continued to lie. "You'll see, I'll do you proud."

John's hasty decision would later cost him dear. He was usually a cautious and steady man. Now he had agreed to repay the additional loan over five years, which ultimately proved to be the most tragic decision of his life. Had Sarah known about her father's reckless decision, she would have done everything in her power to discourage him extending his mortgage.

***

"I'm not looking forward to the wedding," said Sarah.

"I am. From the first day I saw you I wanted to marry you. I'm not going to let anything spoil our special day," Paul replied.

"Did your father say anything?"

"You mean, did he apologise? Mum tried to apologise on his behalf. But I told her it wasn't good enough. It's you he should say sorry to, otherwise our relationship is broken."

"He sounded pretty clear he didn't want a Jewess for your wife. I'm dreading seeing them again."

"You'll hardly see them at the wedding. The Regent Palace Hotel is large and will be filled with all our friends and family. Big enough for Dad to ask all his golfing pals."

"Why can't we have a quickie registry office wedding?" suggested Sarah.

"I don't want a hole-in-the-wall wedding. I want a proper reception with family and friends. Anyway, it's too late now to cancel. If we do what you want, it will look like Mum and Dad have won."

"There's another thing. I can't see how Dad can possibly afford to spend so much on our wedding. He always says money's short and they never have proper holidays."

"Has he taken out a loan?"

"I don't think he'd do that. Mum wouldn't want him to have a loan. She hates the thought of being in debt. He claims he's been putting money aside for years to pay for my wedding."

"So, you've got nothing to worry about."

"I suppose …"

"I'm fed up talking parents and money. Did you ask Rona and Jennifer about being bridesmaids?" he asked.

"Yes. They're really pleased. We're going to look for dresses next week."

"Rona must have some good contacts."

"She suggested John Lewis department store. She worked there after leaving the hospital. Don't you remember?"

"No, I never had anything to do with Rona."

"She said John Lewis have a huge selection of brides and bridesmaid dresses. She knows what's in fashion. And if we don't find what we want, the store will make up dresses to order, so we can be original and select our own styles."

"You wouldn't get to wear such elaborate dresses if we got married in a registry office," said Paul.

"That's true."

Chapter 20

The wedding day dawned, and the sun shone.

Sarah was a radiant bride. She wore a stunning satin ivory maxi wedding dress. The front neckline was 'V' shaped. The back had a deep scoop to just above her tiny waist, and finished with a bold organza bow. The soft folds of the satin skirt accentuated her shapely body. A six-foot-long detachable floating organza train trailed behind her, under the watchful eyes of bridesmaids, Jennifer and Rona. The girls wore champagne coloured satin mini dresses and five-inch-high skyscraper boots. The boots were covered in the same champagne satin to match their dresses. All the dresses and accessories were designed by Rona.

At three o'clock the county registrar married Sarah and Paul in the Regent Palace Hotel. At four o'clock a rabbi and a priest jointly blessed their nuptials.

In spite of previous ill-will, the day went smoothly and there was no visible acrimony between the families. Sarah and Paul enjoyed their wedding day. Everything went to plan. The meal was sumptuous, the ball exquisite and the guests had a good time.

Edith and Albert were impressed, and somewhat surprised, John could afford to pay for a wedding in such an illustrious hotel, in the heart of Piccadilly, in London's fashionable West End. The venue was large enough for Albert to invite, and impress, all his golfing friends!

Sandra still wondered how John had managed to save such an enormous amount of money to pay for the hugely expensive wedding. She never asked him how much the function cost. She estimated it to be several thousands of pounds.

The Coles and the Michaels barely spoke a word the entire day. Until they came face to face on the ballroom floor, when Sandra gently tapped Edith on the shoulder to remark,

"John and I are so happy the day's going so well. Don't you think Sarah makes a beautiful bride?"

To which Edith sharply replied, "All brides are beautiful."

The hurtful comment felt like a punch in the stomach. Four little words Sandra would remember for the rest of her life.

***

"That was one amazing wedding. I do love you so much," said Paul. It was their wedding night and he was looking forward to spending it as husband and wife in their new marital home in Edmonton, north London.

"Can you believe it? With all the family problems and everything, we forgot one most important thing?"

"What's that?" asked Sarah.

"Our honeymoon."

"I never thought about it either. When we got engaged, Rona asked me where we were going for our honeymoon, then it went completely out of my mind."

"Well give it some thought," added Paul. "Where would you like to go?"

"We always said we'd go hitch-hiking around Australia before we got married."

"We've grown up a bit since those dreams. I'll take you to Australia for our twenty-fifth wedding anniversary! We've got a house to fix up first."

"I'm keen to start the renovations. Are you sure we can afford a honeymoon?" Sarah asked.

"We can't get married without a honeymoon. The house will still be here when we get back. Leave it with me I'll surprise you. Do we both agree Australia will have to wait?"

Chapter 21

Paris – the city for lovers. Paul discovered a quaint little hotel in the Latin Quarter close to many places of interest, including the Louvre, Notre Dame, Luxemburg Gardens and several museums. He told the proprietor he and his wife were coming to Paris to celebrate their honeymoon and was thrilled to be greeted with a complimentary bottle of champagne on ice and an exotic basket of fruits and chocolates waiting for them on the coffee table.

The honeymooners walked everywhere by day and made love by night. They shopped in tiny boutiques, trawled the markets and dined in romantic restaurants by the side of the River Seine.

Sarah insisted on visiting the upmarket department store, Galleries Lafayette.

"Only to look," she assured Paul. "I imagine this store's like our Harrods."

She gazed at the luxury goods and designer clothing and dreamed of buying something expensive.

"I can see I'll have to wait until you become a rich consultant," she laughed.

Wonderful aromas of baked goods and coffee lured them into the vast food hall. Sarah was bewildered by the abundance of unfamiliar exotic Caribbean and Mediterranean fruits and vegetables she couldn't identify and presumed hadn't yet reached the shores of England.

They had lunch in the store's bistro and ordered French specialties, *soupe à l'oignon (onion soup)* and *croque monsieur* (ham and cheese toasted sandwich).

"Excuse me," said a smartly dressed middle-aged English woman seated at the next table. "I could hear you speaking English. Is this your first trip to Paris?"

"Yes. We're on our honeymoon," replied Paul.

"Congratulations. Paris is my favourite European city and Galleries Lafayette is my favourite store," she replied.

"Yes, Paris is an exciting city. Do you live here?" asked Paul.

"No. I work for a large fashion manufacturer in London and come here twice a year to look for designs I think will work back home. My name is Dolly."

Sarah and Paul introduced themselves and shook hands with Dolly.

"That sounds very exciting. I hope one day I can afford to buy something here," said Sarah.

"British women never understand that buying an expensive suit or coat is an investment that will last them for years," Dolly replied.

"I think that's truer for the mature woman. I like to keep up with the fashion," said Sarah.

"Yes. The mini changed all that for young girls," Dolly agreed, before turning her attention to Paul.

"Are you enjoying your onion soup?"

"It's very good," he nodded.

"You haven't tasted the real *soupe à l'oignon* until you visit Les Halle Markets. The place is a bit shabby, but the soup's to die for. One thing I would never miss when I come to Paris."

"Friends told us about Les Halle. We'll try and go there. Thanks for the tip," replied Sarah.

Dolly handed Paul her business card.

"If you're ever in London or Paris, you can always contact me."

"We live in London. We might just do that," said Sarah.

Dolly stood up to leave.

"Nice to meet you," she said and was gone.

"What an exotic and charming woman," said Paul.

"I might just contact her when we get back. She could be a good business contact for Rona," Sarah added.

After lunch they climbed the art nouveau staircase to the roof terrace and sat on a bench holding hands, imbibing the sights of Paris. The terrace was cooler than the streets below. Sarah began to shiver. Paul took off his jacket to place over her shoulders and pulled her close.

Galleries Lafayette terrace sat high above the chaos of streaming traffic in the streets below. It was a peaceful oasis for the young lovers to just sit and soak up a birds-eye view of the city. In one direction they could see the Opera House, the Eiffel Tower, and Montmartre. In the other direction, the Sacré Coeur.

"I'm glad we came to Paris to celebrate our marriage. It's been more than I ever imagined," he said, adding, "The honeymoon, of course, but also Paris is pretty fantastic."

"It's been magical. I'll remember this for the rest of my life," Sarah replied, kissing him on the lips. "I'm so pleased you persuaded me to have a honeymoon. The house will still be there long after we've gone."

"If we hadn't done it now, we would have had to wait until our children had grown up," said Paul on the flight home.

Chapter 22

24 Magnolia Gardens, Edmonton, north London.

They arrived home from Paris to find the house stripped bare. The builders were way behind schedule. Clearly, they had taken advantage of Sarah and Paul's absence. Floorboards were up for re-plumbing, re-wiring, and the installation of central heating. The house had no inside running water. The only remaining water tap was in the draughty outside toilet.

Paul stood in the hallway looking downcast surveying the chaos.

"I can't let you stay here."

"Oh, yes you can." Sarah was excited to see her new home, regardless of the lack of progress.

She went upstairs.

"Our king-size bed's arrived," she called down excitedly from the bedroom. "I need to make up the bed. Can you get some scissors so I can take off the cellophane?"

"I'm coming up," called Paul from the kitchen. "Did you see the red mosaic terracotta floor tiles in the kitchen?" he asked.

"I haven't been in the kitchen."

"I never knew they were under that ugly lino. I wasn't interested in the house when I was younger."

She followed him downstairs into the kitchen.

"Don't you think the red terracotta tiles are classy? They should polish up a treat," said Paul.

"Why would anyone cover beautiful tiles with linoleum?" asked Sarah.

"Fashion goes in cycles I suppose. I think they're gonna look great."

They cautiously wandered from room to room, avoiding the debris and open floorboards. She picked up a pair of scissors.

"Leave the cellophane on to protect the bed. We can't stay in this mess."

"I am. The builders need shaking up," Sarah replied.

"They've cut off the water."

"There's water in the outside toilet, although it needs a thorough clean. I pulled the chain and it still flushes."

"It must be at least one hundred years old," replied Paul. "I can't wait to get this place cleaned up."

***

There were exciting decisions to be made. They trawled the Oxford Street stores for ideas, and visited the Design Centre in the Haymarket. The early post-war utility fabrics of the 1950s were lacklustre and uninspiring, a far cry from the burgeoning 1960s styles of exotic fabrics in vibrant experimental colours. The new sleek Scandinavian chic furniture was innovative and becoming very fashionable. Heavy dark walnut wood furniture was being replaced with new lighter teak and bleached wood. Sarah decided to blend the traditional with the modern. She chose a fresh primrose yellow kitchen and bathroom and tiled the walls in milky cream.

***

Five generations of the Michaels family had lived at 24 Magnolia Gardens, Edmonton, London, including, Paul's father Albert Michaels. The mid-Victorian house was built in the 1870s. The rooms were large and airy with high ceilings and huge bay windows. It still had the original dado and picture rails in the living rooms and bedrooms, on the ground and first floors, together with the original fireplaces.

Cyril and his wife Alice had three children, Albert, Emily and Dorothy. Albert was their only surviving child. Cyril had happy memories of the house buzzing with children. Before the Second World War he converted the small fifth bedroom into a bathroom. Other than that, the house had scarcely changed since early in the century. There remained a draughty toilet in the back yard, and an asbestos air-raid shelter built during the Second World War at the bottom of the garden.

After Alice died five years earlier, and during his last illness, Cyril's one dream was his beloved home should remain in the family for at least another five generations. Towards the end of his life, he used only two rooms. He closed off the spare rooms, which remained unheated and full of clutter.

Paul was his eldest grandchild and secretively Cyril's favourite. He always believed Paul would make a first-class doctor because he was naturally caring, and in spite of his busy life, Paul regularly visited his elderly grandfather.

Chapter 23

Sarah's relationship with her in-laws had begun badly. Now Edith and Albert weren't going to inherit the house, she was anxious to find a solution to improve their relationship. She waited until after their honeymoon before bringing up the difficult subject.

"I didn't want to put a jinx on our honeymoon, but I want to clear the air with your parents."

"You can't," Paul replied curtly.

"Do you think we could lose the house? I'm worried after we've made all the changes the lawyers will give it to your parents."

"They won't. We've got to carry on as normal. Call their bluff. I had a suspicion Grandfather might change his will. You saw the letter his doctor and Mr Bentwood signed saying he was of sound mind. He was of sound mind, I saw that. I did everything for him. He changed the will after meeting you."

"I'm flattered."

"He told me he liked you and wanted us to have the house. That's all there is to it. My parents shouldn't have taken it for granted."

"They were banking on having the house. Why didn't your grandfather tell them he was leaving it to you?"

"He couldn't bear rows. And they hardly bothered to see him."

"I just want to make things better."

"So you think I should give them the house?"

"No."

"Dad and Grandfather always argued. Trust me, leave well alone. This has nothing to do with you."

"Okay."

"He knew my parents were relying on the house for their retirement. When he was in hospital, he told me he wanted to keep his home in the family and didn't want it sold. He'd lived in the same house his entire life. Can you imagine being born and dying in the same house?"

"No."

"If my parents had been a bit nicer, I expect Grandfather would have left it to them. As it is, they're going to be short when Dad retires. That's their problem."

"I was worried this could come between us."

"I will never forgive how they treated you, not accept you as my wife. Why are we even discussing them? Move on. I have to."

"I still feel responsible for you falling out with your family."

"It's got nothing to do with you. I don't think they would have approved of any girl I married. Not even a nice Catholic one. I've bent over backwards for them. Even your dad came up trumps with the wedding. Dad said how much his golf cronies enjoyed it."

"Do you think they'll get the will revoked?"

"They might try. But I don't think they'll succeed."

"I'd like to give them one more chance to clear the air."

"Dad needs to apologise to you first. In fact, I think he should grovel after everything he said. But that's not in his character. He's a stubborn old mule. I've never known him to say sorry."

"I was thinking we could give them some compensation … how much do you think the house is worth?"

"Why?"

"I want to offer them an olive branch. Prove I'm not just a gold-digger."

"I don't know. Around £20,000. Possibly in good condition, it could fetch £25,000."

"How about we give them £2,000?"

"I haven't got that kind of money sitting in my bank account. No, they burnt their bridges. They'll have to live with it. They were always too busy to go and see him."

"I just want us all to get on."

"Stop repeating yourself. Don't you think I do?" he shouted. "It's their loss. We've just got to get on with our lives. And nothing's going to change until they say sorry."

***

"Sarah, what's the matter? Are you ill?" Paul called from the bedroom.

She slipped back into bed.

"It looks like I brought up all of tonight's Chinese dinner. My stomach and head hurt," she replied. Then, for a second time, she climbed out of bed.

"You better not go in there, it stinks," she said returning to bed.

The next morning Sarah had her head back over the toilet bowl.

"I'm going back to bed. I can't go to work today."

Sarah was two months pregnant.

***

Suzy and Sam's son Stuart was six months old when they moved from Rory's old attic room in 250 Grosvenor Gardens into an apartment to be close to Sarah and Paul's new home, 24 Magnolia Gardens, Edmonton. The girls also negotiated transfers to work in the local hospital.

Meanwhile, Sarah looked after Stuart during the day whilst waiting to give birth. Emma was born in 1965.

Chapter 24

1966

Sandra didn't want to see the film *The Spy Who Came in from the Cold*. She didn't like spy films. She said it was a man's film. She preferred musicals.

That Thursday morning, John left home at eight o'clock, as he had done every morning for the past thirty years, with his briefcase tucked under his arm, sandwiches packed, but today he had nowhere particular to go. Three months earlier, John, who was an accountant for a building company, was sacked from his job. A routine annual audit discovered irregularities. £1,500 was missing.

In order to impress Paul's parents, John had taken out an additional loan of £3,000 on his mortgage to pay for the wedding. At the time he was so desperate for funds he paid scant attention to the small print and the high-interest rate he would have to pay.

Even before he lost his job John struggled to keep up the payments, and now the loan had grown out of control. He kept a letter from the bank in his briefcase threatening to re-possess his house unless he resumed paying the mortgage. But, with no income, and mounting final demand bills landing daily on his doormat, he was quickly running out of time and money.

John was sacked on the spot when he unable to explain to his directors how the money went missing. He was lucky the company decided not to prosecute. And during the entire time Sandra remained oblivious of the situation and her husband's transgressions.

The day of John's demise was a cold and gloomy one. It was the middle of March. Drizzly rain. Not sufficient to open an umbrella, but enough to drench him. He wandered aimlessly around the shops in Harrow with nowhere to go. By ten o'clock his bones were beginning to ache. He walked into Debenhams department store to buy a cup of tea and nibble on his sandwiches.

The Spy Who Came in from the Cold was showing at the Odeon Cinema. John counted his pennies and bought a ticket. He had read the book, and the film was well-reviewed in the papers. Now he wanted to see the film. With just a few people in the audience for the early screening, the cinema felt vast and unwelcoming. But with the rain now bucketing down outside, this was somewhere to keep warm and dry.

When the film finished, John silently left his seat and went to the men's room. He locked himself inside a stall and used the toilet. He then calmly reached into his pocket for a new packet of razor blades, peeled off the paper, and cleanly cut the arteries on his wrists. He screamed with panic as he watched his blood drip from his veins and escape under the door. John passed out and hit his head on the stall door as he fell.

He lay motionless. His blood dripped soundlessly under the door and out towards a drain gulley under the washbasins.

A twelve-year-old boy walked into the mess and screamed when he saw blood flowing from under the stall door. John was lying lifeless in a pool of blood. The manager called the emergency services, but by the time the police and ambulance had arrived John had passed away.

***

"A policeman said they'll have to be an autopsy and an inquest. Will they expect me to go?" Sandra spoke in a monotone voice. Sarah couldn't be sure it was her mother speaking.

"Mum, is that you? What the hell are you talking about? Where are you?" she screamed down the phone.

"It's your dad … it happened in Harrow. That's why they took him to Harrow Hospital. A policeman came and took me to the hospital in a car. They're taking me home now."

"What's happened? Where's Dad?"

"He's been in an accident."

"A traffic accident?" asked Sarah.

"He was dead when they got him to the hospital." Sandra avoided telling Sarah the full truth.

"Oh, my God. Go straight home. I'll meet you there. Grab some clothes and I'll take you home with me," Sarah instructed.

Sandra wasn't listening.

"I don't understand why he was in Harrow. I thought he went to work as usual this morning. I'll have to tell his boss tomorrow," Sandra droned on.

"Listen to me, Mum. I'm coming over to get you. You can stay with us. Don't worry about Dad's boss."

Sarah panicked. What to do first? She asked a neighbour to look after Emma and Stuart then she drove to her mother's home.

***

A young policewoman was comforting Sandra in her front lounge. The whole scenario felt unreal. John had left home, as usual, to catch the eight-thirty train that morning, and now he was dead. It all seemed implausible, dreamlike. Sarah pinched herself. If she was dreaming, then this was some gruesome nightmare. She suffered nightmares when she was stressed. Soon she'll wake up.

"What happened?" Sarah screamed.

"They couldn't do anything. He was dead when they got him to hospital," Sandra was mumbling through a curtain of tears.

"Did he have an accident?" Sarah was devastated.

Sandra was trying her best to soften the ultimate horrendous news of her husband's death, but she could barely understand the grim event herself. The ghastly truth of John's suicide. She painfully choked out the words.

"He seemed perfectly normal this morning. I knew he had problems at work. He told me last week. But he didn't seem depressed. They found him in the cinema toilets in Harrow ... very odd, being an ordinary workday. He never said he wasn't going to work this morning ... and you know your father never misses a day's work."

Sarah listened anxiously, trying to piece together what had happened.

"The policeman said he slashed his wrists in the gentlemen's toilets."

"Oh my God."

"He cut his veins and there was a lot of blood. A young lad saw blood running under the stall and called security. Dad was already dead when they got him to the hospital. He cut his veins and there was a lot of blood."

"I never knew he was so unhappy," Sarah wailed. "Did he say where he was going this morning?"

"I thought he just went to work as usual. As I said, he told me there were problems at work, but quite honestly I didn't understand."

"It's horrible to think he was so unhappy and couldn't tell you."

"I feel so ashamed. What are people going to think? Am I that bad he had to bottle up his misery and not tell me? What kind of wife am I? If it's suicide they won't bury him in consecrated ground in the cemetery. Where will he end up?"

"It's too soon to think about all that. Would you like another cup of tea?" Sarah put a comforting arm around her mother's shoulder.

Sandra shook her head.

"I left Emma and Stuart with a neighbour. I must ring Paul and ask him to collect the children. Mum, why don't you have a lie-down?"

"Your mum's doctor's already been and left her some sleeping pills and she's got an appointment to see him tomorrow at four o'clock," said the policewoman.

"You should take one and rest on your bed," suggested Sarah.

"I'm not going to bed now."

"Then take one tonight before you go to bed," replied Sarah.

"No. You know I don't like pills … don't you think it's a coincidence?"

"What, Mum?"

"This lovely young police lady is also called Emma."

"Would you like another cup of tea, Emma?" Sarah asked.

Emma smiled, "No, thank you."

"Mum, do you want to come home with me tonight? Or, if you prefer, I can stay here. Either way, I want to go with you to the doctor tomorrow."

"You go home. I'm better off in my own bed."

"I'm not happy leaving you here alone. I'd rather you come back with me."

"I'll be fine. Don't worry. I'll do what you said, and take a sleeping pill."

"Okay. I'll be back first thing in the morning," replied Sarah and gave her mother another comforting hug.

Chapter 25

The following weeks brought more bad news. The official inquest concluded John had committed suicide. He died as a result of self-harm. He had slashed the veins in his wrists and taken his own life.

Another bombshell landed when John's boss told Sarah he had sacked her father for stealing. John couldn't afford the extra payments on the additional £3,000 bank loan. He had originally agreed to pay off the debt over five years. When he fell into difficulties the bank manager agreed to extend the loan to ten years. But with no income, and his savings depleted, his payments dried up.

John never confessed to Sandra he pilfered the money, and was in denial over losing his job. For three long months he followed his usual routine. Up at seven o'clock, prepared his sandwiches and caught the eight-thirty train to the West End. This was a tragic deception. John then walked the streets of Harrow, rain or shine, and returned home at six o'clock in the evening. Sandra was trusting about their financial situation. She was never curious. Catastrophically, over the past months, she had remained that way, oblivious and ignorant of his desperate state of mind.

***

John kept his study door locked and the keys to the room and filing cabinet in his briefcase at all times.

"I need to get into the study to find the will," said Paul.

"Do you have the key to Dad's study?" asked Sarah.

Sandra looked shaken.

"I think he kept them in his briefcase. You can't open his filing cabinet."

"Why not?"

"It's got all his private things in it," she replied.

"Precisely. He won't need them anymore," Paul replied sarcastically.

"No, I suppose …" Her voice drifted off, trancelike.

"The policeman gave me his briefcase. But there weren't any keys," she continued.

"I assume the will is in his study," said Paul.

"I never went in there."

"Then I'll have to break the lock," replied Paul.

"Can't we get a locksmith?" asked Sandra.

"Not worth paying for one. There's no reason to keep the room locked now," Paul replied.

John's study was a drab little room with just one desk a chair and a filing cabinet. He kept it scrupulously clean and his private papers securely locked inside the filing cabinet. Nobody was allowed into his study. When the house was recently decorated, the painters were told to stay out.

"Just as I expected, the filing cabinet's locked too," Paul was despairing.

"Is there a will?" asked Sarah.

Sandra looked agitated.

"If he made a will, it should be in there," said Sarah.

"We don't even know if he made a will," replied a frustrated Paul.

"He never said. I did think about asking him sometimes, but I never got round to it," replied Sandra apologetically.

"What kind of man was he?" Paul mumbled, away from Sandra's earshot.

After Paul struggled to break the lock on the filing cabinet the third bombshell hit the family. The will was in a folder stuffed with final demands. Bank statements deep in the red, a statement for a compound interest loan of £6,000 and multiple letters from the bank. One stating the house was going to be repossessed. Sandra had two weeks to move out. The bailiff was coming in two weeks to lock her out.

"Did you know about this?" Paul was getting more exasperated by the minute.

Sandra looked through the documents.

"I don't understand."

"Your house is about to be repossessed." Paul was now angry. "Didn't he tell you anything?"

"He seemed a bit stressed sometimes. He never told me anything about money. I just don't know," Sandra burst into tears. "What's going to happen? What am I going to do?"

"You are going to lose the house, that's what's going to happen. Why the hell didn't he sell it and pay off his debts? Do you have your own bank account?" asked Paul.

"No," she replied.

"I suggest you start packing," said Paul. "I've got a friend whose company is transferring him to Germany for a year. He's looking to rent out his flat. It's tiny, but it will be a stop-gap until you get yourself sorted. The only problem is it's in south London. I hope you have at least some equity left in the house to buy a small flat. In the meantime, I'll do whatever I can to help you."

Chapter 26

Dear Mum and Dad   17th August 1966
I expect this letter will come as a big surprise. I hope you are both keeping well. It's just we haven't seen you since our wedding and I wanted to tell you, you are now proud grandparents to our beautiful daughter Emma. Sarah and I are doing fine but hate what happened to cause such bad feelings.
Can we talk? I'm very worried about you. Both Sarah and I would like you to come for tea and see your beautiful new granddaughter.
Love, Paul

Dear Paul,   25th August 1966
Your letter was a surprise, but I'm glad to hear you're doing well. I'm thrilled you have a daughter. I would love to meet Emma. You know how stubborn your father is. He's still angry. He read your letter and I'm not sure if he will agree to see you. I'm so happy you wrote to me.
Love, Mum

Paul looked down and hesitated. "This is difficult. I've done something that might make you very angry."

"Spit it out." Sarah looked alarmed. "What have you done?"

"I wrote to Mum and Dad and told them about Emma and invited them for tea."

"I'm not angry. Did they reply?"

"Mum wrote, saying she would like to come, but she's not sure about Dad."

"I think you did right. It's going to be difficult, but you did right."

He leaned over to kiss her.

"You know, you're a wonderful girl. You don't bear grudges."

"I don't know about that. But I do hate bad feelings, and your mother isn't that bad. If your father doesn't come, it's his funeral."

Paul hesitated. "There's something else I want to ask you. If you don't agree, just tell me to shut up."

"What's that?"

"Do you remember when you suggested we give my parents some money from the inheritance? At the time I thought you were crazy, but now I'm earning more money, I feel we could share some of it. How would you feel if I gave them an allowance each month to make up for their loss?"

"It's up to you, it's your money. When I suggested it, I thought your dad would apologise for all the hateful things he said. I didn't think for one minute they'd shut themselves out of our life."

"I agree. But I want to help Mum. I don't want her going short of anything. It's because of her I'm trying to patch things up with Dad. He's a stubborn old fool and he'll probably be too proud to take any of the money anyway."

"Make the offer and see what he says. I'd like to help your mum. And I want her to see Emma."

"I'm glad I got this off my chest. I've been worried to speak to you about it because I know how horrible they were to you."

"I'll never forgive him. But they're still your parents," Sarah added.

***

Edith agreed to the visit. Albert was still deciding whether to join her. Sarah cleaned the house until it gleamed and baked a Victoria sponge cake and chocolate brownies. Paul told her Edith would appreciate home baked cakes. Emma was just walking and looked adorable in her new dress bought for the occasion. The table was laid and Sarah panicked.

"Is your dad coming?" she asked Paul.

"I don't know."

The doorbell rang. Sarah tweaked her hair and makeup in the bedroom mirror then rushed down the stairs.

Albert stepped into the hallway ahead of Edith who trailed behind. His eyes darted around the hall and living room while he silently assessed the changes.

"This is Emma," said Paul, holding her up and offering her to Edith. Emma whimpered and Edith declined.

"She's still a bit sleepy from her afternoon nap," said Sarah apologetically. "You can hold her later."

"How was the journey?" asked Paul.

"The traffic on the North Circular Road is always busy. Everywhere you go there are bloody road works and more road works. Why do they always dig up roads at the weekends?" Albert grumbled.

"Because offices are closed and traffic's lighter over the weekend."

"They forget about all those shoppers clogging up the roads," Albert added.

'More people have cars. You can't stop them using them. I'm sure you're both be ready for some refreshments after your journey. Sarah's been busy baking."

Paul sensed this was going to be a difficult reunion. Sarah called from the kitchen, "Tea or coffee?"

"We like builders' tea, strong and hot," replied Edith.

Albert looked around the living room. "I can see you've made lots of changes."

"Sarah's in charge. She's very skilful. I'll give you a tour while she makes the tea," replied Paul.

"I think it's been over-modernized," Albert growled as they returned to the living room. "It's a 1870s house which she's tried to transform into the 1960s and it doesn't work."

"I think we've been very sympathetic to the period. Of course, we've got new appliances and central heating. We've taken down dado rails and taken out some of the fireplaces, but all in all I'm happy with the refurbishments."

"I think you've done a good job," said Edith trying to clear the air.

To fill an awkward silence, Paul said, "We like it. Sarah's taking an art class on Wednesday evenings. She's learning a lot about co-ordinating colour schemes and modern decorating materials. The teacher was very complimentary. He said she's got a good eye for design, and it's a shame her talent hadn't been discovered at school."

"How does she manage when you're at the hospital?" asked Edith.

"Sarah looks after her friend Sam's baby during the day, and she helps Sarah out when I'm not around."

"I'm glad she's got support. Looking after a baby is hard work," Edith replied.

They seated themselves around the dining room table. Emma was already in her highchair. Sarah brought in the tea.

"There's something I've been wanting to discuss with you for some time. It was originally Sarah's suggestion and I've given it a lot of thought," began Paul. "Because you were so disappointed you didn't inherit the house, we would like to make you an offer."

"What kind of offer? You've already got the house," said Albert.

"Now I'm earning more money, we can afford to give you an allowance each month to make up for any shortfall in your pension."

"Shortfall!" yelled Albert. "What the f...k are you talking about?"

"We know you were banking on getting the house, and we don't want you to struggle ..."

"Struggle!" Albert shouted. "That's a damned insult. Did you hear that Edith? They want to give us *an* allowance!"

"I'm sorry if I used the wrong words. It's just we don't want you to go short of money."

"Short of money. You really don't know, do you?"

"Know what!"

"I thought as much. I thought you asked us over here to discuss my lawyer's letter. I've been pestering that man for weeks, but he still proceeds like a snail. He thinks I've got grounds to get my father's will revoked."

"I haven't received any letter. Everything I said today was in good faith."

"I've never been so insulted in the whole of my life!" Albert yelled. "Come, Edith."

***

Paul attempted to put the disastrous tea party to the back of his mind. The offer had misfired and Albert had other ideas. He was taking the legal route to gain possession of his father Cyril's home.

The following week the unpleasant telephone call came from Edith presenting her well-prepared speech.

"I'm so happy for you. You're a clever man. You've now got a beautiful home and a beautiful baby. But you'll never understand how much you insulted your father. You said it was your wife's idea to give us *an allowance* when it wasn't her money to give. If she wasn't Jewish, she'd be a lovely girl. I know her race is clever with money, but I'll never understand their mentality."

For a second time Paul decided it was wiser not to share with Sarah the latest unpleasant conversation with his mother.

Chapter 27

The unexpected telephone call from Edith came three months later.

"Sarah my dear, is that you?"

Sarah shivered in fear. The voice sounded familiar. Could it be Edith Michaels?

"Mrs Michaels?"

"Yes, my dear. Call me Edith. How are you, my dear?"

"Fine." Sarah was stunned.

"I was wondering if we can meet for coffee. There are important things I want to discuss."

"I'm not sure Paul will agree to meet you."

"Paul can be as stubborn as his father. It's you I want to talk to first; woman to woman so to speak. I'm sorry our relationship began so badly and I want to make it up with you. Also, Albert's had a very bad year health-wise, which I think you and Paul should know about."

Sarah was shocked and could only reply, "Oh."

"Bring Emma. I'd love to get to know her better. How about next Thursday morning at eleven o'clock at Maxie's Coffee House? It's only a few streets from you."

"I know Maxie's."

"I've got important things to tell you."

"Okay …"

"Good, that's settled. I'm looking forward to seeing you again, my dear. It'll be easier to talk without the men around. Albert's got health problems he doesn't even know he's got. Of course, that doesn't excuse his behaviour. See you next Thursday."

"We'll be there," replied Sarah. Still shaking, but also feeling vindicated. She wondered what important things Edith wanted to tell her, other than Albert's deteriorating health.

***

Edith was already seated at a corner table when Sarah wheeled Emma into Maxie's Coffee House. A gigantic teddy bear, in a gigantic paper bag, sat under the table awaiting Emma's arrival. Edith enthusiastically whipped out the bear, which was larger than Emma herself, and placed it on the little girl's lap then bent down to kiss her granddaughter. Simultaneously, the bear fell sideways to the floor and Edith lost her balance, tripped over the bear and left an unsightly smudge of bright red lipstick on Emma's cheek.

Sarah looked on with surprise at her mother-in-law's ungainly entrance.

"Are you okay?"

"Yes." Edith took off her coat and smoothed down her dress.

"The bear's incredible. Thank you ever so much," said Sarah breathlessly. She whipped out a handkerchief and wiped Emma's face.

"Emma looks delightful. I hope she likes it."

"She loves teddy bears."

"Perfect." There was a short pause before Edith continued, "She looks so pretty. How old is she now?"

"Nearly two."

"How are you, my dear?" Edith asked.

"Fine."

"And Paul?"

"He's fine," replied Sarah.

"That's good. Would you like some food? They make a good toasted sandwich?" asked Edith.

"It's a bit early. Just a coffee please."

"Would Emma like something?"

"I have a drink for her."

Edith ordered.

"You're looking very well, my dear. Is the hospital keeping Paul busy?"

"He's always busy."

"I've come with an olive branch, my dear," said Edith, with a condescending edge to her voice. "We were wrong. We are very happy to see Paul has a good marriage and a beautiful baby daughter."

"You hurt Paul very badly."

"The world's changed so much since the war," replied Edith.

Sarah was confused.

"What's the war got to do with it? That was twenty years ago."

"I feel very ashamed. We always describe ourselves as *pre-war people*, which is very silly. We should have moved with the times," said Edith.

"Yes, you should have. You also upset my parents."

Edith ignored Sarah's remark and continued, "Albert's ill. He's always been highly strung with a short fuse, but he's got much worse. It's creeping dementia. He gets very frustrated when he can't do things and quickly loses his temper."

"I'm sorry. When was it diagnosed?"

"About a year ago. He began behaving strangely around the time you got married. At first he kept losing things and got angry. He accused me of hiding things. I was at my wits end and I didn't know what to do."

"Why didn't you tell Paul? He's a doctor."

"I was embarrassed, and Dad had caused you too much trouble."

"Paul could have helped you find a good doctor," Sarah added.

"I told him but he never listens and I didn't want to trouble Paul."

After an embarrassing pause in the conversation, Edith continued, "You mentioned your parents. How are they?"

"My father died and Mum had to sell the house."

"I'm very sorry."

"That's okay," replied Sarah.

She didn't want to discuss her parents.

"Tell Mr Michaels if he needs any help he can rely on Paul."

"You're a good girl. I can see now Paul's a lucky man. I didn't tell you because our relationship began so badly ... and it seems you had a lot going on."

"Paul needs to know his father's ill."

Emma began pulling on Sarah's skirt.

"Mummy biscuit. Mummy drinky."

"You'll be pleased to hear I've persuaded Albert to drop the claim to revoke Cyril's will. He was very angry when the house went to you. But things have moved on, and now with his illness ... I want an easy life ... although it's always good to have more money we're not short and Albert's got a good pension from his company," Edith said with a weak smile.

"Paul will be pleased."

Edith then said something so utterly bizarre, which, earlier in their relationship would have felt like a stab through Sarah's heart. Edith described how she was brought up in a white middle class Catholic bubble, utterly oblivious, and totally unconcerned, about anyone who wasn't like herself. She confessed she had never been curious to learn about other religions and cultures. The words were difficult for Sarah to hear, but she recognised this was her mother-in-law's way of making an apology.

Edith continued, "Then the war changed everything. People are very different now. I must be honest, I was very blinkered when Paul brought you to meet us. I could never have imagined he would marry a Jewess. But now the country's being flooded with people like you and other foreigners I've got to move on and be more opened minded and change with the times."

Without a hint of visible resentment Sarah boldly replied,

"Yes, you must. It was a hard lesson for Paul and me to learn. You rejected me out of hand, without knowing me, just because I'm Jewish. I look like an English woman. I have white skin. I was born in England, only I have a different religion to you. I'm human and I hurt just like you, but I'm the wrong religion. Regardless of skin colour and religion, we all want to be loved and respected for what we are."

The words spilled out. Sarah wondered whether she had said too much and feared how Edith would reply. But she smiled and reached for Sarah's hand.

"I feel humbled. I wish we could begin again. Can we be friends?"

Sarah thought for a moment. This had certainly been an emotional meeting. For Paul's sake she nodded. She lifted Emma from her pushchair and sat her on Edith's lap.

"What would you like Emma to call you? Do you want to be called granny, grandma or nanny?"

Edith wiped away her tears, and kissed Emma on the cheek for a second time.

"I don't care. Whatever you say. I'm just so happy to be with you both."

"Granny it is," said Sarah. "Emma, give Granny Edith a kiss."

Chapter 28

"Did you get to see my mum today?" asked Sarah.

Paul was in south London this morning to deliver a paper to a British Medical Association conference in a hotel very close to his mother-in-law, Sandra's flat.

"I went during my lunch break. She was pleased to see me. Although I should have phoned first because she was still in her dressing gown when I got there at two o'clock."

"She depresses me when we speak."

"I asked her over this weekend. Emma can cheer her up. She said she'd come, but won't stay over because she prefers her own bed."

"I got a telling off because I've only been to the flat once in three months," said Sarah.

"She still blames me for sending her to south London. But after losing the house, I had to act fast. We had no choice."

"You did your best," Sarah replied.

"We've got to move her closer to us. We can't leave her languishing in Clapham. The flat's very tiny and dark. It's okay if you're out at work all day. But she never goes out … you wouldn't like it."

"Can she afford to buy a small flat near us?" Sarah asked.

"We won't know until probate's sorted. It depends on your dad's debts. I hope she's left with some equity in the house to buy a small flat."

"When will you know?"

"Probate's always long-winded. I'll call the lawyer again to see what's holding things up."

"How was the conference?" asked Sarah.

"Good. My paper seemed to go down well. I had some good feedback."

***

With Sandra's problems still whizzing around in her head, Sarah decided to wait before telling Paul about her meeting with Edith.

"You won't believe this."

"What's that?" replied Paul, his mind full of other things.

"I met your mum for coffee."

"How come?" Sarah now had his full attention.

"She phoned and asked to meet me for coffee and wanted to see Emma."

"What did she want?"

"She apologised for your father's behaviour. She excused it by saying he's not well. The bad news is he's recently been diagnosed with dementia."

"That's no reason to be so aggressive."

"She said it was the dementia talking."

"I thought he wasn't well. I'm sorry to hear the bad news," replied Paul.

"I said you'd do whatever you can to help. And ... the good news is ... they're dropping the case. They're not going ahead to try and get your Grandpa Cyril's will revoked."

"Maybe now they'll let us help them financially."

"She made it clear they're not short of money. Your dad's got a good pension."

"That's a relief."

"She gave Emma that enormous teddy bear. Remember? You asked me where she got it. I said it was a hand-me-down from a friend," said Sarah.

"You've done well," replied Paul. "Somehow you've discovered her softer side."

"I don't know about that. She's an oddball. She said some very strange things about being *pre-war people* and never knowing, or mixing with anyone from other cultures."

"It was like that before the war. People didn't mix. My mother has always been a snob. She likes to think she's a pre-war aristocrat. She used to imagine herself as one of the Mitford sisters. Get her in to conversation about the Duchess of Windsor and she'll tell you how badly the royal family treated her."

Sarah laughed. "She reminds me of the Duchess of Windsor, skinny and haughty."

"Believe me, she's got nothing to be snooty about, her parents were working class. I can't imagine where she got her airs and graces."

"She told me they don't like change. They thought the world was a better place before the war. In an odd kind way, I began to understand her a bit more."

"My father has always been a narrow-minded racist."

"Isn't there anything nice you can say about them?"

"You shouldn't have gone without me."

"I'm glad I did. You wouldn't have been so tolerant. Your mum did say one nice thing. She's happy you and I have a good marriage and she was clearly pleased to see Emma. And don't forget she took the trouble to buy that huge teddy for Emma."

"How was it left?" Paul asked.

"We didn't arrange to meet again, if that's what you mean."

"I'm sorry Dad's got dementia. I'll speak to her and see if she needs any help, if that's what she wants, but other than that our life has moved on and I don't want to get sucked into their narrow little golf club world. I've got a lot going on at the moment and there's something more important I need to discuss with you. I don't want my parents adding their pennies worth and trying to destroy us for a second time."

"You won't see them?"

"I guess the answer is no. I'm not going to let them bully me ever again. We have our little family. As far as I'm concerned, they've burnt their bridges. I've cut them out of our lives. If they need me professionally, I'll help them, but I want to keep them away from you."

"I almost felt sorry for her. She's lived such a sheltered life. She admitted they had never met a Jew and didn't like change. I think your mother can now see how they messed up. Shouldn't we give them another chance?"

"I can't believe you said that. They're toxic. I think they want to destroy our marriage. I'll deal with them."

Chapter 29

"Emma and I took Mum out for lunch today. She said she doesn't know a soul and hardly ever goes out," said Sarah.

"She must've been pleased to see you."

"She said we brightened up her day. She's coming over again next weekend. Is that okay?"

"Of course. You see what I mean about the flat. We've got to move her out."

"She asked about probate. She wants to make plans to move."

"The lawyer should finally have the paperwork ready for signature next week. I'm very annoyed it's taken so long. I suppose he has to justify the fee."

"Can she afford to buy a one-bed flat closer to us?" asked Sarah.

"The lawyer told me something in confidence, so don't say anything to mum until we know for sure. He said your father's debts pretty much wiped out the equity in the house. I don't think she'll be able to afford to buy anything. One positive is, your father had a small life assurance policy, but it's not enough for her to continue living independently until she gets her state pension. And if your mum continues to rent, the money will soon run out."

"She'll be devastated. What can she do?"

"How old is she?"

"Fifty-five."

"She can't claim her state pension until she's sixty. She'll have to find a job."

"She's not trained for anything."

"If things are as bad as I think they are, there's only one other possibility. It's more a business proposition, and I don't even know if you'll agree ... because I know your relationship hasn't always been the best. But ever since your dad died, I've been giving it a lot of thought. What if your mum comes and lives with us? This house is too big for us. We can convert the upstairs into a fully self-contained flat. What do you think?" asked Paul.

"You're not serious?"

"Very serious, she could live here on your father's life assurance policy, without getting a job, until she reaches pension age. I won't expect her to pay rent. Otherwise, she's destitute."

"That's it."

"She won't find worthwhile employment at her age without training. See what she thinks about my idea at the weekend. If she comes to live with us, we can still have our privacy and she can have hers. She can even have a lock on her door if she wants and help you with Emma and Stuart."

"What about your parents. What if they find out?"

"Forget about my parents. This idea has been bubbling about in my mind ever since your father died. As soon as I looked through his papers, the day after he died, and saw all the creditors and letters from the bank, I've been searching for a solution. Give it some thought. It could work well."

It was a risky offer from Paul, given the fact that Sarah and her mother Sandra were both strong characters and still argued over petty differences.

***

Sarah always believed marriage was a partnership. With neither partner having complete control. When she was a teenager, she accused her mother of being timid because she resented her father's dominance. A wife's sole job was to please her husband. That was her father's mantra. Years later she realised how wrong she had been to judge her parents' lifestyle, and find fault with something she didn't understand.

Sandra was shaken when she learned about the state of her finances. There was little equity remaining from the sale of her home. No money to buy her dream flat. However, Paul explained if she moved in with them, she could live on John's small life assurance pension for five years until she reached retirement age of sixty. The money would meet her needs, but no more.

***

Sandra was pleased to leave the dingy little flat in south London and move in with her family. After John died, she dreamed of buying her own flat. But that wasn't going to happen. She insisted on paying towards the costs of the renovation work and enjoyed shopping trips with Sarah to choose furniture and fittings. But as soon as Sandra moved into Sarah and Paul's home she gradually went into a spiral of deep depression.

Sarah's life also changed the day her mother moved into her newly converted upstairs flat. Sarah had imagined coffee mornings and trips to the shops and park with her mother and Emma and Stuart. But Sandra just craved peace and quiet and wallowed in her own company. She was content to spend entire days alone upstairs, even refusing to join the family at mealtimes.

"What am I doing wrong? I ask her down for coffee with the children, but she just wants to stay up there," she asked Paul one morning.

"Sounds to me she's still mourning her past life," he replied. "Be patient. It's hard to lose your husband, especially the way your father died and lose your home. Give her time to settle. Things will get better."

Chapter 30

"How's your mum settling in?" asked Sam.

"Confidentially, not good," replied Sarah.

"When I last saw her, she was so excited about the move. What's happened?"

"It all gone sour. She loved the idea of coming here. We had lots of fun buying things for the flat. But now she's moved in, she stays upstairs and wants to be by herself. I don't think she'll ever get over losing her home and Dad leaving her almost penniless. Even Emma doesn't seem to cheer her up."

"She's got too much time to think," replied Sam.

"I can't do anything right and she's bringing us all down with her."

"Time will heal. She'll soon see how lucky she is to have you and Paul."

"I'm beginning to think we should never have asked her to live with us."

"What does Paul say?"

"It was his idea in the first place. He says she's still grieving," Sarah replied.

"You've got to be patient."

"She bottles everything up. It would help if she would talk to me."

"Would she consider bereavement counselling? They have good counsellors in the hospital." suggested Sam.

"Paul reckons she should get herself a part-time job, it would keep her mind off things and meet new people, but she hasn't worked for years."

"She's still very fragile. She was so dependent on your dad and after the way he died …" Sam trailed off. "Have you thought about going back to work?"

"Maybe when Emma goes to school. We're lucky we don't have a mortgage or rent to pay. But we could certainly do with the extra money after all the spending on the flat conversion."

Sarah hadn't intended to discuss her mother with Sam. They would have to work through the problem. Theoretically, she had everything she ever dreamed of – a husband whom she loved dearly, and who loved her, a beautiful daughter and a lovely home they could never have afforded to buy.

But the ghost of Paul's grandfather, Cyril, still hung heavily over her. She had lately come to the conclusion that living in his house rent-free was a high price to pay for falling out with her in-laws. There were times she wondered whether Paul would be amenable to selling the house, splitting the proceeds with his parents, and buying something smaller. But in her heart of hearts, she knew Paul would never agree to give up the house that had been in his family for five generations. And it wouldn't solve the problem of her mother living upstairs. Grown up life was complicated.

"The house is looking great. I didn't know you were so artistic," said Sam, breaking the silence. "I don't know how you manage to juggle caring for the children and decorating."

"Decorating's very therapeutic. I do it mostly in the evenings and weekends." Sarah smiled. "I love my Wednesday evening art class. I'm learning lots about modern products and new ideas about colour co-ordination and fabrics. You'd be amazed at the colours they're mixing together now. Colours we would never have dreamed of using together years ago."

"Sounds exciting. A wonderful way to take your mind off babies," joked Sam.

"My teacher said I've got a flair with colours."

"Anything's easier than nursing."

"I still love nursing. But I must say, I was chuffed when he said that," Sarah replied.

"Have you ever thought about becoming an interior designer? You could be your own boss and work your own hours."

"That's not a bad idea. But at the moment I've got things to sort out at home," replied Sarah.

"If you're successful you can earn pot loads of money."

"Maybe."

"I was wondering, with your mum, and everything, if it's still okay for you to look after Stuart?"

"Stuart's family. See how well they play together."

"Let me know if things get too tough."

"We love having Stuart. I promise I won't be shy if things change."

"Can I go upstairs and say hello to your mum?"

"She's at the hairdressers. She'll be back soon." Sarah paused then continued, "Mum and Dad were an odd couple. Dad dominated her. He always chose things for the home. I don't think she had much of a say about anything. They never went to the cinema or the theatre or have friends over."

"That was the war generation. Things are more equal now. Your mum's still young enough to get married again. She's still an attractive woman. How old is she?" Sam asked.

"Fifty-five. Nah, she's too sexually repressed. But stranger things have happened. Would you like to see her flat?"

"If she doesn't mind."

"No. She's proud of it and her new furniture. Come up now before she gets back from the hairdressers."

Sandra was very house-proud. A place for everything, and everything in its place. The walls were off-white. The lounge furniture was stylishly modern teak *'G' Plan*. The fitted cupboards in the kitchen were bright orange. The smell of fresh paint and newly laid carpet still lingered.

"It's lovely. I never thought she'd choose such modern furniture. When things settle, she's going to be very happy here," said Sam."

"I hope so."

"One thing occurs to me. If you've only got two bedrooms, what happens if you have another baby, and it's a boy?"

"We're not planning on having another baby. But if we do, we have a huge attic and, when Paul becomes a rich consultant, we can build up there, like lots of the neighbours around here have done."

There were footsteps on the stairs. Sandra stood on the landing smiling.

"Hello Sam," she said. "How nice to see you."

"I hope you don't mind, Sarah's been showing me around your beautiful flat."

"Of course not. Paul and Sarah have done a wonderful job, don't you think?"

"I think it's brilliant," replied Sam.

"Mum, your hair looks lovely," said Sarah.

"Thank you, my dear."

"I hope you have many, many years of health and happiness living here," said Sam.

"All thanks to my wonderful daughter and son-in-law," Sandra smiled.

Chapter 31

The first time Sarah saw George she was with Paul in the DIY store, Homes-Are-Us. The humongous stores were emerging in most towns and cities in post-war Britain to satisfy the appetites of the new middle-class homeowners. Sarah was looking for paint to match her newly ordered curtains.

"I'll meet you in the paint department," Paul said and went off to buy a new toolbox. Sarah felt lost clutching her small swatch of material.

"Can I help you, madam?" The young man smiled and gave a familiar wink.

"I'm looking for the paints."

"No trouble. This is your lucky day. Come with me. I work in paints."

"Thank you very much." Sarah felt her face blush. Had he just made a pass? Her heart skipped a beat. It seemed a long time since a man had found her attractive. Not since before her pregnancy. But that was probably her fault. Paul frequently told her to buy pretty clothes. But what was the point when she was at home all day looking after children?

***

The following week Sarah was back alone in Homes-Are-Us, ostensibly to look for light fittings, but also to search for the handsome young man who had served her in the paint department the week before. She spotted him talking to a customer. He caught her eye, waved and mouthed the word *wait*. She moved further down the aisle.

"How can I help you today," he asked.

"I'm looking for light fittings," she replied.

"Aisle 20. I'll be over to help when I'm finished with my customer."

He joined her in aisle 20.

"They all look lovely. I can't decide what to buy," said Sarah, after the young man had taken the trouble to demonstrate most of the stock.

"I'll take some light bulbs and come back later," she added apologetically.

"No problem. I have a break in ten minutes. Would you like to join me for a coffee next door?" he asked. And that was the beginning of something that would change Sarah's life forever.

***

George was twenty-two years old with a slim athletic body and black curly hair. He told Sarah he was re-taking his *'A' level* exams and hoped to go to university to study engineering. He described himself as a *late developer* and was now ready to better himself. His parents divorced when he was ten and he shared a flat with his friend Benny.

Their first date was a trip to the cinema. George chose the film *Alfie* in which young actor Michael Caine plays a roguish young man addicted to young women.

"Did you enjoy the film?" asked George as they were exiting the cinema.

"I thought the film was going to be a comedy. I like Michael Caine but the back street abortion scene was barbaric," Sarah replied.

"I agree."

"I feel particularly sensitive because I'm a nurse and I see what happens when back street abortions go wrong."

"You've seen the grisly results."

"You could say the film is topical, with the controversial abortion act going through Parliament," she said.

"Would you like it passed?"

"Of course. There are too many butchered abortions and young girls and women dying," Sarah replied with some emotion.

"We should have seen another film. I never intended to get so serious on our first date."

"No. I'm glad I saw it."

"Let me cheer you up. Will you come back to mine for dinner?"

"I've had a lovely time, but I must get home."

"What about just coffee?" he pleaded.

"I'm married and got a baby. I've never gone out with another man before."

"When I saw you in the store you looked so miserable. You know you're very beautiful when you laugh."

"I've never been unfaithful. Thank you for this evening. I must go."

"When you smile you look like a teenager. How old are you?"

"Twenty-six," Sarah replied.

George reached for her hand. "Come back to mine for dinner. I'm not a bad cook you know. I'm good with chicken."

"I can't believe I'm doing this. I don't even know you," she said, limply following him.

"You trusted me in the coffee house the other day. You can trust me now. I don't bite," he said with a twinkle.

George had clearly expected her to join him at home for dinner. His flat was small and clean. The dining table was laid for two with a crisp red and white cotton gingham tablecloth. A candelabra with eight red candles stood as a centre-piece on the table. He struck a match and flames flickered and danced throughout the room. A vase of fresh red roses sat on a large coffee table.

"I'm so pleased you agreed to come. Otherwise, my dinner would've been ruined."

"Don't think I'm in the habit of going back to strange men's flats."

"When I saw you in the store the other day, I could see you were special."

"I can't accept flattery when you don't even know me."

"I can read your heart," he replied whimsically.

Sarah ignored his reply. She turned away from him. Her cheeks burned. She looked around the room and changed the subject, "Nice flat. Who's your flat-mate?"

"Benny, but only for the next two months. He's marrying Suzanna."

George slipped away into the tiny kitchen. A wonderful aroma of cooking wafted into the living room. He called from the kitchen,

"Do you like gazpacho soup?"

"What's that?"

"It's Spanish. I had it in Spain last year. It's a cold soup with tomatoes, cucumbers, peppers, garlic, and ice cubes. Delicious. Would you like to try?"

He placed two bowls on the table. She sipped it.

"It's very good. I like spicy food."

He uncorked the wine. "Then you'll like what's coming next."

He cleared the bowls and returned with two plates of steaming teriyaki chicken with peppers. Another new taste experience.

"This is delicious," she said, greedily wiping the plate clean with some crusty bread.

"You're an amazing cook. Where did you learn to cook like this?"

"Books and recipes from friends. I did think of becoming a chef before deciding on engineering."

"Well, I love it. You must give me the recipes."

George was gregarious, but also modest.

"I'm glad you enjoyed it. I hope we can do it again."

They cleared up then relaxed on the sofa sipping coffee and chatting. His hands rubbed the back of her neck and gradually worked down to her shoulders.

"You're very tense. What's up with you?" he asked gently.

"Things and children."

"You have children?"

"I thought I told you I'm married with a daughter, Emma. I also look after a friend's baby whilst she works."

"You're too young and beautiful to be a mummy."

She stood up. "I have to go. This is not right. Please let me go."

He pressed his hands firmly down on her shoulders, forcing her to sit down on the sofa and began to massage the back of her neck and shoulders again.

"My, my, you're in a bad way. Let's lie on my bed, we don't have to do anything. I've got strong hands and can relax you."

"Where's your flat-mate?"

"He's with Suzanna. He won't be back for ages. It's okay."

Her cheeks still burned and her head spun from two glasses of wine. She followed him meekly into the bedroom.

They lay side-by-side. His hands continued to massage her shoulders then moved down her entire body before successfully searching out, kissing and stroking her sensitive areas seemingly all at the same time. She was ready for him when he slid effortlessly into her. She gulped and screamed as he seemed to hit every erogenous nerve. Like a bolt of electricity shooting through her entire body. It felt sensational.

He lit two cigarettes and handed one to her. They smoked them silently, immersed in their own thoughts. He finally inhaled deeply, stubbed out the butt then rested his head on Sarah's chest.

"You're quite a girl. I didn't expect this."

She was shaken.

He slipped off the bed and returned with two cups of coffee.

"Did you feel the earth move?" he teased.

"I can't believe this," she replied, responding to his kiss.

"Can I see you again next week?" he asked.

"I'm not sure."

***

The weeks flew by. Sarah made numerous excuses to slip out of the house to meet George. One day they fell asleep on his bed and woke up at midnight. Paul was working at the hospital and Sandra was at home looking after Emma.

"Oh, my God. Do you realise the time?" yelled Sarah. "Mum must be going crazy with worry. Can I use your phone?"

"Mum, is that you?"

"Who do you bloody well think it is – the Queen Mother?" replied Sandra angrily. "Where are you?"

"I'm glad you're there."

"Where the hell do you think I'd be at midnight? Down the dance hall. I've been sick with worry. I couldn't sleep. Have you been in an accident? I phoned Paul because I was so worried."

"You shouldn't have done that Mum. I'd have phoned you if something was wrong."

"I've had too many nasty shocks lately. I imagined you lying in the road in some traffic accident."

"I'm fine. It's just, I'm staying at Rona's tonight. We fell asleep watching television and I missed the last train home, so I'm stuck out in Hackney."

"You promised you'd be home so I could go to my Kalookie card game. You know how much I enjoy it."

"I'm really sorry. I'll be back first thing in the morning. How's Emma?"

"She's been a good girl. Tell that Rona from me, she can't be trusted," grumbled Sandra.

"Yes, Mum."

Chapter 32

"Rona's invited me to her sister's wedding next month. Would you mind if I stayed overnight?" Sarah asked.

"I didn't know she had a sister. Where's the wedding?" Paul replied.

"Somerset. It's too far to go for the day. So we thought we'd stay over Saturday night. Her sister Suzanna is getting married to Benny. His parents live in Somerset."

"Why wasn't I invited?"

"You were. But you've always said you don't like Rona, so I made the excuse you work most weekends."

"I might have liked a break in Somerset. I can always swap my shift," Paul added.

"Do you want me to tell her you're coming?"

"No, you go and enjoy yourself. Check with your mum that she can look after Emma. I'll probably be on weekend duty next month anyway."

'Phew. That was a narrow escape!' Sarah thought.

***

Sarah was looking forward to Benny and Suzanna's wedding in Somerset. She could hardly wait to spend an entire night with George in the luxurious wedding hotel. The affair would have to end when he went to university.

At the end of the evening they fell into bed, euphoric and tipsy. Lying beside George, Sarah had no inhibitions and felt free again, with no responsibilities. Tomorrow there will be guilt. But tonight was her night of shameful self-indulgence.

"I've never done this before," said Sarah.

"Done what," asked George wearily.

"Slept with another man. Paul's the only man I've ever slept with. He was my first real boyfriend. You believe me, don't you?"

"I'm not interested in Paul."

"I lied to him about coming here. I've never been disloyal before."

"Shut up, stop talking. We've got the whole night," he groaned into her ear, then rolled on top of her.

Waking up with George beside her the next morning, she felt a mixture of exhilaration, guilt and sadness.

***

After the wedding, Sarah avoided Homes-Are-Us until she was certain George had moved on. Benny told her George had obtained good grades in his exams and been accepted at Bristol University to start in September.

At the end of the affair Sarah reflected over her scandalous behaviour. She was shocked how easily she had succumbed to pure lust, and how she had embarrassed herself by falling for George's youth and charisma. In the decades to come she imagined George would just be a whimsical interlude.

She had risked her marriage and Emma's happiness. And yet … she will always remember how George made her feel so special. They laughed a lot. He was fun, funny and sexy. Sex with Paul had decreased to almost zero since Emma's birth and Sandra's move upstairs. She told herself she must never again be tempted into another affair.

There were painful gremlins at work inside her head. The affair had forced her to re-evaluate what was important. One thing was certain. Paul was important. She loved him and had shamefully betrayed him. She didn't deserve his love and would never again risk destroying their relationship and Emma's security and respect.

***

Paul couldn't understand why Sarah was still unhappy. Sandra was now settled into her flat upstairs. She was taking Italian lessons and had begun to meet new people. Sandra also helped with Emma and Stuart, allowing Sarah free time for herself. Paul continued to search for answers. He remembered with pleasure the early days of their marriage, before Emma was born, when every evening they discussed their workday and hospital politics. Lately Sarah showed little interest in his work. Irritability had replaced her old *joie de vivre* and had dulled her enquiring mind. When Paul asked Sarah why she was still unhappy, she replied with obscure excuses, then quickly changed the subject.

"You know I've never been happy in Grandfather Cyril's house. It's never felt like a real home. The rooms are too large and cold, even in summer. The more changes we make, the more I fear the curse of your parents and the ghosts of your ancestors consuming me."

Before their marriage Paul was troubled about Sarah's reluctance to move into his grandfather's home. However much he loved their home, if this was the cause of Sarah's depression, he would sell it and move on. He had loved his grandfather, and felt privileged to live in the house of his antecedents and to proudly tread the same floorboards. The vision of them was still one of esteem and pride. But he was also confused. In spite of Sarah's protestations, her actions contradicted her words, while she continued to work on the house renovations and decorations.

"If you feel so strongly, we can sell it," said Paul.

"We can't move Mum again."

"If you're unhappy here, we'll have to move," he replied.

***

It was during the time of Sarah's affair, Sandra received an unexpected telephone call from Doris, an old neighbour who had recently moved nearby. She was a sociable widow, of a similar age to Sandra, who craved company. She introduced Sandra to the card game Kalookie. John never approved of card games. The women also joined an Italian class.

"I've always wanted to visit Italy, but my late husband was never interested," Sandra told Doris. The women also joined a book club that met regularly in members' homes. So Sandra's circle of friends began to expand.

With her new-found freedom, came a surge of new energy. Now the genie was out of the bottle Sandra was making up for lost time after all the years she stayed at home with her husband John, who had no appetite for outside company. After decades of loneliness, Sandra was turning into a *new woman*, enjoying new experiences, meeting new people and now Sarah had a new mother. A mother, who was also a best friend, who joined her on shopping trips and afternoon walks with the children in the park. This was Sarah's dream come true, which had taken almost a lifetime to achieve.

Chapter 33

Paul was due a week's holiday. He decided this was the perfect opportunity to give their marriage a much-needed boost. Their last holiday was their Parisian honeymoon. Sarah had been house-bound, looking after two young children and busy fixing the house, for too long without a break.

"I think we all deserve a holiday." He handed her the holiday brochure.

"You've been stuck at home looking after Emma and Stuart for too long, and I certainly need a break from the hospital. There are some good hotels on Majorca and Emma will love the beaches."

"Going abroad. Can we afford it?" Sarah flicked through the brochure.

"The new package holidays are good value. We all need some sun and sea. I'm excited just thinking of Emma playing on the beach. She'll love it."

"I don't know," she pondered. "The hotels look lovely. Sam will need to find someone to look after Stuart."

"I'm sure she can find help for a few days. We need to get away, just the three of us. We've got too bogged down in routine and don't talk or laugh anymore."

***

Majorca was as beautiful as the brochure pictures. Sarah had never seen such deep blue skies and exotic Mediterranean plants and flowers of deep reds and blues. They gazed in amazement at the growing fruit; pineapples, figs, and watermelons.

The hotel stood proudly on a wide sandy beach of soft white sand. The sea was clear and brilliant turquoise. Emma enjoyed precious days with both her mummy and daddy. They frolicked on the beach, made sandcastles and paddled in the sea.

One evening, after Emma was safely tucked up in bed on the fifth floor of the hotel after a busy day making sandcastles, Sarah and Paul enjoyed a romantic dinner on the roof garden restaurant, perched high over the sandy beach and glossy black Mediterranean Sea.

"I always thought you looked good in red," said Paul. He reached for her hand. "I believe you're blushing."

"It's too much sun and sangria," she giggled.

"I think you look amazing. Just like the first day I saw you."

"I wasn't in red then. I was in my nurse's uniform."

"You know what I mean. We've only been here two days and it's clear it's doing you a lot of good," he said.

Stars twinkled. Lights around the bay shone in harmony. The warm, humid evening gave Sarah a sense of well-being.

"I wasn't sure about this holiday, but it's perfect. Thank you," she said.

The atmosphere oozed romance. The restaurant was bedecked with candles. Large coloured lanterns hung from ceiling joists.

"This is the ideal place to be with the one you love," she said, placing her hand on his.

"I knew you'd like it."

"I'm sorry I've been so miserable. I've had too many things buzzing around in my head. My father's suicide; and it seemed to take forever to get Mum settled and I still feel responsible for what happened with your parents."

"It wasn't your fault."

"It's because of me you don't see them."

"Forget my parents. It's you I love, and I want us to be together," he replied.

"Your mum and dad won't see Emma growing up."

"We've both been under enormous strain, me at the hospital, you a new mum and coping with everything at home. There's never time to talk."

The holiday cleared the air and was restorative for both of them. Sarah had time to enjoy Paul and Emma. They walked in the sunshine, breathed the clean air, laughed and loved. In spite of spending money they could ill-afford, they both agreed it was a magical week.

Sarah returned home bronzed, relaxed and positive her future was with Paul and Emma. Never again would she risk destroying a good marriage. She had come very close to losing the best man she could ever have wished for.

"Thank you," she kissed Paul. "Now we have our precious Emma, Majorca was even better even than our honeymoon."

But Sarah's happiness would be short-lived. Soon she would discover she was pregnant again. And the one thing that would haunt her for years to come was ... *who is the father of my child ... Paul or George?*

Chapter 34

"How do I get a passport?" asked Sandra.

"Are you going somewhere?" replied Paul.

"I've already told you, I'm going to Rome with Doris and my Italian class at the end of term."

"You can pick up a form at the post office."

"I have a special friend I'd like you to meet," she continued.

"Why don't you ask Doris over for tea on Sunday?" replied Sarah.

"Thanks. Incidentally, it's not Doris. His name is David Fineberg. We met in my Italian class, and he's coming on the Italian trip."

***

David Fineberg turned out to be a charming American from Washington D.C, where he was employed on high-security projects at the Pentagon. He currently worked at the American Embassy in Grosvenor Square, London where he was mid-way through a two-year secondment. He explained when he returned home there would be other important projects requiring his attention at the Pentagon.

"I sold my apartment in Washington before coming to London, so I no longer have a home there. When I know precisely when I'm going back, I'll instruct my agent to find a suitable property for me to buy so Sandra and I will have a good home to move into."

Paul thought, 'What on earth is he talking about.'

"How interesting. We've never been to America. But I know they're steaming ahead in my profession," Paul replied.

"And what's that?"

"Medicine … interesting – I've just read in a medical journal about an American surgeon who has successfully performed the first lung transplant into a convicted murderer." Clearly no one was listening to his prattle. He felt foolish and silently thought, 'they didn't hear a word I said.'

David ignored Paul and continued speaking.

"It seems Sandra hasn't told you."

"Told us what?" Sarah and Paul replied in unison.

"That Sandra's agreed to be my wife."

They were speechless.

But Sandra remained relaxed and smiling. "David asked me to marry him, and I accepted."

"It's all discussed and agreed. We're now formally engaged," added David. "Aren't you going to wish us *mazeltov*?"

"You're Jewish?" said a surprised Paul.

"Of course, David's Jewish. With a name like Fineberg? We met in our Italian class, and we're going to Rome together. Isn't that romantic?" replied Sandra.

Paul enthusiastically shook David's hand, and Sarah kissed him on the cheek.

"*Mazeltov, mazeltov*. That's incredible news," added Sarah, wondering why Sandra had kept David a secret until now.

David spontaneously broke the awkward silence.

"Thank you for your good wishes. I'm a lucky man. Your mother makes me very happy. Believe me, I wanted to end it all after my wife Diane died five years ago. Your mother is the best thing that's happened to me. I promise I will look after her and love her."

"Have you set the date?" asked Sarah.

"It's all a bit complicated," answered Sandra. "David, I think you should explain."

"Sandra's agreed to wait until we can get married in America. First of all, I need to tidy things up here. My contract at the embassy has about a year to run. We're not teenagers. So there's no rush."

"That gives us time to get to know you," said Paul.

"It seems Sandra hadn't told you about me. So I must be a big shock."

"You certainly are. My first thoughts were my mother's lost the plot. But I must say, I've never seen Mum looking so radiant," replied Sarah.

"Doesn't she just. Don't you think a man can look radiant too? Because Sandra makes me feel radiant." David smiled.

"I don't see why not," joked Paul.

"I will do my very best to care for her for the rest of our lives."

"It's amazing what you can pick up in an Italian class," smiled Sandra.

Whilst David chatted with Paul, Sarah took Sandra aside and whispered in her ear.

"Why did you keep David a secret?"

"I wanted to make sure I wasn't making a mistake."

"Did I hear right? You're getting married in America?" Sarah now addressed David.

"Yes, my sister Doreen and her family moved from Washington D.C. to Tampa in Florida and Sandra has agreed we marry there. Doreen has two grown-up children, Marcia and Spencer. Marcia has two children. Lyla who is seven and five-year-old Eli."

"And you're going to live in America," said Sarah.

"I love London. But I have to go where my work takes me. If they find me work here, I'll happily stay," David replied.

In an attempt to add a little lightness into the conversation, Sandra said, "David says Tampa has the best beaches in the whole of America and we'd like Emma to be our beautiful bridesmaid with Marcia's daughter Lyla."

"Where's Tampa?" asked Paul. "Is it near Miami?" The question sounded trite.

"No. It's on the Gulf of Mexico, the other coast. Miami's on the Atlantic about two hundred and fifty miles away."

"America's a wonderful country. Who knows, one day you may all come and join us. As you said, Paul, it's the perfect place for medical research," added David.

***

After David left, Sarah vented her frustrations.

"How could you plan all this without telling us?" She was angry her mother hadn't prepared them for meeting David.

Sandra rarely cried. Now tears rolled down her cheeks.

"I'm sorry. I should have told you sooner. It's just … it's not David that's the problem. I love him. It's just … I don't want to live in America," she snuffled.

Sarah cuddled up to her mother for the first time in a very long while.

"Tell him the truth."

"I wanted you to meet David to see for yourself what a wonderful man he is. We met last September in our Italian class, we've only recently been seeing each other on our own."

"I like him and clearly he thinks the world of you, but we don't want to lose you to America," said Sarah.

"I hope he can stay here. I've lived in London all my life. I've got my family here and I've made some really good friends now."

"David doesn't seem in a rush to go back to America. Didn't he say his contract's got a year to run," added Paul.

"He wants us to get married in Florida. He's got a special hotel planned."

"Sounds exotic. I'm not going to grumble about a holiday in Florida. First of all, get yourself a passport, have a lovely holiday in Rome. Enjoy each other's company. Who knows? As you say, his plans could change, and he might even stay here," said Sarah.

"Wouldn't that be a wonderful ending," sighed Sandra.

"We don't want you moving to America. I've only got one mother and I don't want to lose you."

Chapter 35

"Mum's getting married," said Sarah.

Sam looked flabbergasted. "I didn't know she was seeing anyone."

"Neither did we. Have another cup of tea and an éclair and I'll explain everything."

"Oh my God." Sam pointed to the remaining éclair. "Split it in half, let's share it. You know how to spoil me, especially with my favourite coffee éclairs."

"His name is David Fineberg. He's Jewish, like us. He seems very nice. He adores Mum and comes from Washington D.C. and works in the American Embassy in Grosvenor Square. They met at night school, learning Italian, and they are going on holiday to Italy together," said Sarah.

"How romantic. I'm not surprised. I thought when she put herself out there with all the middle-aged singles someone would snap her up. She's still a very attractive woman," replied Sam.

"She's certainly looking more relaxed. Clearly David's done her a lot of good. The problem is he's got one year left on his contract and then wants to take her to live in America."

"How does she feel about living in America?" asked Sam.

"Not happy. David likes London and it's just possible he could get a permanent job here."

"Let's hope so for your sake."

"I don't want her to go to America. After the bad start we're now getting on really well, and I would miss her. And I know how much she's looking forward to the new baby," said Sarah.

"How's the morning sickness?" asked Sam.

"I'm over it and feeling great. I only hope she doesn't make a hasty decision she'll later regret," added Sarah wistfully.

"How things have changed. I remember how unhappy you both were," said Sam.

"I know. Now she's out of the clutches of my father she's, like, twenty years younger. I'm pleased she's met someone. I always thought of her as a caged bird, and now the bird's taken flight, but I'm not sure she'll fly as far away as Washington."

"You are funny and very poetic. I would say your mum's making up for lost time. She's not getting any younger, and suddenly she's seen the light after being controlled by your dad for so long. That's one big decision she has to make. But she can come back for regular visits," replied Sam.

There was a short pause in the conversation while Sarah began the washing up.

"Something's come up I want to talk to you about in confidence."

"Anything wrong?"

"No. It's to do with my adoption."

Sarah paused to collect her thoughts.

"You'll think I'm crazy, but ever since I was pregnant with Emma, I've been worried about having the perfect baby. Remember I told you about my brother?"

"Brian. Of course I remember. You're not crazy. Every pregnant woman has those thoughts."

"After Brian died, Mum and Dad never talked about him."

"You must be thankful you don't carry their genes. I imagine your birth parents were young and healthy."

"That's the problem. I don't know anything about them. How do I know if there were birth defects in their family?"

"Because Emma's perfect," Sam replied reassuringly.

"I'm worried, if I have a boy, he could be like Brian. Boys are more prone to be born with birth defects. I've never spoken to Mum about my birth parents. I didn't want her to think I was being disloyal. But last night, after a couple of glasses of wine, I plucked up the courage and asked her."

"What did she say?"

"She doesn't know much, only they were both Jewish and not married. So that makes me illegitimate!"

"You knew that."

"When I say it out loud it sounds awful,"

"You've got nothing to apologise for. It's not your fault. What else did she say?"

"They wanted a Jewish baby and they looked after me for a whole year before the adoption was final. During that time my birth mother could have changed her mind and taken me back. She said everything that happened during that time was a blur because she was worried sick she could lose me. But she did have the name of the adoption society and I've got an appointment next week. Can I ask a favour? Will you come with me?"

"Of course."

"Mum was so understanding. David's obviously good for her. We cried together and she cuddled me. I can't remember when she ever spontaneously cuddled me. You will keep this to yourself. You can tell Suzy. About the adoption and my brother. No one else needs to know. You understand?"

"You can trust me."

"Mum didn't think I was being disloyal. I said I just wanted to know about my birth parents now I'm expecting number two, but I'm still scared about what they'll tell me. Is that silly?"

"No, quite natural. I think you're doing the right thing."

Chapter 36

Paula Green, a Senior Counsellor at the Adoption Society, shook Sarah's hand.

"This is my friend Sam," said Sarah. "She's come to give me support."

"Please sit down and make yourselves comfortable. Would you like some tea?" Mrs Green asked.

"Yes please."

She rang for tea then bent down into her briefcase and placed a large file on the table between them.

"So many of our files were destroyed during the war. You're in luck," she smiled. "The building was bombed in 1944 and several of our storerooms were destroyed," she paused. "Don't look so serious. I tell all the young men and women I counsel – knowledge is power."

"I was scared what I might find out," said Sarah.

"You mustn't be. Remember, your mother gave you the gift of life. She was a brave young woman."

Sarah nodded.

"Is there any particular reason why you want to know about her now?"

"I'm expecting a baby and want to know if you have any information about my birth mother's medical history."

"That's a strange one. I don't think I've been asked that question before. In those days it was usual to carry out health checks on the birth mother and baby before adoption, but I don't think mother's medical history would have been available. Also, you've got to consider the health of the unknown father, and we don't have anything on him. Has something upset you?"

"I'm scared of having a boy. I've already got a little girl called Emma and she's perfect. I've been told more boys than girls are born with birth defects."

"If you have a perfect little girl, I see no reason to think you'll have a problem with your second."

Mrs Green swiftly shuffled through the papers.

"In 1941, when you were born, they didn't know much about hereditary diseases. Try and think logically. You're a healthy young woman with a healthy child. There's no reason why your next baby shouldn't be healthy. Are your adoptive parents still alive?"

"My mother is."

"Have you spoken to her about your concerns?"

"She doesn't know anything about my birth parents. She said I should ask you."

Mrs Green took out a sheet of paper.

"Before we go through your file together, there's a routine question I ask everyone who wants to know about their birth parents."

"What's that?"

"Do you remember when you were told you were adopted?"

"I've always known. When I was little, they told me I was chosen, not born to them."

"So it never came as a shock?"

"No. When I was little, I always wanted a baby brother or sister. I can still remember Mum and Dad telling me I would have a new baby for Christmas. That was when my brother Brian was born."

"They sound good parents."

"The tragedy was Brian was born with lots of health issues and died when he was four."

"I'm so sorry. Why didn't you tell me about Brian at the beginning of our interview? Clearly he is the reason for your fears now you're pregnant again."

"I loved him and missed him a lot when he died."

"Brian would have had a tragic impact when you were growing up. But remember you don't have their genes, so there's no possible reason why you should have a disabled child."

"I know. I've got a perfect little girl and a wonderful husband."

"What does he say?"

"I should stop worrying and get on with life."

"I think that's exactly what you should do. Soon you'll have another perfect baby and you'll forget all about this," replied Mrs Green.

"I'm a twenty-seven-year-old mature woman and want to know who my birth parents were. I won't look for them yet. I just want to know their names. I want know who gave birth to me, if she was in good health and why she gave me up for adoption. Then I'll probably leave it at that. Certainly until after my baby is born."

"I think you're sensible to take things slowly. Beware ... I've known birth mothers who don't want to be found. Think, for example, if a young unmarried girl has an illegitimate baby. Then a few years later she marries and never tells her new husband about her past. Such traumas can tear families apart. But I'm sure you understand all that."

"I could have half-brothers and sisters and not know them. I hadn't really thought about that."

"You must be careful. Wouldn't you be upset if you contacted your birth mother and she didn't want to meet you?"

Mrs Green handed Sarah an envelope.

"I think yours is an extraordinary case. Before you go through the paperwork, I think you should read this very special letter which explains why your mother went ahead with the adoption, and how she looked after you for almost a year. It was very unusual in those days. Sadly, we couldn't identify your father."

The fragile paper was brittle and yellowed with age. Sarah read the heart-breaking letter slowly with tears rolling down her cheeks. Sam put a comforting arm around her friend's shoulders.

16th September 1942
To My Darling Daughter
I hope one day when you are a grown woman, you will read this letter and understand that everything I did was

with your future happiness in mind. I believe your new parents may change your name. But that's unimportant. What is important is that you have a good life. I want you to know how much I love you and will continue to love you even though we will be living apart. I sincerely believe the adoption is in your best interests and you will be loved and cared for by a good family.

Your father, Simon, and I did intend to marry but there is so much confusion at the present time and I don't believe this is now going to happen. Simon came from Germany, he was a Jewish refugee. He is a good and loving man.

He went missing one night before you were born and we haven't been able to trace him. We believe he was picked up by the police and taken away. The Government is suspicious of all Germans, even Jewish refugees! I never heard from him again.

There's so much stigma attached to being an unmarried mother so I gave birth to you in a mother and baby home. I love you so much I didn't want to give you away. I looked after you for nearly a year but it became clear it would be impossible for me to care for you single-handedly. It was then I decided you deserved a proper mother and father.
You will always be a special person to me, and I know you will grow up to lead a happy and fulfilling life. It was a privilege to be your mother.
With love.

"Are you okay?" asked Paula Green.

Sarah nodded.

"Take your time. Would you like more tea?"

"Thanks."

"My mother must've been very brave. I have a three-year-old and expecting another soon and I couldn't imagine giving them away."

"Don't blame your mother. Life was very tough then."

Sarah picked up her original birth certificate. In the space allocated for *mother* was the name, *Julie Shaw*. The space for her father's name was left blank. Place of birth was Denby Hall Mother and Baby home in Norwich, Norfolk.

"Be kind to your birth mother. You'll see, when you read the letters, her family lived in east London which was, and still is, a Jewish area. It was a close community and her parents would have been very embarrassed by the pregnancy and sent your mother away to a mother & baby home to give birth. It wasn't uncommon in those days."

"How cruel. She said in her letter they were going to marry …"

"It's probably true your parents planned to marry. I think an explanation for your father's disappearance could be he was sent to an internment camp. She wrote he was German, and all enemies were sent to internment camps, even Jewish refugees from Germany. He may well have spent the entire war in a camp and your mother would never have known."

"Why do you think my mother didn't put my father's name on the birth certificate?"

"She was probably advised not to by the Home. After all he was still considered enemy."

"Oh my. Like *Romeo and Juliet*. Wouldn't he have tried to write to her?"

"You're talking about Germans and World War Two. Letters from the enemy were probably destroyed."

Sarah sighed.

"If that's the case, what a sad story. Do you think my mother got married later and had a family?"

"More than likely. But mark my words, she would never forget you, and mourn you all her life. Especially every year on your birthday."

Sarah looked wistful.

"How would I go about finding her?"

"Through births, deaths and marriage registries. We know where she lived, from the letters on file. You know her name is Julie Shaw. That's a good starting point."

"If she's made a new life, she might not want to be found. How would she find me?"

"She'd have to search through adopted children's registers."

"I don't think I'd want to find her if she's got a husband and family. I'm glad I know her name. One day I might try to find out where she lives, even if I never meet her."

"This is your file to take home and keep. It's full of letters and interesting documents. Contact me again if I can help."

"Thank you so much." Sarah and Sam stood up, shook Mrs Green by the hand, and left the office.

"Are you okay?" asked Sam as they were leaving the building.

"That was some pretty emotional meeting. What am I going to do now?"

"Tomorrow we'll sit down and study the pile of letters and documents. Tonight, I'm treating you to a slap-up meal and your favourite black forest gateau. Your mum will take care of Emma."

"What have I done to deserve a friend as good as you?" replied Sarah, tears dripping down her cheeks.

***

The next day, Sarah and Sam spread the many precious documents on the dining room table. There were handwritten letters from her birth mother, Julie Shaw, to the Adoption Society, and typed carbon copies of replies from the kindly manager, Mrs Rosenthal, updating Julie on Sarah's progress with her new parents, Sandra and John Cole.

Attached to Sarah's original birth certificate were letters from Sandra and John Cole with updates on Sarah's progress. One letter said, they didn't want to confuse the child any further, and decided to keep her original given name, *Sarah*.

There were health and psychiatric reports on Julie and Sarah. And something very precious, a professional photographer's picture of a healthy baby Sarah, taken at about nine months old. She remembered early photographs, taken by her new father, John Cole, shortly after the adoption, when she was scrawny and covered in spots after being neglected in the care of a foster mother. Just a few short months later, Sarah had grown into a healthy and beautiful little girl.

From the wealth of letters and information, it was clear Julie Shaw was heartbroken to give her daughter away for adoption.

Chapter 37

In 1941, nothing would have ruined a young girl's reputation more than having a baby out of wedlock. That's what happened to Julie Shaw when her daughter Sarah was born on 15th September that year. This was an exceptionally sad saga. Unbeknown to Julie, her fiancé, Simon, a Jewish refugee from Germany, was arrested and shipped to an enemy aliens' internment camp on the Isle of Man. It was decades later before she discovered the truth about Simon's disappearance. As an unmarried, pregnant girl from an Orthodox Jewish family, Julie was ostracised and forced to leave home to give birth.

1941: Denby Hall Mother & Baby Home, Norwich, Norfolk

"What would you say if I decide to keep my baby?" Julie asked Mrs Dunstan, manager of the Home a few weeks before her baby was due.

"It's very unusual. Unmarried girls normally hand over their babies immediately after birth."

"I want to keep my baby. I still believe my fiancé Simon will come home, and when he does, how will I be able to tell him I've given his baby away?" Julie replied. Tears welled up in her eyes as she sat shredding her handkerchief into tiny pieces.

"If things don't work out, and Simon doesn't come back, have you thought how much harder it will be to give your baby up for adoption after you've looked after him or her?"

"I haven't stopped thinking about it. If my parents won't let me take my baby home, can I stay here until I find somewhere else to live?"

"We have a small room you can use for a few weeks. I can see if it's available. After that you must move out and find somewhere else to live. Now's not too soon to start asking around in the village. You've got to realise it will be tough managing on your own. You'll need a job and enough money to pay someone to look after your baby. Have you thought how you're going to do all this?"

"Not really. Only that I must keep my baby. That's what Simon would want me to do."

The room Julie and Sarah used had one small fanlight window and was no bigger than a largish storage cupboard with barely enough space for a bed and cot. For six short weeks Julie was a devoted mother and Sarah, her new-born, was a contented baby.

When it was time to leave the security of the Home, Julie had only one offer of accommodation. A spare bedroom in Mrs Campbell's house. Nasty Mrs Campbell, an old woman, who in reality was still in her fifties, stank of body odour and cheap perfume and her small, damp, draughty house smelled of over-cooked cabbage.

Julie worked two part-time jobs. One, in the local library cataloguing books and the second job working as a ledger clerk for Mrs Dorothy Martin, bookkeeper, of the Denby Hall Mother & Baby Home.

Baby Sarah was unhappy each morning when her mummy went to work. She cried most of the day when Mrs Campbell left her in a cold bedroom hungry and in dirty nappies.

Every evening when Julie came home, Sarah felt warm and secure again and responded with smiles and chortles. Mummy smelled of sweetness and roses.

Mrs Campbell enjoyed criticising Mummy. She said things like, "You're doing it all wrong. Cuddle baby and spoil baby."

This unpleasant woman made Mummy cry and when Mummy cried Sarah cried.

However much she tried, Julie reluctantly came to the conclusion her dreams of bringing up Sarah alone wasn't working. She disliked and distrusted Mrs Campbell, but they had nowhere else to go. With a heavy heart, Julie began to make plans to return to London.

***

"Mrs Campbell doesn't like us," said Julie.

"I'm sure that's not true. She's always telling me what a good mother you are," Mrs Dunstan replied.

"I've been asking around the village to find somewhere else to live, but no one will take the two of us."

"The villagers can be unfriendly."

"Believe me, I am trying to make it work with Mrs Campbell …" Julie took out a handkerchief to wipe her eyes, then continued, "Her house is dirty and she doesn't keep Sarah clean."

"Would you like me to find someone new to look after Sarah?"

"No. We both need to get away from Mrs Campbell. I'm living from week-to-week and never have enough money. Did she tell you she wants to put up my rent? I'm struggling to pay the current rent. I keep our room clean and clear up whenever I see a mess. I don't think she ever does any cleaning. You must see the dirt when you go there."

"She takes me straight through to the living room and keeps the curtains drawn. I've noticed she covers the furniture with sheets," Sheila Dunstan replied.

"I want to buy Sarah nice things. I also want to go to night school to learn bookkeeping." Julie had a natural skill with figures. After Sarah's birth, Mrs Dorothy Martin, the bookkeeper at the Baby Home gave Julie paid employment as a ledger clerk with training.

"Mrs Martin said I should learn bookkeeping and do the exams. But I can't leave Sarah with Mrs Campbell all day long and again in the evenings. We must get away from Mrs Campbell."

"I didn't realise things were so bad. Mrs Martin told me you're a good worker. She'll be sorry to lose you. Have you changed your mind about adoption?"

"No, I'll never do that."

"What will you do?"

"I don't know. Mum won't have us. She won't even speak Sarah's name. My only hope is my brother David. I've written asking if he and his wife Tilly will take us in. Mrs Martin said she'll give me a good reference. I'll need a job." Julie paused. "I was hoping you could help me find someone in London to look after Sarah when I'm at work."

"I'll do my best."

"Believe me, I want to make it up with Mum. I'm going to ask David if he thinks I should take Sarah to see her. Dad was the one who was most hostile. Now he's dead I thought mum might want to see us. Wouldn't you think she'd like to see her granddaughter? A lot of water's run under the bridge since Dad died."

"I think David should speak to your mum first. So she's prepared. You don't want to surprise her with Sarah," suggested Mrs Dunstan.

"I will."

"Have you told Mrs Campbell you want to leave?" asked Mrs Dunstan.

"No. I'm waiting to hear from David first. If he says we can stay, we'll go as soon as possible."

"I won't discuss our conversation with Mrs Campbell. What you've told me is confidential and a warning for any future placement."

"I really appreciate everything you've done. You and Mrs Martin have been amazing. I'll miss you both," replied Julie.

***

Sarah and Julie moved in with her brother David and his wife Tilly. Julie quickly learned the East End of London was an unhealthy and unenlightened environment to bring up an illegitimate Jewish child. She was snubbed by people she'd known all her life. She overheard mutterings such as, "Disgusting, that child needs a secure home with two parents."

Julie never bonded with her sister-in-law Tilly. She was critical of her brazen style of dressing. Her heavy makeup and bright red lipstick. Tilly dyed her hair bright orange and piled it high on the crown of her head in the style of the wartime movie star, Betty Grable.

But makeup and hairstyles are skin-deep, and first impressions can be wrong. Tilly proved her true abilities when she was promoted to director of the family's dress factory business after her brother joined the army during World War Two. Before the war, straight out of school, she had a minor role in the company modelling suits and dresses and sold to the trade. Tilly loved clothes and was a natural saleswoman. She instinctively knew what women wanted to wear and styled the clothes to fit wartime shortages. Her ability and acumen belied her looks. Somewhat strangely, it never occurred to Julie she could be jealous of her sister-in-law's success.

Julie felt lost and defeated when Tilly announced she was pregnant. Finally, with nowhere else to go, Julie moved in with her mother, Esther and placed Sarah with a foster mother to await formal adoption.

Julie was now spurned by her family for a second time. She could see no viable way forward to keep Sarah and herself, with no support, no money and no love from her family. Until her dying day Esther denied her granddaughter Sarah's very existence.

Chapter 38

London, 6th April, 1968

"It's a boy," Sandra Cole told her Kalooki-card-playing friend Doris over the telephone. "They're calling him Stephen."

"Congratulations. How are mother and baby?" Doris asked.

"Doing fine. Sarah just wants to come home."

"How much did Stephen weigh?"

"A healthy 8lbs and he's gorgeous. We took Emma to see him. We're not sure how much she understands. I've decided to give up some of my classes to help Sarah. You do understand?"

"Of course."

"I still want to keep our weekly Kalooki game going. I find it takes my mind off things," added Sandra.

"Good. Would Sarah mind if I come to see her and Stephen?"

"I'll let you know."

"She'll need a lot of support now with two young children," said Doris.

"Yes," replied Sandra.

"I'm glad things are working out. Send Sarah my best wishes. See you soon. Goodbye."

***

"How's David. We haven't seen him lately?" asked Paul.

"He's doing fine. He was called back to Washington to fix some important business," Sandra replied. "I thought I told you. I told Sarah, but she's got more important things on her mind at the moment."

"Have you set the wedding date?"

"Not yet. It's highly possible he could be offered a permanent job here. We're hoping he'll know before he comes back."

"We'll keep our fingers crossed…"

***

Sarah returned home from hospital with Stephen, tearful and disorientated. Since his birth, her feelings of guilt had intensified. She had nightmares. In the dreams she saw the faces of Paul and George consecutively superimposed over Stephen's face. During the day she studied Stephen's face endlessly while he slept in his cot, but was incapable of picking him up for a cuddle.

The question she dreaded to think about during her pregnancy now constantly tormented her. Who is Stephen's father? Who does he resemble? *Paul or George*? Currently neither. He was just baby Stephen. For the time being no one could possibly suspect. But Sarah was petrified of the future. Who will Stephen grow up to look like in two, five or even ten years' time?

***

"Have you noticed a change in Sarah since Stephen was born?" Sandra asked Paul.

"She's very frail and weepy. We've just got to keep supporting her. It's exhausting feeding every three hours," he replied.

"It's more than that. She's not looking after herself. I don't think she's washed her hair since she's come home, and yesterday I had to tell her to have a bath."

"I know. If I say anything she just flares up. I'm just as concerned," he replied.

"It's not normal. She never cuddles Stephen. She feeds and changes him then puts him back in his cot. I pick him up to give him a cuddle."

"If it goes on much longer, I might suggest she sees someone."

"A therapist."

"Yes."

"I don't want to give you more worry, but can I be blunt? I don't think she wanted Stephen," said Sandra.

"Stephen came a little sooner than we planned. We did talk about another baby when Emma starts school, but now he's here, give her a few weeks and I'm sure things will improve."

"I hope so. Why is she so tearful? I read an article in *Woman's Own* only last week about *baby blues*. Do you know about it?"

"She's just exhausted."

"Emma's been a handful since Stephen came home. Yesterday I found her trying to stuff food into his mouth. I told her babies can't eat proper food."

"I think this is more out of love for her brother than being naughty. As for Sarah, I'm sure this will all be forgotten in a month or so," replied Paul reassuringly.

But he was much more concerned about Sarah's mental health than he admitted to Sandra. He'd seen postnatal depression, and how badly it can affect women. It was still too soon to discuss his concerns with Sandra. He hoped it was just *baby blues* as Sandra put it. Postnatal depression was something far more serious.

Paul suggested Sarah should buy some new clothes and have her hair re-styled. He was fed up seeing her in the same old baggy maternity clothes.

***

"Sam, I must see you before I go mental," Sarah yelled down the phone. "Paul's on late shift tomorrow. Can you come over for some supper?"

Sam was barely through the front door when Sarah blurted out,

"I don't know if Paul is Stephen's father. I've been going crazy for months."

"What on earth makes you think that?"

"Remember last summer, and the problems when Mum moved in? She made me depressed and you said things would work out. Well … I had an affair with George."

"Who's George?"

"I met him last summer, just before we went Majorca. He was working on the paints counter in that big DIY store, Homes-Are-Us. He chatted me up and I was taken in by his flattery. I was having a hard time at home and made any excuse to get out of the house. Paul knew I was depressed and I think that's why he booked the holiday."

"You came home looking fantastic."

"Paul never understood how difficult Mum was."

"I didn't know things were so bad. Suzy and I could have helped with Emma to give you a break."

"I didn't want to tell anyone I felt an utter failure. And George made me feel wonderful. The whole affair is now a nightmare."

"Did you have sex with Paul on holiday?"

"Of course. But how do I know if Stephen's Paul's son? If I tell him about George, he'll go ballistic and want a divorce."

Sam couldn't think of any words of reassurance.

"Can you imagine what my mother would say? She'd call me a whore. Funny, isn't it? I've been thinking, like mother, like daughter. Stephen could also be illegitimate."

"That's ridiculous. I can't believe Paul's not Stephen's father. I think you're worrying over nothing."

"But what if Paul's not his father?"

"You said you fell pregnant in Majorca – didn't you?"

"I don't know. My period was a bit late when we went. What should I do?"

"Say nothing. If you tell Paul, you'll upset everyone and it will probably be for nothing. Are you still seeing George?"

"Of course not. It was over almost before it began. It was in July, just before we went to Majorca. So the dates match. George never knew I was pregnant and Paul and I didn't have sex for months before our holiday."

"You're quite a girl," said Sam.

"A stupid girl. George was working in the store to earn some money before going to Bristol University to do an engineering degree. He went off to Bristol in September and I never saw him again."

"Keep calm and say nothing. See if Stephen grows up to look like Paul. Sometimes secrets should remain secrets."

"I can't do that. Paul trusts me. And Stephen deserves to know who his father is."

"Paul will always be his father. He will bring him up and love him."

"That's not right. I must tell Paul, and eventually Stephen must know the truth."

"But you won't know the truth and you could be worrying for nothing," added Sam.

Logical words from Sam – maybe. But Sarah couldn't imagine a lifetime of deceit, watching Stephen grow up knowing there was a chance the boy Paul loved, and called his son, was the child of another man. She envisaged, with horror, Stephen maturing into manhood and still uncertain of his true paternity. The deception would eventually drive her insane.

***

In the 1960s, before DNA testing, there was no definitive method for determining whether Stephen was Paul's son. Finally, after many attempts to speak to Paul about her concerns, Sarah decided to wait for a more convenient time. But there was never a convenient time and she remained silent. Sarah convinced herself to believe, as Sam had suggested, there was every probability Stephen was Paul's biological son, and her fears and anxiety was groundless.

Chapter 39

3rd June 1968

For over an hour Margaret watched the women enter and leave the ladies' changing rooms in Selfridges department store, whilst the baby slept peacefully outside in his pram. She wondered how a mother could leave a small baby unattended for so long. Could she have suddenly taken ill and now lay unconscious on a cubicle floor? Margaret went to check the changing rooms. They were all occupied. She called out,

"Is that your baby outside?"

Two women simultaneously pulled aside the cubicle curtains.

"I don't have a baby," said the first woman.

"Neither do I," added the second.

"Did you see anyone leave the baby?" asked Margaret.

"No," said the first woman. "There was small baby outside in a pram when I arrived. I've been in and out of this cubicle for well over an hour trying on dresses. In all that time I haven't seen anyone with the baby. I'm looking for something special for my sister's wedding and I must have tried on the whole shop by now."

"Thanks. I'll check the changing rooms over by the cocktail dresses," Margaret replied. "If I can't find the mother, I'll take the baby to the security office."

But Margaret never intended to go to the security office. She swiftly wheeled the pram out of the store and into a nearby shop to buy baby clothes and formula. She fed and changed the baby and wheeled him back to her home.

***

That evening, Sarah was resting on the sofa when Paul arrived home at five-thirty. He bent down to give her an affectionate hug. She swiftly stood up.

"You look great." He was thrilled.

"Mind my hair."

"I have my old Sarah back. You look fantastic. I can see your day out has done you lots of good."

She twirled around. "Like my dress?"

"Fabulous – I always said red suited you. You look fantastic. I hated those frumpy old maternity clothes. We're gonna have a wonderful evening. I'm just going up to say hi to your mum, read Emma a quick story and get changed."

"Have you booked the taxi?"

"Six-thirty. That gives me nearly an hour to get ready and kiss the children good night."

Paul climbed the stairs to Sandra's flat. He was pleased Sarah and Sandra were now reconciled. Sandra was a good grandmother and the children loved her. Emma was freshly bathed and curled up on the sofa watching television. She was too absorbed on the small screen to even notice Paul had come into the room. Emma clearly enjoyed spending time with Sandra. It had taken a long time, but Paul was now convinced they had beaten all their gremlins and Sandra was happily settled into her flat.

"Hi, chummy. You be a good girl whilst Mummy and Daddy go out tonight. Grandma will stay in our part of the house with you until we get home."

"Has she been a good girl, Grandma?"

"Good as gold, as always."

"Good."

Paul kissed his daughter on the cheek, blew a kiss and left the room. He went into Stephen's room. His cot was empty.

"Where's Stephen?" he yelled running down the stairs. "Stephen, Stephen, our son. He's not in his cot."

"What?" Sarah looked bewildered.

"Read my lips. **Where is Stephen? HE'S NOT IN HIS COT**."

Sarah fell, crumpled, onto the sofa in tears.

"I don't know."

"Did you take him out with you today?"

"I think so."

Paul, the doctor, now forced himself to think rationally. I mustn't shout. It will only upset Sarah more.

"Stay there. Don't move. I'm sorry I shouted. I'll be back in a minute."

He rushed up the staircase two at a time. Maybe Sandra knows something.

"When did you last see Stephen?"

"This morning, before they went out." Sandra looked confused. "I offered to look after him, but Sarah said she wanted to take him with her."

"On the train to Oxford Street?"

"Yes. What's this about?"

"Have you seen him since they got home?" Paul asked.

"No. Thinking about it, I haven't heard him cry, which is unusual. I normally can hear him crying. Is something wrong?"

"I can't find Stephen."

"That's ridiculous. I'll come down."

"No. You stay with Emma. I'll come up if I need you."

Sarah was lying flat on her stomach, her face in a cushion.

"Where did you go today?"

"Oxford Street."

"Did you take Stephen?"

"I think so."

"I don't understand. You think so! Was he with you when you had your hair done?"

"I think so. I did things the wrong way round. I had my hair done first before looking for a dress. So I had to put the dresses over my head."

"Where did you have your hair done?"

"Renee's in Regent Street, where I normally go."

"Give me the number. I'll ring Renee. Where did you buy your dress?"

"Selfridges."

"Was Stephen with you then?"

"Yes, I think so."

"You think so. Did you take Stephen into the cubicle when you tried on the dresses?"

"There wasn't enough room. I think I left him outside. I was confused. When I came out, he wasn't there. So I thought I left him at home with Mum."

"You were confused?"

"I was in the cubicle trying on dresses when I felt dizzy. I think I passed out. When I came round I was very confused and forgot what I was doing. When I couldn't see Stephen's pram I decided to pay for the dress first then look for Stephen. It's a funny thing – I seemed to lose my memory. It was only when I got home everything that happened came flooding back to me."

"Where's Stephen?"

Sarah burst into tears.

"Stop questioning me. I don't know."

"Oh my God, you really don't know."

Chapter 40

3rd June 1968

"Had a good day?" asked Wills. "Did you apply for that job?"

"Yes, and I bought a really smart suit in Selfridges for the interview," Margaret replied.

"Bit ahead of yourself, aren't you?"

"No, it's not always easy to find an outfit that's just right."

"You look a bit flushed. Are you feeling okay?"

"Excited about the interview and my new suit. I'll show you."

"Shush," whispered Wills and opened the sitting room door.

"Turn off that music," he ordered. "Can you hear that noise? It sounds like a baby crying."

"Didn't I tell you, I agreed to look after Alison's baby?"

"Who's Alison?"

'Why is he crying when he's just been fed?' Margaret mumbled to herself.

"Is there a baby in our bedroom?" questioned Wills.

"I told you, Alison asked me to look after him for a few days when they go on holiday."

"No, you didn't. And who's Alison? We know nothing about babies."

"A friend I worked with. She went on a last-minute business trip with her husband to New York."

"Lucky you're not working right now. What's his name?"

"Who?"

"The baby's," Wills replied irritably.

"Err ... William."

"This doesn't seem right to me. We should have talked it over first."

"It's just Alison was let down at the last minute and needed someone quickly. I'm sorry."

"Doesn't sound right to me," said Wills.

Margaret picked up baby William and handed him to Wills. The baby chortled and smiled.

"That could be wind," said Margaret, demonstrating her baby knowledge.

"He's a beautiful baby. He warms your heart. But we don't know anything about babies. Doesn't seem right to me." Wills repeated.

"I told you it was very last minute."

"Well, I suppose there's nothing else we can do."

"Thanks ... it's only for a few days."

Margaret breathlessly changed the subject.

"Look, about the job. I went to see the personnel department this morning and they're writing a new job description which will definitely be on a higher pay scale. Unofficially they said I will be on the interview list. It's exciting and, if I get it, I'll be earning lots more money."

"I'm not sure we should be looking after this baby. We haven't a clue what he needs," sighed Wills.

10th June 1968

A week passed.

"I'll get that," Margaret rushed to answer the ringing phone.

Wills still couldn't understand why Margaret agreed to look after some stranger's baby so soon after her last miscarriage. And, how strange she hadn't spoken to him about the baby before bringing him home. She was still very fragile. A month earlier, Margaret's boss told her to go home and take three months unpaid leave to recuperate after suffering her third miscarriage. She was four months pregnant when it happened and the doctors could give no explanation why she miscarried. Since then a position had become vacant in another department which would also mean promotion, and she was invited to apply. But Margaret and Wills still hadn't discussed the very delicate question of whether she wanted a full-time career or whether they should continue to try and have a family. They were still recovering from a painful third bereavement.

"Who was on the phone?" asked Wills.

"Alison. Isn't it amazing how you can phone across all those miles? They're still in New York. She asked about William."

"When are they coming home?"

"She didn't say. She asked if we could have William a bit longer. Her husband's been offered a job in New York and they want to look at houses before coming home."

"Bit of a nerve. We've already had him a week."

"I told Alison he's no trouble. I asked her if they'd read about the missing baby in London. I said the baby is about the same age as William. She said they hadn't. They don't get much news from England. She said, just don't let him out of your sight."

"Did Alison give you any money to look after him?" asked Wills.

"She gave me £30."

"I checked our bank account and there's less money than I expected."

"I bought the suit, remember. It was more than I would usually pay. But I am going for promotion."

"I reckon I'm at least £50 short."

17th June 1968

Two weeks passed.

"I love William dearly and I'll miss him when he goes home. But when **IS** Alison coming back?" asked Wills.

"She phoned yesterday. They're buying a house in New Jersey and have a flight booked for next Wednesday."

Wills began to think that Alison was never coming home.

"Alison's never coming home, is she?"

"Of course she is. She's coming home next Wednesday, I just said so."

***

Wills was now beginning to think Alison was a figment of Margaret's imagination. She was deluded, and he had been duped. She truly believed she was caring for Alison's baby. But if Margaret had taken the missing baby, it would appear she was also suffering from complete memory loss about the abduction. Margaret was a good woman and would never deliberately wish to cause pain to another woman by taking her child. However, the story of Alison going to New York, and leaving her baby with a comparative stranger, made no sense. This also explained the missing money. Clearly, the money had been spent on clothes, toys, and formula.

Wills had a dilemma. If he had reached the wrong conclusion, it could be the end of their marriage. On the other hand, if William was the missing baby, Margaret was certainly in denial. He decided to have a confidential talk with their doctor. He would know what to do.

Chapter 41

4th June 1968

"The police want a statement from Sarah. I told them I gave her a sedative and she's sleeping. They're going to send a lady detective inspector tomorrow morning," Paul told Sandra.

"Hope she does better than us."

"I phoned Renee's Hairdressers. The girls remember Sarah and Stephen. They made a huge fuss of him when she changed and fed him. From there she would have walked to Selfridges and bought the red dress. What we don't know is whether she went into any other stores en route."

The phone rang.

"Mr Michaels, I'm Detective Inspector Sophie Griffin. I've just been handed your case. How's Mrs Michaels?"

"Very distressed. I've given her a sedative and she's sleeping."

"Can I come and see her tomorrow morning at ten o'clock?"

"Yes, I'll be here," Paul replied.

"Good. This is a tragic situation. Usually it's a young woman who snatches a baby. Often, she can't conceive or suffered miscarriages. They usually treat the baby like a precious doll, and rarely keep them long. The baby's then left in a prominent place to be found."

"Let's hope Stephen's found soon," replied Paul. "Incidentally, I don't know if you've been told I'm a doctor, so I do have some understanding of the mind-set of the kidnapper."

"No, I didn't know Dr Michaels ... Oh, one more thing. Can you come to the police station this afternoon at about two o'clock? I've got some questions for you before I speak to Mrs Michaels tomorrow."

"Okay."

"Can someone stay with your wife? It's important she's not left alone when you come here."

"Her mother is here."

"Good. See you this afternoon at two o'clock."

***

Detective Inspector Sophie Griffin and Paul Michaels shook hands.

"Thank you for coming. This is my assistant, Detective Mary Rose."

Paul nodded.

"We usually tape interviews. Do you have any objections?"

"No."

"Then let's get on with it."

"*2.10pm, 4th June 1968* – Interview Room 2B. Interviewer D.I. Sophie Griffin. Interviewee Dr Paul Michaels, with Detective Mary Rose in attendance," announced D.I. Griffin.

"Can you give me Stephen's full name and birth date?" was D.I. Griffin's opening question.

"Stephen Robert Michaels born 6th April 1968."

"So he's two months old. Correct?"

"Correct."

"Does Stephen have any distinguishing marks, birthmarks?"

"He has a mark on his left thigh almost like a heart."

"What was he wearing?"

"You'll have to ask my wife."

"Do you have any other children?"

"Emma, who's three."

"I'm somewhat confused," began D.I. Griffin. "You reported Stephen missing at six o'clock last evening, 3rd June. I spoke with the proprietor of Renee's Hairdressers this morning and she confirmed your wife attended her appointment yesterday at ten-thirty and had Stephen with her. Renee said they left at about twelve-thirty. Mrs Michaels told her she was going to Selfridges to buy a dress. We need to know what happened between twelve-thirty, when she left the hairdressers, and six o'clock, when you reported the baby missing. And if Stephen was snatched in Selfridges, why didn't your wife report him missing? What happened? Why did she wait until you got home from work?"

"You'll need to ask her. All I know is, my wife told me she felt unwell in the changing room and thinks she may have passed out. She remembers buying a coffee and a sandwich in the café. She had a receipt for the dress dated yesterday, timed at two-thirty in her bag. I also found a receipt for the sandwich and coffee in her coat pocket, timed at one o'clock, also with yesterday's date. Which, to my mind, is proof enough she was in Selfridges yesterday lunchtime. When I got home last night, she told me she was scared and confused to the point she wasn't sure if she'd taken Stephen with her."

"Your baby is very young to be taken to the West End. Did you try to discourage your wife?"

"No. Sarah told me the girls in the hairdressers were looking forward to seeing Stephen, and I know she was excited about our night out. After his birth Sarah seemed depressed so I booked a table at the Savoy for dinner to cheer her up. We were supposed to go there last night. I'm shocked at what's happened. I'll arrange a full medical check-up for her as soon as possible."

"Has Mrs Michaels suffered from depression before?"

"The whole family went through a bad time after my wife's father committed suicide a few years ago, and Sarah's been pretty low since Stephen's birth, but I thought it was just *baby blues*. Her father left Sarah's mother almost penniless. She now lives with us."

"I'm so sorry. In your opinion, from a professional point of view, do you think your wife was clinically depressed after her father's suicide?"

"So much happened during that time, I suppose I could have missed important signs. After the tragedy I concentrated more on her mother. She lost her home. That's why we converted upstairs into a flat for her. The suicide was a terrible shock and totally unexpected. He was an introspective man, but we didn't expect that."

"I appreciate your honesty."

"One other thing comes to mind. I know Sarah still misses the structure of having a job. She was a nurse. That's how we met, in the hospital. It took time for her to reconcile being at home all day."

"How was Mrs Michaels yesterday morning?"

"She seemed back to her old self. I genuinely believed we were working through things together."

"Thank you for being so open. The most likely outcome is Stephen was taken by a sad person who will bring him back safe and well. Mrs Michaels lives in a caring family. I can't see her abandoning her baby. But we have to check all avenues. You understand?"

"Of course."

"Can you think of anything else out of the ordinary that has happened recently?"

"Not really." Pause. "One thing could be relevant. Sarah was adopted during the war. When she was pregnant with Stephen she saw a counsellor about her birth parents. It all seemed a bit odd to me. Suddenly she became obsessed about hereditary diseases. She mentioned it occasionally when she was pregnant with Emma, but as soon as she found she was expecting Stephen, she became almost neurotic."

"You've given me a lot to work on. I certainly won't discuss any of this with your wife. Especially if we discover Stephen was taken by a passing man or woman, then none of what you've told me in confidence will be relevant."

"She found it tough after Stephen's birth. But that's normal with two small children. Her mother's a huge support. Sarah wouldn't harm Stephen. She loves him."

"I'm sure we'll find Stephen safe and well very soon. Thank you for your time. Please remind Mrs Michaels I will come to see her about ten o'clock tomorrow morning."

***

The police released a statement.

Baby Disappears from Selfridges Department Store.

Two-months-old Stephen Michaels disappeared from the store yesterday lunchtime (3rd June). He was in his pram, outside the ladies' changing room, close to the cocktail dresses, on the third floor. We are appealing for witnesses, who may have seen the baby's grey and cream pram, to come forward. Telephone Whitehall 1212.

***

By late afternoon, news coverage of Stephen's disappearance was all over the media. Television and radio stations asked the public to phone with any information.

Two women came forward giving almost identical statements. Both were in Selfridges' changing cubicles, around the time of the baby's disappearance, when a woman questioned them about a baby in a pram outside the cubicles. Both women gave independent reports, and placed the time to be somewhere between one and two o'clock.

They reported seeing a baby in a small pram when they arrived. However, by the time they left the dress department, the baby and the pram had gone. The woman who approached them in the changing cubicles said she was going to take the baby to the security office. However, she clearly did no such thing. She and the baby subsequently disappeared without trace.

The woman was described as being in her mid-thirties to early forties, attractive with shoulder length dark curly hair. She wore dark heavy-rimmed glasses and was smartly dressed in a black business suit. Both women emphasised her heavy foundation makeup and bright red lipstick.

5th June, 1968

D.I. Sophie Griffin arrived at the Michaels' home at ten o'clock precisely.

Paul opened the front door. "I'd like to speak to your mother-in-law first. I understand she saw Mrs Michaels on the morning of Stephen's disappearance," D.I. Griffin requested.

"Why would anyone take a baby?" asked Sandra tearfully.

"That's what we need to find out."

"Before we begin, can I have your full name?"

"Sandra Phyllis Cole."

"Before I speak to Mrs Michaels, I need to ask you a few questions."

"Yes."

"In your opinion, was Mrs Michaels behaving normally on the morning of 3rd June?"

"Yes. She was looking forward to a day out and a special dinner with her husband in the evening. I helped her get Stephen ready. She went to get her hair done and buy a dress for the evening. Her hair appointment was ten-thirty. She said she wanted to get there early and they left home about nine o'clock."

"What time did she get home?"

"I'm not sure exactly. She normally pops her head around the door when she arrives home. I was with Emma, my granddaughter."

"Before Mrs Michaels went out that morning, did she give you any indication when she'd be back?"

"No. I didn't think she'd be out that long because she had Stephen with her. I think I heard the radio on downstairs at about four o'clock. I didn't go down because I was cooking Emma's supper."

"You said she normally comes up to your flat to say she's home?"

"Yes, she always does. It never occurred to me something could be wrong," Sandra sighed and wiped her eyes.

"There's no reason why you should."

"I did offer to look after Stephen, but she said the girls at the hairdressers wanted to see him. Should I have insisted?"

"No, you did right."

"Do you think you'll find Stephen soon?"

"We've got our best staff on the job. You've been very helpful. I'm going to talk Mrs Michaels now," replied D.I. Griffin.

"I'll be in my flat. Call if you need me."

***

Sarah dragged herself out of bed. Her hair was matted and her eyes red and swollen.

"Any news?" she asked the detective inspector.

"It's still early days. I'm confident Stephen will be found soon. It's all over the television and newspapers. We want the public to be very nosey and report anything suspicious"

"Paul showed me the *News Chronicle*," Sarah replied.

"I know how painful this is going to be ... but can you take me back to the day before yesterday?"

"I took Stephen to Selfridges and left him outside the changing rooms in his pram. Then I felt ill. I think I passed out and don't remember anything."

"Didn't anyone help you?"

"No. When I came round I was sitting on a chair in the changing room, and for a short while I think I lost my memory. It was only when I got home everything came flooding back and I panicked."

"Why didn't you ring the police?"

"I should've, but I just panicked," she was crying.

"I'm sure we'll find Stephen safe and well very quickly," reassured D.I. Griffin, handing Sarah a wodge of tissues. "Do you remember if you went in to any other shops before going to Selfridges?"

"No. I only went to the hairdressers. I planned Stephen's feeds and worked out if I fed him at eight o'clock, he'll need another feed when I'm at the hairdresser. I remember the girls making a big fuss of him. I got to Selfridges around lunchtime."

"Who's your hairdresser?"

"Renee's on the corner of Regent Street and Oxford Street."

"After the hairdressers you're sure you didn't go into any other shops other than Selfridges?"

"I didn't go anywhere else. I've bought dresses there before. I didn't want to be out too long. I needed to get home to give Stephen and Emma their tea and have a bath and get ready. We were going to the Savoy Hotel on the Embankment for dinner and Paul had a taxicab booked for six-thirty."

"When you discovered Stephen was gone, what did you do?"

"I wasn't feeling well. I was confused and my head was spinning and when the pram wasn't outside the changing cubicles, I couldn't remember if I'd brought Stephen with me. So I went home to wait for my husband."

"When did you remember taking Stephen with you?"

"Later, when I got home. I was feeling ill and just wanted to get home. I was confused. I didn't know what to do."

"Why didn't you go to the security office, they would have called the police?"

"I don't know. It was all a blur. I thought he was at home."

"Is your head clear now?"

"Yes." Sarah looked embarrassed. "Immediately I got home I had a bath and a rest and dressed ready to go out. I think I was in the bath when everything came flooding back to me."

"Why did you wait for your husband to come home before contacting the police?"

"I was scared because I still didn't know what happened. I can't even remember my journey home. I was scared I had a sudden loss of memory. I still don't understand how I could have forgotten taking Stephen with me to Selfridges."

"You remember you were in Selfridges?" asked D.I. Griffin.

"Not really. Just, I must've been there, because I have my new dress and a dated receipt from the store. I'm scared. Where is he?"

"I'm sure he's safe and will be returned soon. Normally when someone takes a baby on impulse, they soon realise the shocking consequences. They don't want to harm the baby and normally return the baby to the place they took him from."

"Do you remember what Stephen was wearing?"

"Nothing particularly special. I think it was a blue jumpsuit and a yellow coat."

"Does Stephen have any recognisable birthmarks?"

"He has a cute little mark on his left thigh, almost the shape of a heart."

D.I. Griffin was concerned about Sarah's state of mind and decided to terminate the interview.

***

A small team of hand-picked policemen and women were selected to investigate the likely kidnapping of Stephen Michaels and interview the public.

"We always believe a press conference has maximum impact if it takes place on the crime site. The managing director has been very helpful. He has agreed we can use the third-floor dress department tomorrow at one o'clock for our meeting with the press, roughly the time Stephen went missing. It could jog memories. Do you think Mrs Michaels is up to reading the statement?" asked D.I. Griffin.

"I doubt my wife will ever go into that store again. But I'll ask her," replied Paul.

"I want to be at the store tomorrow, and I want to read out the statement. I'm sure it will encourage more people to come forward," implored Sarah.

D.I. Griffin handed her a typewritten sheet of paper. "This is a draft. If you have anything more to say I can make changes."

"I'm happy with the way it is," replied Sarah.

"If you change your mind, I'll read it for you," said Paul, and put a comforting arm around Sarah's shoulder.

Chapter 42

17th June 1968

Two weeks passed.

"I can't take any more anti-depressants. It's worse than morning sickness," cried Sarah.

"Dr Elliott said it could take a couple of weeks before you begin to feel better," replied Paul.

"How can I start feeling better when I've lost my baby?"

"I'm meeting D.I. Griffin this afternoon to get an update."

"They would have told us if there was any news. I'm scared to eat or drink. Everything comes up. You can smell sick all over the house. I've lost seven pounds in two weeks."

Sarah flushed the remaining anti-depressant pills down the toilet.

"Why did you do that?" Paul remonstrated.

"I can't go on like this. Can't you ask Dr Elliott to give me something else?"

"I'm not sure what else he can give you."

"They said they would have found Stephen by now," she sobbed.

"I'm sure we'll get him back."

***

Paul, who, in his doctor's capacity, passed on bad news to his patients with sensitivity and empathy, had no easy words to say to Sarah. He tried to stay calm for the sake of the family. However, his nerves were in tatters with the worry of Stephen's disappearance and Sarah's state of mind. He was beginning to think he too should be taking anti-depressants.

With one final solution on his mind, Paul decided it was time to discuss the very delicate subject of therapy.

"I have a very caring colleague who's a psychiatric doctor. How would you feel about having a confidential chat with her?"

"Can't I try another anti-depressant?" Sarah mumbled.

"You said they make you ill. You heard Dr Elliott say he's reluctant to give you anything stronger. I'm thinking of alternatives. I hate seeing you so sick."

"I don't want to see a shrink."

"I would like you to talk to Maria Stoven. I've been reading up on ECT (electroconvulsive therapy). It could help. I also think it's worth discussing the procedure with Dr Elliott. See what he has to say."

***

23rd June, 1968

Dr Maria Stoven was an ample-sized woman in her forties, kind-hearted and concerned about Stephen's abduction and Sarah's state of mind.

"This is a shocking situation. Every mother and father in the country will be praying Stephen is found safe and well." Dr Maria tried to reassure Sarah.

"I just want Stephen back," cried Sarah.

"I'm sure you'll have him back soon."

"That's what the police keep telling me. They said I'd have him back by now. He's been gone three weeks …" Sarah's voice trailed off.

"The police are professionals. They know what they're doing," replied Dr Stoven, an arm around Sarah's shoulder.

"Can you explain electroconvulsive therapy?" Paul asked, anxious for Dr Stoven to speed up the interview.

"Yes, of course. One thing you must know is that if Sarah decides to go ahead, she will need several sessions."

"I've read up on it. What's unclear, is whether it's carried out under local or general anaesthetic?"

"It's done under a general anaesthetic. Outcomes are generally good, and the procedure safe. But being a doctor, you'll know we always warn our patients there are risks with all kinds of procedures and anaesthetics."

"Can you explain the procedure?"

"Small currents of electricity are passed through the brain which triggers a brief seizure. ECT causes changes in the brain that quickly reverse symptoms of certain mental health conditions, in particular depression."

"It sounds dangerous to me," replied Sarah, unconvinced.

"You will be well looked after. Look, I don't want to put you under more pressure now. Wait a while, see what happens with Stephen. Discuss this between yourselves."

"I told Paul I want to try a new anti-depressant first. If I get Stephen back, I won't need pills or treatments," Sarah mumbled.

"The bad thing about anti-depressants is they're hard to wean yourself off. After a few ECT sessions you should feel much better. It's no longer regarded a radical treatment. I can assure you outcomes have much improved since the 1950s," replied Dr Stoven.

"I'll think about it," replied Sarah petulantly.

"Read this leaflet. If you decide to go ahead, I can come back and explain the procedure in more detail."

"Thank you, you've been very helpful," said Paul.

"Paul will tell you that before any operation the doctors need to know you're in good physical health. So if we go ahead you'll need a full medical check-up, a psychiatric assessment and echocardiogram. I think it's always good to have regular health check-ups regardless, don't you?" added Dr Stoven.

"I'm not sure I could put myself through all that," said Sarah.

"That's why I say don't make a hasty decision. I'm sure Stephen will be found safe and well then you can forget you ever met me."

"Thank you for coming," said Paul, as he walked Dr Maria to the front door. "We have to hope and pray this all ends well."

2nd July 1968

Paul lifted the ringing phone.

"We have a white male baby, about three months old, we believe to be Stephen. He is being rushed to the Middlesex Hospital in Mortimer Street, London, as we speak for a medical assessment," announced Detective Inspector Sophie Griffin.

"WHAT?" Paul screamed.

Sarah pushed Paul aside and grabbed the phone.

"Where was he found? How is he?"

"Earlier today a Caucasian male baby was reportedly left in a pram in the male toilets of Selfridge's department store. The store put an announcement over the public-address system and no one came forward claiming to be the baby's parent or guardian."

"What does he look like?" asked Sarah.

"He fits Stephen's description. He's clean and well nourished. Would you like me to send a police car to take you to the hospital?" asked Sophie Griffin.

"Thank you. Just one quick thing. Do you know if the baby's got a birthmark on his left thigh? Our baby has a birthmark on his upper left thigh – a cute little heart. Oh my God I can't believe it," said Sarah crying down the phone.

"I haven't seen the baby. All I know is what I've told you."

"Tell D.I. Griffin we don't need a police car. We're on our way," said Paul.

***

Margaret and Wills had grown to love baby William. Margaret proved to be a good surrogate mother. Especially now, when it appeared unlikely she would ever have a healthy baby of her own.

A month passed and Margaret's story of Alison's trip to America sounded more implausible by the day. Wills was beginning to think Margaret was now too content and cosy staying at home looking after baby William.

Two weeks earlier Wills accidently eavesdropped on a telephone conversation between Margaret and a colleague in the personnel department. She was clearly being encouraged to apply for the job that would give her promotion, extra money and senior status in the company. Margaret told Wills a director intimated she was an ideal candidate. But the job application form remained in the kitchen cabinet drawer and the expensive suit, Margaret bought in Selfridges for the interview, was gathering dust in the wardrobe.

"Didn't you say Alison was coming home this week?" Wills asked.

"They have to wait to sign the sales documents for the house before they can come home."

"So you still don't know when they're coming back?"

"I can't bear it when you nag me," Margaret shouted, then ran upstairs and locked herself in the bathroom.

Wills had finally made up his mind. Above all William must be kept safe and warm, but he also had to protect Margaret. He remembered reading press reports about the baby who went missing from Selfridge's store. Didn't Margaret say she bought her new suit in the store on the very day the baby went missing? This had to be more than a coincidence.

Early on, Wills gave Margaret the benefit of the doubt, but deep down he had misgivings. If Margaret had taken the baby, it was because of confusion, and the belief that she had been asked to look after her imaginary friend Alison's baby. Since the miscarriages, Margaret occasionally drifted into an alternative world. Her mind played tricks. Wills reproached himself for not fully understanding the full extent the psychological and physical damage her three miscarriages had triggered.

The baby with a small heart-shaped birthmark on his upper left thigh was returned to Sarah and Paul healthy, happy, if not a little plumper, and he passed all the health checks.

Chapter 43

Paul always preferred the early shifts, so he could be home in time for the children's tea and bath time. He read Emma a bedtime story and settled them down for the night.

He let himself into the house and first checked on Sarah. She was fast asleep on their bed, as she was most evenings. Sandra welcomed him home. Her flat radiated comfort and warmth and, as always, emanated an appetizing aroma of cooking. Sandra was feeding Stephen in his highchair while Emma played contentedly with her dolls.

"How's she been today?" he asked.

"She slept most of the day. I think she's worse now she's back on the anti-depressants. I don't think they're working. When she's awake, she complains Stephen's not her baby. She's convinced they switched him. She says he looks different. His hair is fairer, he's bigger and his clothes are different," Sandra replied.

"We know that's ridiculous."

"When I asked her, who *they* are, and why they switched him, she says they gave Stephen to another couple and she was given some unmarried mother's baby who wasn't wanted."

"She's hallucinating," said Paul. "She says she's having nightmares. I don't think she can tell the difference between dreams and reality. Sam's coming over tomorrow. She was a psychiatric nurse and I value her opinion. Maybe she can fathom out what's going on in Sarah's head."

"She trusts Sam. She says I'm in collusion with *them*. It's so sad, and we were getting on so well," added Sandra with a deep sigh. "I wish she'd trust me."

"It's not just you. She doesn't trust me," Paul replied. "I've asked Sam to give me her professional opinion about electroconvulsive therapy (ECT). I've read some controversial articles, and I don't want to put Sarah through it if it's risky. I've also asked Dr Stoven to come back. I'm not sure how much Sarah understood the last time. I'm still not ruling out ECT."

He bent down to give Emma a hug.

"And how's my little lady?"

She beamed up at him.

"And what have you done today?"

"I went to the park with Grandma and Stephen. I missed Stephen when he wasn't here."

"We all did, sweetheart. What's for supper, Grandma? I'm starving," asked Paul.

"Fish pie," replied Emma.

"Um, my favourite."

***

Sam's visit was a disaster.

The following week Paul was in Sandra's kitchen having coffee.

"I've given it a lot of thought. I've decided if she doesn't get better soon, I may have to get her sectioned."

"Not that! You know, what upsets me most is how she ignores Stephen. She won't have anything to do him. She doesn't look at him, or even try to bond with him. I worry what it's doing to Emma," Sandra replied.

"Her behaviour is extraordinary. I worry how all this is affecting Emma. I just want us to be a happy family again. Very young children are sensitive to what's happening around them. We've got two beautiful children, and if Sarah's not careful they could both be taken into care and our family could be split up forever," replied Paul.

"That would never happen when the children have got us. Would it?" Sandra was alarmed.

"I hope not. But with me working long hours, it's hard on you."

***

"Last night I warned Sarah if she doesn't get any better, I'll have her sectioned." Paul was at the end of his tether.

"What did she say?" asked Sandra.

"Not a lot. Wait and see what Dr Stoven has to say next week," replied Paul.

"That ECT treatment sounds barbaric. I just want her well again," said Sandra.

"Don't we all? I must admit I don't understand depression. I'm at my wits end."

***

"Stephen's a beautiful bonny baby," declared Dr Maria Stoven.

Sarah gave a weak smile.

"I thought I'd feel better when I got him back, but I'm worse than ever on the new anti-depressants. I sleep most of the day and they give me nightmares. I dreamt they gave me the wrong baby. I don't think I have my Stephen back. This baby's fatter and was wearing different clothes," Sarah replied in tears.

"You've been through a terrible trauma," replied Maria, gently taking Sarah's hand.

"This is our Stephen. She's crazy." Paul was irritated.

"This baby's bigger, and his hair looks different," protested Sarah.

"Your husband says this baby's your son, so why are you so convinced he isn't?" asked Dr Maria.

"A mother knows her own son. He looks different," Sarah was adamant.

"So ... he's put on some weight and wearing bigger clothes, that's all," replied an exasperated Paul. "What do you expect? He's four weeks older. I keep telling her tiny babies can put on as much as half of their birth weight by three months."

"That's true. Did the police find who took Stephen?" asked Maria.

"I don't know. I didn't follow it up. We're just happy to have him back," replied Paul.

"Of course you are. Thankfully the person who took Stephen took good care of him, so he's put on some weight. They loved him and bought him new clothes. That's all. Babies change every week."

Dr Maria addressed Sarah with more words of comfort.

"You said Stephen had a small heart-shaped birthmark on his upper left thigh. Does this baby have the same birth mark?"

"Yes, he does," Paul replied.

"Surely then, this must convince you. I can't see any reason to believe he's not your Stephen."

But nothing would persuade Sarah she had her son back.

"Postnatal depression is rarely discussed, but it's more common than you'd think and recovery can take a long time," Dr Maria tried to reassure Paul.

"I don't want you to have a wasted visit. Can you tell us about ECT again?" asked Paul.

"Does Sarah agree?" asked Dr Maria.

She nodded.

"Very well. As I explained last time, it's carried out under general anaesthetic. A strong electric current is sent through the brain. Be reassured, throughout the process nurses check the heart rate and blood pressure. Sometimes when patients regain consciousness, they feel euphoric. Some suffer memory loss, and tell me they can't remember why they were depressed in the first place."

Sarah managed a forced laugh.

"I don't want to know the gory details. It sounds horrible. I just want to forget everything," she said.

"We want you to get better. And I promise you will," replied Dr Maria.

"How many sessions will I need?"

"We normally recommend two or three procedures over about a week. Depending on the hospital. You can elect to be day-care or an inpatient."

"Three, that's a lot. It sounds scary. But I can't carry on like this."

Paul sat quietly by Sarah's side and reached for her hand. She was sick and disorientated from the antidepressants and he hoped she'd remember the meeting.

"If you agree to go ahead, I think you'll be more comfortable as an inpatient. I would suggest three sessions in the first instance. Then we can review. You might not need any more," said Dr Maria.

"I must get better for my family," said Sarah.

'That's the first sensible thing she's said in weeks,' thought Paul.

"Think about it and let me know what you decide," replied Dr Maria.

Chapter 44

Wimbourne Psychiatric Hospital was hidden deep in a remote part of the Sussex countryside. Paul gave a huge sigh of relief when they drove past the sign - Wimbourne Village five miles.

"At long last! I thought I'd missed the road."

Paul had had second thoughts about their rushed decision to travel so far from home. Sarah was assessed by Mr Barrett in London. He also practised in Wimbourne, Sussex, where his charges were significantly lower than at his Harley Street, London address.

Mr Barrett had told Sarah to expect to have at least three electroconvulsive therapy (ECT) sessions over the first week. She may need more later on. Paul arranged a few days leave and booked himself into a local hotel to be with Sarah. He had to be back at work the following week.

It was a hard drive from London. Heavy traffic, together with torrential wind and rain made driving very stressful. Paul's eyes began to sting. The final five miles were the most challenging of all. He had to navigate the car along narrow country lanes that wound sharply to the left then to the right, with barely sufficient room for cars to pass in the opposite direction. He waited for the onset of another migraine.

"What earthly reason did the doctor refer you down here?" he moaned.

"Don't you remember? We already discussed it. Mr Barrett's fees are lower outside London."

It was still only three o'clock in the afternoon and black thunder clouds blocked out most of the September daylight. A strong wind forced the torrential rain to fall almost diagonally across the car, while the windscreen washers struggled to clear the deluge. Hedgerows swayed back and forth and Paul had to avoid broken tree branches strewn across the roads.

"This last five miles seems like twenty." Paul carefully navigated every bend in the road just in case an approaching car took a curve too quickly.

"There must be another sign soon," he mumbled.

It was early autumn. Sarah agreed to begin treatment as soon as possible and Paul had anticipated a relaxed and tranquil drive to the country.

"Look, look," shouted Sarah. "I think I just saw a sign to Wimbourne Village."

"Did it say how many miles?"

"Two, I think."

"Thank God for that."

Wimbourne Psychiatric Hospital was originally a neat Georgian minor stately home built around 1820. It was occupied by the Fitzgerald family for six generations. In 1916 the family converted part of the building into a hospital for returning injured soldiers from World War One. In the 1930s the property was sold to a large corporation who erected outbuildings and transformed the house into an elite boarding school for boys. The house finally metamorphosed into Wimbourne Hospital in the 1950s when six brand new annexes were added. The hospital now consisted of ten, ten-bed wards and thirty, two-bed semi- private rooms.

Paul left Sarah at the front door and went to park the car. The rain was still heavy and a blustery wind made it impossible to shelter under his umbrella.

Paul met Sarah inside the grand hallway. She had registered at the reception and was waiting to be shown to her room. After a few minutes, a young nurse came hurrying towards them.

"I'm Nurse Patton. I'm sorry to keep you waiting. Let me take your bag."

"It's okay," Paul mumbled.

They followed the nurse along a long corridor and up two flights of stairs. The room was clean and bright with a large window and two empty beds.

"That's your bed. The other lady will be back shortly. Make yourself comfortable. Would you like some refreshments? Sandwiches, tea?"

"Cheese sandwich and coffee would be nice," Sarah replied.

"Mr Michaels, would you like some refreshments?" asked Nurse Patton.

"No thank you. I must check into my hotel soon. I'll be back later."

"Mr Barrett will be in to see you soon," she said to Sarah. "He's ordered a repeat of the medical checks you had in Harley Street to make sure everything's in order for tomorrow. An echocardiogram, blood pressure, blood tests, nothing to worry about."

"Okay."

The door opened and a woman lying on a trolley was wheeled into the room and lifted on to the adjacent bed. The curtains around her were hastily pulled closed.

"I think I should go," whispered Paul.

"Okay."

"I'll check into the hotel and come back later." He kissed Sarah and left.

Sarah's next visitor was her psychiatrist, Mr Barrett.

"How are you today, my dear?" he asked.

"I'll be happy when it's all over."

"You'll be fine."

He placed a consent form on the table beside her.

"Please read and sign this."

Whilst she signed the form, he continued,

"Nurse Patton has probably told you, you'll be having a repeat of the pre-med tests we did in London. I need to make sure your heart is strong enough for the treatment. Also, you'll have blood tests and blood pressure. You were fit and healthy last time, so there's nothing to suggest anything's changed. A nurse will come for you shortly … and about tomorrow. I want to reassure you the treatment has a proven good outcome and should quickly reverse all your symptoms and depression. Do you have any questions?"

"Last time I saw you, you said you'll pass electric currents through my brain to trigger a brief seizure. I've been worrying about that ever since."

"You'll be under a general anaesthetic and strictly monitored. Just like any operation ... you'll be fine." He gave her a gentle pat on her hand.

"You may feel a little nauseous and confused when you come out of the anaesthetic, but that will quickly pass."

"I just want to get it over with."

"Of course you do. We'll do the first three procedures this week."

"How many will I need?"

"Depends. We normally review after three. Don't worry. You'll be fine, dear," he said, patting her hand for a second time. "I'll see you early tomorrow morning with Mr Brown, my anaesthetist. And remember, nil by mouth from 6.00 a.m."

The curtains around the bed alongside Sarah were pulled open. A young woman lay on her side fast asleep.

Sarah undressed and waited anxiously for the nurse to take her down for the tests. Just as well the bathroom was adjacent to the bedroom. Her bladder played nasty tricks on her when she was nervous. Whilst she waited for the nurse, she felt the need to pop into the bathroom almost every fifteen minutes to empty her bladder.

The medical tests went smoothly. The results were well within range. Sarah was a healthy young woman. However, the long journey and the procedures left her exhausted, and by the time she returned to her room dinner time was over. Sarah closed her eyes and slept for the next eight hours. She was fast asleep when Paul returned to the hospital that evening after checking into his hotel.

She slept soundly until eight o'clock the next morning. Still drowsy from sleep, Sarah was aware of a woman standing over her.

"Hi, how are you?"

She slowly opened her eyes and peered around. It was the woman from the next bed.

"Okay. I don't know whether they gave me a sleeping drug, but I had an amazing night's sleep."

"The stress and the tests make you exhausted. I saw you move. I hope I didn't wake you."

"No. What's the time?"

"Eight o'clock."

"I haven't slept that long for years," Sarah replied.

"Are you having your procedure this morning?" asked the young woman.

"Yes."

"I'm Margaret. What's your name?"

"Sarah ... I saw them bringing you back yesterday. Did you have the same treatment?" she replied sitting up.

"You having ECT?"

"Yeah. Is it really horrible?"

"No, nothing to worry about."

"Mr Barrett's booked me in for three this week. I hope I don't need anymore."

"I'm getting over a breakdown. I've had three miscarriages and an ectopic pregnancy. I can't seem to keep a baby for more than five months. I'm going home today and don't want to see this place again."

"Are you feeling better?"

"Too soon to say. This is my third time back here. I think the worst thing is memory loss, but maybe that's a good thing. Some things you don't want to remember."

Sarah smiled for the first time in weeks.

"Do you live locally?" Margaret asked.

"No. Edmonton in north London," replied Sarah.

"That's a coincidence. I live in Muswell Hill. We're almost neighbours. Why don't we meet for coffee sometime to swap notes?"

"I'd like that."

"What's your phone number? I'll leave mine on your bedside table. My husband Wills is coming to take me home so I'll probably be gone when you get back. Although

I still need to be discharged, and that can take all day. Good luck. Hope all goes well. See you in London. Oh, and by the way, the food's good. Tell your husband he can eat here."

"Thanks."

Nurse Patton arrived. Sarah climbed onto the trolley and was wheeled away for her first treatment.

***

"Mr Barrett said you were a good candidate. Indications are it went well," said Paul.

Sarah looked across to Margaret's empty, freshly-made bed.

"Has she gone?"

"About ten minutes ago. Her husband came."

"I'm sorry I missed her. She was nice. She lives in Muswell Hill and we arranged to meet for coffee when I get out of here. Did she leave her telephone number?"

"It's here. How are you feeling?"

"A bit dizzy. Glad it's over."

"I've been here for over an hour. Mr Barrett popped his head around the door about ten minutes ago and said you did very well. I've ordered you some sandwiches and coffee."

"Thank you."

The brief conversation left her exhausted. She closed her eyes and fell into a deep sleep.

Paul

Paul was deeply affected by Sarah's illness. In spite of being a doctor, he knew very little about mental health and how best to care for her. Looking after the family, together with working long hours in the hospital, was taking its toll. They were no longer a team and he didn't like the role of carer. He was also beginning to question their relationship, and whether he was still in love with Sarah, although he still wanted their marriage to survive, and the children needed them both. He was concerned about the procedures, but pleased Sarah had taken the initiative and decided to go ahead. As the day of the first procedure came closer, Paul was anxious they had made the right decision to go ahead with the ECT therapy. He would support her in every way possible.

Sarah had had her first session today and Mr Barrett reassured Paul it went well. But should he agree to put her through this for a second and third time, or call it a day and take her home? It seemed a radical treatment ... and what happens now if it doesn't work? If it makes her physically ill? Finally, he came to the conclusion, Sarah, alone, must decide whether she wished to continue. He just wanted his wife back.

Sarah

The sleepless nights and stress of waiting was over. The treatment was underway and soon she would be better. She was blessed with a wonderful husband and two healthy children and was determined not to throw it all away. But she sensed even Paul's patience was wearing thin. He deserved better. Once this was all over, she was determined to work hard at their marriage and make it a success. But the question of Stephen's paternity would remain in doubt for years to come. Whether his father is *Paul or George*?

***

Sarah was relaxing in the armchair beside her bed when Paul arrived the next morning.

He bent down to kiss her. "How are you feeling?"

She looked up and smiled. He hadn't seen her smile since before Stephen went missing.

"Good."

"Mr Barrett's very pleased with you," Paul replied.

"I know. He spoke to me during breakfast."

"How do you feel about having more treatments?" asked Paul.

"Now I'm here, I've got to go for it."

"That's great."

"I'm having two more. On Thursday, and Saturday. If all goes well, I can go home on Sunday."

"I can't get over how calm you look," Paul commented.

"I feel a weight's been taken off my shoulders and I've got my appetite back. I had an enormous breakfast of eggs and bacon and I've ordered salmon for lunch. Margaret said the food's good. Her husband Wills ate here. I can order you salmon for lunch if you want. But I think you'll have to pay."

Paul was delighted to see the change in Sarah. He was relieved the first procedure was successful and she was prepared to continue with the treatment. He was looking forward to having his old Sarah back.

"What did Mr Barrett say about the anti-depressants?"

"I can throw them away. Isn't that wonderful?"

He bent down to hug her. "You look amazing, and after only one session. I think you made the right decision to come here," he replied happily.

"Margaret had ten sessions."

"Judging by today, you won't need anything like that."

"She said she was going home feeling better," said Sarah.

"I can't believe how positive you are. I've got my old Sarah back," he exclaimed.

Nurse Patton put her head around the door.

"Would you like to join us for lunch, Mr Michaels?"

"Thank you ever so much. I'm told I can have salmon."

"Yes. Boiled potatoes and peas okay?"

"That would do a treat. And coffee?"

He took hold of Sarah's hand.

Chapter 45

Paul checked out of the hotel in Wimbourne Village early on Friday morning. He stayed with Sarah all day at the hospital and began his drive home late afternoon. He planned to spend all of Saturday with the children and return to the hospital on Sunday morning to bring Sarah home.

It was a hard drive from Wimbourne that Friday afternoon. The roads were always busier on Fridays, and as dusk fell the wind and rain began to whip around the car. Paul's thoughts drifted to Sandra. She had turned out to be a phenomenal mother and grandma and David helped her with the children on his days off.

By early evening Paul was beginning to tire and feel hungry. As he reached the outskirts of south London he decided to stop for a hot meal and a beer. He remembered reading about a public house called *The Drunken Donkey*, which he just happened to be passing on his route home. It was well-reviewed in *The Good Food & Pub Guide,* and he had promised himself to take Sarah there one day for a meal. Alongside the pub was an attractive looking hotel with ivy climbing up the walls. Both buildings stood in substantial grounds of lawns and trees.

The pub was always busy on Friday nights with diners and drinkers celebrating the end of the working week. Tonight, it looked as if the whole of south London was in the pub enjoying the convivial atmosphere with friends and work colleagues, good food and a glass or two of wine. He recalled the *Pub Guide* recommending the mile high steak and ale pie as probably being the best in London.

Paul ordered his food and grabbed a high stool at the bar. He was tired and closed his eyes to avoid the heavy cigarette smoke which was beginning to sting his eyes. He sipped his beer and was looking forward to enjoying the famous steak and ale pie, when he felt a tap on his shoulder. Paul was a stranger to the area. He swivelled around on his stool, and to his surprise, Rona stood behind him smiling.

"Paul?"

"My goodness. Rona, is that you?" He kissed her on the cheek.

"How are you?"

"Good. How did you see me in all this crowd?"

"I saw you come in," Rona replied.

"How are you?" he asked.

"Keeping going. Are you living down here now?" she asked.

"No. We're still in Edmonton. What a lovely surprise. Are you with someone?"

"No. Just popped in on my way home from work to pick up some food," she replied.

"Why don't we grab a table? You can eat it here." Paul suggested.

"Okay. I didn't see Sarah?"

"She's not with me."

Paul blinked. Rona looked amazing. Her hair was cut short in the fashionable geometric *Mary Quant* style bob. As usual, she was stylishly dressed in a black and purple hounds-tooth check pinafore dress, the hem rose inches above her knees, matched with fashionable and sexy white shiny patent leather boots that reached to her thighs. All this was covered in a voluminous short red leather coat. They pushed their way towards a vacant table.

"So … how are you? Where's Sarah?"

"She's not with me."

"You on a business trip down here?"

"No." Paul was being cagey. He didn't want Rona gossiping about Sarah's illness.

"How's your daughter?"

"Emma. She's doing well. We also have a son, Stephen."

"Lucky you."

"When did you last see Sarah?" he asked.

She looked thoughtful.

"A long time ago ... three years maybe, can't remember. With everything that's been going on in my life ... I've also lost contact with the girls. Are you visiting family?"

"No ... well. I wasn't going to say anything. But you might as well know ... Sarah's been having problems. After our son Stephen was born she had severe postnatal depression and she's in hospital in Wimbourne, Sussex. I'm on my way home from seeing her."

"I'm so sorry. Give her my love."

"We've had a terrible time. Stephen was kidnapped and she went into a deep depression."

"It was your baby who was kidnapped! Oh my God! It never occurred to me it was anything to do with you."

"Why should you?"

"I didn't know you had a son. Did they find out who took him?"

"The police never got back to us and we had other things to deal with," Paul sighed and paused. Rona reached for his hand.

He continued, "Thank God Stephen was returned to us safe and well. You can imagine the nightmare almost destroyed the family. I wanted to forget it happened but it had a lasting effect on Sarah. Please don't let on about Sarah's illness if you see anyone."

"Trust me. I'm a hermit. I've lost touch with everyone. I'm taking out all my frustrations and disappointments working all hours."

The waitress came with their food. There was an embarrassing silence whilst they ate. The pie was delicious, and with every mouthful Paul felt his anxiety lift and his strength return.

"This is the best ever pie I've ever tasted," he commented.

"So I hear. If I had the pie, it would put inches on my hips." She forced a laugh.

"Does that mean I can't persuade you to join me with something sumptuous from dessert trolley?"

"You can force me. They say the crème brulee is pretty good."

"You've got it!" replied Paul. "What have you been up to since we saw you last."

"After I left nursing, I got a job in John Lewis department store. Then I had a lucky break and got taken on by Mary Quant. That was before she became famous. I think I was already working for her when you got married."

That accounts for Rona's very modern outfit and *Quant-like* hairstyle Paul thought.

"I learned so much from her. Three years ago, I opened my own boutique on the King's Road in Chelsea, in competition with Quant. The shop's doing really well. I'm selling similar lines but cheaper." Her eyes shone.

"I can see the excitement in your eyes."

"Last year I won a contract with Terence Conran to design curtain fabrics for his shop. He also works with architects and designs interiors for the rich and famous, and I'm getting contracts for exclusive curtain designs from his rich clients. I'm now working more in fabric design and constantly looking for good staff to manage the shop and assist with the fashion design side."

"We always knew you were artistic. In truth, I never thought nursing was for you."

"Not really. That was a mistake. But all experience is good experience. Working and getting on with the public," she smiled.

Rona's young customers loved her short shifts, mini-skirts, hot pants all at affordable prices. She was an immediate success. But she was not so lucky in love.

"Are you with someone?" he asked.

"Married? No, I'm single again. Did you meet Neil?"

"No."

"We were married for two years. Bought a flat together. That's when I moved from Hackney. He's an actor and went away for weeks on tour. We spent so much time apart. I was busy building up my business and working all hours. I never knew when he was coming home. Then he had an affair with a blonde actress and we just drifted apart. We divorced. I think he married his blonde bombshell."

"I'm sorry," Paul replied.

There was a pause in the conversation.

"I'd like to see your shop. Sarah needs cheering up. I promised to buy her some pretty nightdresses."

"If you like we can go to the boutique tomorrow. That's if you've got time. I have some really sexy nightdresses. In fact, why don't you come back with me tonight and we can pick out some nightdresses for Sarah together tomorrow."

Chapter 46

Rona lived a bright new two-bedroom apartment on the London Road in Croydon, south London. Her choice of furniture and furnishings were straight out of *Ideal Home* magazine and Terence Conran's new *Habitat* store on Tottenham Court Road.

Her ultra-modern flat was filled with beech wood Scandinavian furniture. She had two stylish sofas in bright red leather and turquoise scatter cushions. The floor boards were stained black and covered with two huge white shaggy wool rugs. The large window was covered from floor to ceiling with stunning multi-coloured curtains in an asymmetrical design. They were so modern, at first sight, Paul thought the fabric had been indiscriminately splashed with turquoise and red paint.

In contrast, Rona's bedroom was decorated in subdued lilac and creams.

She guided him gently into the bedroom. He was exhausted after months of suppressed tension. Suddenly he became emotional and weepy. His body began to shake and he cried like a baby. Rona took him in her arms and let him cry on her shoulder. Then she slowly eased him gently on to the bed. They snuggled up together and Paul slept.

The stress and tension of the past months gradually began to fade away. He craved love and support. After years of the occasional one-night stand, which left him impassive, he feared falling in love with Rona. Caring for Sarah had taken its toll and had left him exhausted. Paul emerged from their love-making in a cosy, exhausted haze. Rona was warm and responsive and wanted to please him. She took him to dizzy heights he'd only previously dreamed of.

***

After the act he was remorseful. What on earth was he doing making love to Rona? For a nanosecond she calmed the stresses of the past months.

It was bizarre to think, that during their student days, he dishonestly told Sarah he didn't like Rona, when, in fact, he was always attracted to her. Paul began to brood over his lost youth. He had watched her on the night of the girls' party, many years ago, in the dank dark Kensington basement flat. The night of the drugs raid. Rona wasn't like the other girls. She stood out from the crowd. His impression was of a frivolous, exotic young woman who craved to be the centre of attention.

"I was wild during my year as a trainee nurse. The night of the girls' party was the first and last time I smoked cannabis. I ended up in a police cell smashed," smiled Rona. It was as if she could read his mind.

Rona was a sad enigma. Her mother was a war widow and an alcoholic and Rona was forced to leave home at sixteen. Her ebullient personality was her window on the world. She desperately wanted to be liked. As she grew into womanhood, she complained she attracted the wrong kind of men. Even her husband Neil had let her down. She remained a generous and vulnerable young woman, still searching for love, loyalty and security. And, as she confided in Paul, marriage and a family.

"When you get married you believe you're going to be happy forever? Then life gets in the way," mused Paul the following morning.

"Marriage works for some people. Men and women are like oil and water. They don't mix. Even on the day I married Neil, I was confused, and wasn't sure it would work. I attract the wrong kind of men. I've never met a man who wants stability and a family," replied Rona.

"That's sad. You'd make a great mum."

"I've always liked you, but early on you took a shine to Sarah," she confessed.

"You never showed any interest in me. I always fancied you, but I never thought you would be interested in a boring conservative junior doctor."

"That was my party girl image. I was only nineteen. I was acting out to hide my insecurities. My father was killed in the war and my mother went out cleaning and there were always lots of men around. I hid it from my friends, but it was just a case of survival."

"You certainly gave me the wrong impression in the nurses' home. I watched the young men sniffing around you. You've certainly changed and matured. Am I being too personal?"

"None of us are what we seem." She moved from her chair to sit on his lap and kissed him on the mouth.

"I don't think that's always true. But there are times we do our best to hide our anxieties," replied Paul.

"Why is it I can confidently run a successful business, but when it comes to a relationship it always breaks down?"

"Personal relationships are the hardest thing. I could have left Sarah many times over before we got married, but I loved her. I had so many rows with my parents. They didn't like Sarah because she's Jewish and we're Catholic. She was very upset. I suppose that's what being part of a family is all about."

"You've got to be firm when family get in the way."

"That's why many couples break up," replied Paul thoughtfully.

"Last night was great, but it should never have happened. Sarah was one of my best friends and I shouldn't have asked you back here," confessed Rona.

"I have to admit I've had the odd one-night stand during our marriage, but I've never been seriously unfaithful before last night. Believe me, and I'm not being glib, you're a breath of fresh air. I'd like to do it again."

Now he'd broken all the rules. Today was Saturday. After a week in Wimbourne he was looking forward to being with Emma and Stephen. Something had gone badly wrong. He'd slept with another woman whilst Sarah languished in a mental hospital – the very same woman he'd told Sarah on various occasions he didn't like. And today Paul planned to shop with Rona for exotic nightwear for Sarah. What kind of man does that?

His marriage was now threatened. After all the family pressures. The early years and the birth of their children. What had gone wrong?

Chapter 47

Paul had promised Emma he'd be home on Friday evening. It was now Sunday morning. He'd spent a second indulgent night with Rona. They enjoyed a luxury breakfast of bagels, smoked salmon and cream cheese in a five-star hotel before he began his drive back to Wimbourne to bring Sarah home.

***

By the time Paul arrived at the hospital, Sarah was packed and ready to leave. She looked well-rested and was pleased to see him.

"You look amazing," Paul beamed. "How were the treatments?"

"Much easier. I can't wait to get home to see the children."

"Me too … " Paul's voice trailed off. He'd let them down badly.

"I bought you these to cheer you up."

Sarah opened the bag. She held the first, then the second, raunchy nightdress up against her body.

"What the hell!" she exclaimed.

"I promised to buy you some nightdresses."

"Not like these. Did you get them from some sex shop? I'll never wear these. Only a whore would wear these. I can't believe you chose them."

Paul looked embarrassed.

"I like them. I thought they'd cheer you up. They're sexy and I'll be the only person to see you in them. I didn't buy them in a sex shop, I bought them in a very upmarket boutique on the King's Road in Chelsea. I'm sorry. I'll take them back and get something more suitable."

Sarah felt humbled.

"I'm sorry I shouted. Thanks for trying. This whole business has wreaked havoc on us both. I keep forgetting how much you've been running around because of me. You must be exhausted," replied Sarah.

"That's okay. This is the last day I'll be doing all that driving … we'll work things out," he replied. He moved over to give Sarah a hug. "I'm just pleased to see how well you look."

"Yes, well, I think we made the right decision to come here. Mr Barrett wants to see you before we leave. He's tied up until two o'clock. Do you mind hanging on?"

"No. I can do with a rest. I've been driving for three hours." Paul hesitated. No more lies! "There's a nice-looking pub a mile or so down the road where I thought we could have lunch. Also, if you're up to it, I like to show you the gardens here before we leave."

"I fancy some pub food," Sarah replied.

"Great. How about I show you the gardens first? You can't see how beautiful they are from your window. The horse chestnut trees make me feel nostalgic … I want to collect some conkers to take home for Emma."

It was a cool late September day. Even by midday the ground still squelched with heavy dew. They strolled around the landscaped gardens hand-in-hand. The sun twinkled on the lily ponds. The lawns were immaculately designed. Intimate family zones were created amongst sunken paved areas with seats strategically placed, shrouded by shrubs and bushes for family and patient privacy.

Paul bent down to select the hard conkers and stuffed them into his pockets.

"Did the boys at your school play conkers?" he asked.

"I played conkers."

"It was a big thing in our school. The best thing was getting them ready for the next big fight. I drove mum mad in the kitchen drilling holes to string them and soaked them in vinegar to harden them up. Mum complained I stunk the kitchen out after I persuaded her to let me dry them out in the oven. I always painted the winners in different colours before I swapped them."

Paul's eyes shone with nostalgia.

"I can just imagine you in short trousers playing conkers and *swapsies*," Sarah laughed.

"I'm so happy to see you laugh. You're looking so much better."

"It's done me good. I told Mr Barrett I'm gonna make sure I don't come back."

"We'll work on it together."

"I don't want to come back like Margaret."

Sarah bent down to pick up conkers.

"I want to show Emma how the girls in my school painted them with nail varnish and made them into necklaces and bracelets. She'll love it. Kids used their imagination in those days. We didn't have expensive toys."

They filled all their pockets.

"You're shivering. Let's take a rest," suggested Paul.

The sun slipped behind a cloud and it began to drizzle. He placed his new camel haired scarf around her shoulders.

She snuggled up to him.

"You know, I love you," he said.

"I'm sorry what's happened. I will get better, I promise you."

"I'm proud you managed this. I know this wasn't easy."

***

The drive home was uneventful. Emma and Sandra greeted Sarah with hugs and kisses, whilst Stephen slept peacefully in his cot. It was a happy homecoming.

Sarah was exhausted.

"You won't mind if I go straight to bed?"

"I'll bring up a light supper," said Sandra.

Sarah lovingly folded Paul's new camel haired scarf and carefully placed it on her dressing table. She hastily undressed and slipped into bed, too sleepy to notice the incriminating stain on the scarf.

***

That evening Paul reflected over his ill-fated and adulterous weekend. He had wallowed in pure lust and was ashamed. But after the events of the past year, he began to think whether he wanted to save their marriage.

The next morning Sarah woke before Paul. Bright sunshine shone through the chinks of curtain. She picked up the scarf, intending to put it into the wardrobe, but shock of shocks, there for all to see were smudges of bright red lipstick. Only yesterday, in the gardens, Paul had placed the scarf around her neck and said he loved her. Who was the owner of the lipstick? Who had he been with while she was in hospital? Her imagination began to run riot. The unpleasant lipstick stain had spitefully acquired a voice of its own, "*You'll see, I've got him now*."

Sarah prodded Paul in the ribs.

"What's this lipstick on your scarf? Whose is it?" she yelled in his ear.

"What the hell? Go back to sleep," he groaned and rolled over.

"The lipstick. Whose is it?"

"It must be yours. The scarf's brand new."

"I haven't worn lipstick since before going into hospital."

"Go back to sleep."

"Who's the woman? Are you having an affair?"

"Don't be silly, I've been with you all the time. Go back to sleep."

Over breakfast Paul was conciliatory. "Couldn't this have waited? Remember what Mr Barrett said. 'We've still got a lot of building work to do'."

"No. What do you expect me to think?" she replied sulkily.

"There's a very simple explanation. I should have told you, but I didn't think it was important. Last Friday, after leaving you, I had a meal in a pub called *The Drunken Donkey* in south London. Remember, I read you the good review in *The Good Food & Pub Guide* and said we'll go there one day. Well, you won't believe who I bumped into."

"Who?"

"Your old friend Rona."

"Oh."

"She was already drunk and tearful when I saw her. She'd just broken up with her latest man and I literally gave her a shoulder to cry on."

"You saw Rona?"

"Did you know she got married?"

"No. I haven't seen her for ages."

"So you never met Neil? They were divorced after two years."

"We lost touch. I'll phone her. Have you got her number?"

"I wouldn't bother her just now. She's a mess. She bored me with all her troubles, about her latest man letting her down and then collapsed in my arms. I'm almost a total stranger and still couldn't get away from her."

"I used to envy her. She was never without a boyfriend on her arm and always the live-wire of the party."

"You wouldn't envy her now. She said how she'd like to find someone steady like me and have children. She said she always attracts losers."

"I should have known there was a simple explanation. Mr Barrett's right. I've got so much to be grateful for: you, Emma and Stephen. As he said, 'I've got a lot of building work to do to get better'. Isn't it funny, Rona probably now envies me. I'm sorry I didn't trust you."

"Everything's going to be fine," reassured Paul.

***

Paul tried his best to follow Mr Barrett's instructions to the letter. On a good day, he had his old Sarah back, but on a bad day she still struggled to bond with Stephen, was uncooperative, and there were days of silence.

He quickly became frustrated with her slow progress and began to spend more leisure time in pubs. He didn't intend to be unfaithful, and explained his adulterous blips as the result of exceptional pressures at home. Paul was a healthy man, and this was the late 1960s, swinging London, the *pill*, and free-love.

Three months passed. After all his encouragement and Sarah's promises, he saw little improvement in her condition. She continued to be withdrawn and immersed herself in domesticity. Paul once told a colleague, "Going home to Sarah was like being in solitary confinement." He kept up the appearance of normality for the sake of the children.

Over the following months, with the help of intensive therapy, Sarah began to make a slow recovery. Gradually there were more good days than bad, and Paul became more optimistic there was a light at the end of a very long dark tunnel.

Chapter 48

"Sam told me the hospital's advertising for returners and part-time staff. Do you think I should apply?" Sarah asked.

"Of course."

Paul was delighted. This was the first positive conversation they'd had in months. She even sounded excited at the prospect of returning to work.

"I think it's a great idea. Sam told me about the new openings. I said I wasn't sure you were ready."

"Do you think I can cope?"

"Definitely. You're a good nurse and you need something other than the children to think about."

"I'll have to do a nurses' refresher course first. Mum said she'll help with the children."

"Things haven't changed much at the hospital. They'll be delighted to have you back. I definitely think you should apply."

"After my last few therapy sessions with Mr Barrett I told him I'm feeling much more confident and he said I should try and do a little job."

"All I can say is, go for it. It's the best thing you've said in months."

Paul was waiting for Sarah to get stronger before passing on his own news. His manager was impatient for a decision but, due to Sarah's ill-health, Paul had procrastinated.

"I wasn't going to tell you so soon," he hesitated, "But I've been offered a promotion. It came out of the blue ... the only problem is ... I wasn't sure you were ready for this."

"With all the work you're doing, I think it's long overdue. Will you get lots more money?"

Paul gave a nervous laugh.

"Yes. But before I finally accept, I need to discuss it with you because the job's on split sites. They're allowing me three months to tidy things up in my current job. But it will mean spending two days a week in Croydon Hospital and three days in the Middlesex Hospital. So I'll be away for two nights each week. I'll get a substantial raise in salary and a generous two-night residential allowance. It's a wonderful opportunity. But I'm concerned how you'll cope."

"I'm not sure … it's true I'm feeling much stronger and I don't want to hold you back. Mum's here to help and David loves the children as if they're his own. Is it permanent?"

"Yes. It will look good on my curricula vitae. If all goes well, I could soon make consultant."

"You've sacrificed so much for me, and if it's something you want to do, I think you should accept."

"I promise I'll come home as much as I can. And Croydon's not that far in case of an emergency."

"I'm very proud of you. You've had so much to put up with from me. I promise I'm not going to let you down again, and once I get back to work, I'll be my own woman with an independent income."

"Atta girl. Now you're talking like my old Sarah."

Chapter 49

Throughout Sarah's long recovery Paul's thoughts frequently drifted back to his magical weekend with Rona. Pondering in metaphors, he compared Sarah with Rona. Rona was champagne, effervescent and bubbly, while Sarah, he described cruelly like flat lemonade.

During these self-indulgent spells he dreamed of a future with Rona. It was on one such day of introspection he called her.

"Hi Rona. It's Paul Michaels."

"I was wondering if I'd hear from you again," she replied sarcastically.

"I'm sorry. It's not what I intended."

"What did you intend?" she asked.

"It's not what you think. I've had a tough time with Sarah. It's been an exhausting six months. Hopefully she now seems to be showing some improvement."

"It's just that I thought we clicked."

"We did," Paul replied. "Why didn't you phone me?"

"I thought about it. But I don't like getting tied up in threesomes. It becomes too messy."

"To be honest, I don't think I would have had the energy. Believe me Rona, there's not been a week gone by that I've not thought about you."

"That's touching."

"It's true. I've been to hell and back with Sarah, but I've got some good news I want to share with you." Suddenly a thought flashed into his mind. Did she have another man?

"You're not with anyone else, are you?"

"No one special."

"Believe me Rona, you've been on my mind for months. I'll never forget our weekend. Can we meet?"

***

Paul arrived at the Clementine Restaurant early that Saturday afternoon and sat at the nearest vacant table to a large bay glass window. He ordered a cup of coffee whilst anxiously watching and waiting for Rona to walk through the door. In a state of heightened anxiety, his fingers began to chip away on the cold hard wax that had dripped and solidified on the side of the chianti bottle candle holder. A regular nervous ritual in times of tension. He then carefully rolled the wax into tiny balls and placed them decoratively around the bottle. Small slivers fell on to the tablecloth, some flakes floated on to his trousers. He began to brush them away. Finally, fussing too much on his trousers, he hadn't noticed Rona approach his table. He looked up and there she was, in all her radiance, towering over him. He attempted to stand up, but she was already bending down to kiss him on the cheek.

"You look fantastic." Paul was pleased to see her.

"You don't look so bad yourself."

"I can't stop thinking about our amazing weekend," he smiled.

"Wasn't it great?"

"Would you like to eat?"

"Thanks," she replied, trawling through the menu. "What's all this good news?"

"I've got a promotion."

"Congratulations. What's the job?"

"Well, it's very interesting and very different. I'm going to be running a department working on two split sites, between Croydon Hospital and north London."

"That's a lot of travelling," Rona replied.

"I'll be spending two days and nights in Croydon. So I won't be that far from you."

"You can stay with me," she jumped in.

"I wouldn't be that presumptuous."

"Hotels are expensive."

"I'll get under your feet."

"I get lonely at nights," she smiled. "What does Sarah think about you staying away?"

"Sometimes I think she'd be happier if I wasn't around. She's planning on going back to nursing. It'll take a little while because she needs some refresher training first. If it works out, the job will keep her busy and her mum's around to help."

"In that case, what's the problem? It's all settled. I'll air the bed," she laughed. "You know, I always envied Sarah. I thought she had it all."

"She said the same about you. My main concern are the children. I'm a doctor but I didn't cope well with Sarah's breakdown. I think I've been wanting a way out for some time but can't leave the children."

"It's good she's going back to work. She'll meet new people and it'll give her a bit more confidence. Also, being apart two nights a week might bring a little sparkle back into your marriage."

"Maybe."

"Sometimes I wish I had children. But I don't think I've ever properly grown up. Never had a long-term relationship. I don't know if I can now," Rona mused.

"You haven't met Mr Right."

***

Paul never intended to fall in love again. Indeed, it created too many complications and too many lifestyle changes. Staying married was the easy option. He recalled the heady days with Sarah, wanting her and loving her.

He began his new job and settled into a busy split family lifestyle. The joy of being with Rona regularly each week quickly became a drug. On his Croydon shift his one thought was the joy of seeing Rona. He ached to be physically close to her warm yielding body – wanting her, needing her. Paul was almost middle aged. Could he be suffering from midlife crisis? Or was the daily drudge of family life getting him down? But surely marriage was wanting to be with the one and only person each and every day? How he missed his beautiful children. And would he ever tire of Rona?

Chapter 50

"I saw the consultant gynaecologist, the one you recommended at your hospital, and he's going to do a stitch in my womb next week," said Margaret.

"I thought he'd suggest that. How many weeks are you?" asked Sarah.

"Twelve, I think. I told him about losing two babies at around four months and one at five. He said the stitch will strengthen my womb and I should be able to carry to almost full term, or at least until the baby's viable."

"Our obstetrics unit is the best in London. How are you feeling?"

"Much more positive."

"I'm so happy for you."

"The downside is the doctor said I will need a lot of bed rest, so I will have to give up work early. We'll miss my wages."

"It'll be worthwhile when you have a beautiful baby," replied Sarah.

"I know. But I almost can't imagine having a baby after everything I've been through."

"I can understand that."

"How are you?" asked Margaret. "Did the ECT work?"

"I think so. I've also had some extra intensive therapy from Mr Barrett. I feel more in control, but I still get bad days and can't risk falling back into a depression again. I've had six bad months and still feel very fragile. I couldn't have come through it without Paul and Mum."

"You look well and you haven't needed to go back for more treatment like me."

"That's true ... but it's not been easy."

"It's never easy," added Margaret with empathy.

"I do have some good news. I'm going back to nursing. The hospital has a new scheme for part-timers, and I've enrolled on a refresher course next term," replied Sarah.

"I think you're amazing."

"I hope I can cope. Mum's at home to help, and if it doesn't work, I'll know I've tried. Paul thinks it's a good idea. He said I need to be with people."

"How soon can you start work?"

"The refresher course begins in September. If I pass the exam, I could start in the New Year. They call me *a returner*. It's an incentive to get young mums back working part-time."

"That's such a modern idea. Good luck."

"Thanks. We've both got a lot to look forward to."

Chapter 51

September 1970

As the day drew closer to the start of the nurses' refresher course, Sarah's anxiety returned. Without Paul's words of encouragement, she probably would have withdrawn.

"This is the perfect opportunity to get your confidence back with little effort. It will be good for your wellbeing and mental health and a mistake to pull out now. And, as for the exam, you can do that standing on your head!" Paul reassured.

January 1971

As Paul predicted, Sarah sailed through the refresher course, and achieved ninety-five percent in her written exam. However, her confidence began to wane when young full-time nurses treated her like a junior straight out of nursing school.

"How was your first week?" asked Sam.

"Challenging. Some of the full-timers are very arrogant. They seem to have a huge chip on their shoulders when it comes to us."

"The hospital's still experimenting with you part-time returners. They don't like change," Sam replied.

"Procedures haven't changed. The hospital's much the same and I'm more qualified than most of them."

"They'll come to their senses when they see how skilled you are."

"Some of them treat me like a halfwit. I try to tell them I was a staff nurse before I left to have a family."

"They see you as a threat. The silly ones think married women only work for *pin money*. You all have rich husbands to keep you."

"That's ridiculous. I want to work because I want to become a better nurse. I haven't got a rich husband yet ... Maybe when Paul becomes a consultant ..." Sarah laughed.

"I'm glad you can see the funny side. Some of the older career nurses lost husbands and fiancés in the war and can be jealous and bitter," added Sam.

"I never thought of that. I just want to add to my skills and work when the children go to school. Some of us part-timers are older women in their fifties with grown up children," added Sarah.

"Don't worry, we know you've got the best of motives. It's good so many hospitals are flexible and employing more people with different skills. The moaners will have to get over it. Soon there'll be lots of returners joining them."

"I had a run-in with Tracy Williams because I peeked at her medication chart and thought there was a mistake with a prescription. If I hadn't pointed it out, she could have given an old lady forty milligrams of a drug instead of twenty. Tracy reported me to Ward Sister saying I was interfering with her work."

"Aren't you on Boden Ward?"

"Yes."

"If you're talking about Sister Llewellyn, she's a mate of mine," said Sam.

"Should I have spoken to Ward Sister first, rather than speak to Tracy?"

"Sensitive situation. It may have been more diplomatic to have had a quiet word with Ward Sister first, but if it wasn't clear when the medication was due, it could have been dangerous. So I think you probably did right. I also think Ward Sister should have told Tracy about your previous seniority and trustworthiness. Tricky one," replied Sam.

"That's basically what Sister Llewellyn said. She spoke to Tracy and me together. She told Tracy I'm a highly qualified nurse, but also said Tracy was rightly cautious of me because she wasn't sure of my ability."

"I'll speak to Susan Llewellyn. See if we can go out for coffee sometime. We had a returner on our ward, and it can be tricky absorbing them. They're normally very good and work twice as hard because they are part-timers and grateful to have a job."

"I certainly am. Going back to work has been my saviour. It's a way of putting all the bad times behind me."

To celebrate Sarah's return, and to clear the air, Sam, Tracy Williams and Susan Llewellyn took Sarah out for an *Angus Steakhouse* dinner.

Chapter 52

"Thanks to you and your consultant, we have a beautiful baby boy. We're calling him Damien. He weighs 6lbs," announced Wills.

"Congratulations. How's Margaret?"

"Fine."

"Did she go full-term," asked Sarah, showing excitement.

"They took the stitch out at thirty-six weeks and Damien was born two days later. So 6lbs is a healthy weight."

"I'll say. When can I come and see them?"

***

Sarah answered the ringing telephone.

"Hi Sarah. It's Wills."

"Is it still okay to come over to see Damien tomorrow?" Sarah asked.

"Margaret's looking forward to seeing you. It's just she's not doing too well."

"What's wrong?"

"Come over. I think you'll be good for her. It's just … I want to warn you that since Damien's birth she's back on a downward spiral. She says you'll understand her depression."

"After everything she's been through," replied Sarah.

"I know. I thought she'd be over the moon. It's awful. This time we've kept her depression to ourselves, but I think you're just the right person to see her."

"I hope I can help," added Sarah.

"I'm worried now she's back on the anti-depressants. I can't be at home tomorrow. I have to go to work for an important meeting."

"Margaret will be okay with me. Trust me."

"Right now, I think you're the only person I can trust," replied Wills. "And oh, she has something important she wants to tell you."

***

"He's beautiful. I almost feel broody again," said Sarah taking Damien in her arms and rocking him.

"The stitch was a miracle. Wills now says he wants more babies," replied Margaret. "You know, he's amazing with Damien – definitely a *new man*. He's really enjoyed his time off work looking after us, and takes turns changing nappies."

"It's also a man's job now," joked Sarah.

But she was concerned. Margaret looked unwell. Her skin was sallow with dark shadows under her eyes.

"I'm glad everything's turned out well. You look great," added Sarah, doing her best to cheer up the occasion.

"I never thought this day would ever come after all the miscarriages."

"Nothing can be more wonderful than giving birth to a healthy baby."

Sarah was doing her best to lighten up the conversation, but she sensed something was clearly wrong. After an uncomfortable silence, Margaret bent her head forward as if deep in thought, and began to fiddle with her fingers.

Sarah took hold of her hand. "What's wrong?"

Margaret began to cry. "I've done something terrible and have a horrendous confession to make." Tears dripped down her cheeks.

"Nothing can be that bad," Sarah replied in an attempt to comfort her friend.

"Oh, yes. I was wicked, wicked, wicked."

Now Sarah was feeling uncomfortable and embarrassed. Was it right that Margaret should confide in her? They had only met a few times in the past year, so Sarah could never describe Margaret as a close friend.

"Does Wills know about what you want to tell me?"

Margaret shook her head and wiped her tears on her sleeve.

"This all sounds very melodramatic. Are you sure?"

"I think of you as a good friend since Wimbourne, and I value your opinion more than my family's. We've talked through the good times and the bad times together, and I know I can trust you."

Long silence. "I must confess something now. Not even Wills knows the truth."

"I still think you should tell Wills first."

"No. I've been thinking about this for ages, and now Damien's born I need to tell you. Wills will never forgive me."

"I'm not sure I want that responsibility if it's that bad."

"It's thanks to you we've got Damien. At the time this happened we never thought we'd have a child. Just try not to be too judgemental …"

Sarah couldn't imagine what Margaret had done, so long ago, that still caused her so much grief she had to beg for forgiveness. Something she couldn't even tell Wills.

"One of the reasons I ended up in Wimbourne is … I took someone's baby. Then, when you told me what happened to Stephen, I realised I took your baby."

The cold hard words hit like thunder and lightning, both striking simultaneously. The world immediately stopped and froze on its axis. Sarah was traumatised. Did she just hear Margaret confess that she had kidnapped Stephen?

"What are you saying?" Sarah replied, astounded.

"I don't know what you mean."

Sarah was horrified. "Why have you waited until now to tell me?"

Margaret was so distressed, wrapped up in her own little world, with her hands covering her face, she didn't hear Sarah's question.

"God forgive me. I saw the baby left all alone and thought the mother didn't deserve to have such a beautiful baby. No mother should ever leave her baby alone," Margaret whimpered.

"You kidnapped my baby?"

"No, I just borrowed him. He was all alone. I wanted to give him a good home. I wasn't going to harm him. I just took him home. I always intended to give him back. I admit I was jealous and desperate after all my miscarriages."

"You took my baby to your home. How did you explain Stephen to Wills?"

"I told him a friend left him with me when she went on holiday."

"You took my baby from Selfridges!" Sarah was incredulous.

"You make me sound like a wicked witch."

"You are a wicked witch. You're right. What you did was beyond wicked. You must have been out of your **bloody mind**," Sarah screamed.

"I know that now. I was on tranquillisers most of the time and didn't know what day it was. After my last miscarriage my boss told me to go home and get better. It wasn't easy."

Sarah rushed out of the room her hand firmly over her mouth.

"Are you going to be sick?" Margaret ran after her.

Sarah vomited into the toilet, wiped herself down then staggered back into the living room.

"You're a mad, crazy woman. I had a nervous breakdown and landed up in that looney-bin just because of you."

"Will you ever forgive me?" pleaded Margaret.

"No. I just wanted to die … For the rest of my life I'll never forget the four weeks Stephen was missing."

"Wills took William back to Selfridges. He was a beautiful baby, we called him William. I never told Wills about your baby, so there's no reason why he should connect Stephen and William."

What craziness was she spouting? Or was she genuinely confused there were two babies?

"There **IS** only one baby, and his name **IS** Stephen," Sarah shouted drying her eyes. "You almost destroyed our family and sent me mad. Why didn't Wills contact the police? Stephen's disappearance was in all the papers?"

"He wanted to protect me. It was an act of madness. Somehow, I lost control. I can't say sorry enough. Will you report me to the police?" asked Margaret.

Sarah took her time to reply.

"No. Too much time has passed and I can't face giving statements to the police. I won't even tell Paul. Thank God Stephen's home safe and well." She reached for her coat, adding, "Well, that's the end of a beautiful friendship."

"Don't go," Margaret pleaded. "You can't drive home in that state. You'll have an accident."

The women stood up, tears running down their faces, then simultaneously, and incongruously, reached out to give the other a comforting hug. Wiping her eyes, Margaret asked, "I suppose you won't stay for some tea?"

After long consideration, Sarah replied in a monotone voice, "Strong and sweet. You're right, I can't drive home in this state. My whole body's shaking."

They sat silently sipping tea, Sarah brooding over Margaret's revelation, when a sudden compulsion became overwhelming. It was now time for Sarah's confession.

"Since you've been so honest with me, I'm going to be honest with you." She coughed and composed herself before continuing,

"I'm also ashamed I've let my family down badly. The day you took Stephen, I was in a bad way. I was suffering from postnatal depression and Paul wanted to cheer me up. I had my hair done and went to Selfridges to buy a new dress. We were due to have dinner at the Savoy that night. Not that we could afford it.

"I can remember being in the changing room, trying on dresses, when I began to sweat and feel dizzy and confused. I think I may have passed out for a few moments. When I came out of the changing room, Stephen's pram was gone and, this may sound weird, I was so confused I couldn't even remember whether or not I'd brought him with me."

"If only I'd seen you in the store, I could have helped. What I did was unforgiveable."

"Yes, it was," Sarah confirmed.

Gradually the sweet tea and biscuits began to calm her nerves, to the extent she now felt a smidgen of empathy for Margaret's predicament and emotional state the day she snatched Stephen from Selfridges.

"Let's try to calm down," Sarah hesitated. "In some ways I can understand what pushed you over the edge to take a baby."

"I'm so, so sorry. I will never forgive myself. I promise I'll make it up to you. I don't want to lose your friendship. I'd die if I thought you'd tell Paul," Margaret beseeched.

"What you told me is horrific, and I promise I won't tell anyone, not even Paul. Believe me, I'm no Mother Theresa. After you've been so honest with me, I want to tell you something which you must never ever tell anyone. It's got to do with my postnatal depression and the day I took Stephen to Selfridges. Can I trust you? Promise me Wills and Paul must never know this."

Margaret thought, 'What could possibly be more sensitive than Sarah forgetting she left baby Stephen in Selfridges.'

"Anything, anything. You can trust me."

"Well, this is also one more reason I ended up in Wimbourne. My good friend Sam knows about this, but no one else. The main reason for my depression and anxiety that day in Selfridges, the day you took Stephen, and why I'm never going to tell Paul and the police that you snatched Stephen, is because …"

Now it was Sarah's turn to cover her face and cry. Sobbing between her words she continued erratically, "I was depressed because … I don't know if Paul is Stephen's father … because I had an affair around the time he was conceived. At one time I tried to tell him but I couldn't find the courage."

"Oh my. What a pair of misfits we are!"

Margaret hugged Sarah.

"I promise I won't tell a soul. Did Paul find out about the affair?"

Sarah shook her head. "Paul would go ballistic if he had any inkling Stephen might not be his son."

"I promise you, your secret's safe with me."

Chapter 53

The doctors said Simon Drew was lucky to be alive. He'd been in a coma on life support for four weeks after narrowly surviving a horrific car accident. Every day his devoted wife, Rosie, sat by his bedside watching and praying for him to regain consciousness.

On the twenty-ninth day Rosie's prayers and patience reaped rewards. On that momentous day, Simon slowly began to come back to life. With all the strength he could muster he tried to force his eyes open. This went unnoticed by Rosie and the nursing staff, and Simon was still too weak to open them and lapsed back into a comatose sleep.

With each passing day Simon grew stronger. On day thirty-two he managed to keep his eyes open for a few seconds, whilst trying to make sense of his strange new surroundings. The following day Rosie was euphoric when she saw Simon's eyes flash open and quickly close. Overjoyed she ran down the middle of the ward, yelling frantically and waving her arms for attention. Simon's recovery now seemed possible. Nurse Sarah Michaels was the first to see Rosie.

"What's the matter?"

"He's opened his eyes," Rosie screamed, jumping up and down with joy.

"Are you sure?"

"Yes – look, he's doing it again. I thought I saw some movement the other day. I'm certain he can see me."

Simon saw a strange woman peering over him and heard her loud voice. He was confused. Who is this woman with the piercing voice? Her scream would awaken the dead. He began to shiver.

"Nurse, why is he shaking? What's the matter with him?"

Simon's thoughts were running apace. 'Who am I? What's my name? The place was anodyne and bleak. Where am, I? Is this a hospital? Was I in an accident? Think, think … who am I? What's my name? Oh my God, I can't remember a thing.'

"Is he going to be all right?" the woman yelled again.

"Shush, keep your voice down. Your husband's recovering from massive injuries and he needs quiet," Sarah replied.

"Mr Drew, can you hear me? Squeeze my hand if you can hear me," said Sarah in a hushed voice.

Simon Drew squeezed her hand in response.

"That's amazing. He can hear you. Does that mean he's going to be okay?" Rosie's voice remained shrill.

"It's a good sign. Keep your voice down. He needs peace and quiet."

Sarah leaned over to adjust an intravenous drip.

Simon was in a coma for over a month. In week two he had had a second brain scan. The consultant said there was some brain activity, but they wouldn't know how badly his brain was damaged until he regained consciousness. Rosie was ecstatic to be by his side as he slowly came back to life.

"Mr Drew I'm leaving you in the competent hands of your wife," said Nurse Michaels.

"Simon, Simon I'm so happy. We've been waiting for this day for weeks. You know you were in a horrible car accident and we thought we'd lost you."

He recollected the high-pitched voice, but he still didn't recognise the woman sitting beside him to be his wife. Even in his frail condition, he wished she'd go away. Every part of his body hurt. He ignored Rosie, closed his eyes and drifted back into a deep sleep. He wished the angel nurse who saved his life would come back.

Simon's physical strength slowly began to recover, but he still remembered nothing from before the car accident. Rosie, and his three children, Philip, Suzy and Gregory remained strangers to him. They may well have been people who'd just walked off the street. And he still couldn't reconcile Rosie as being his wife. Yet he was convinced he recognised the angel nurse who'd saved his life from before his accident.

Rosie was anxious to restore his memory. She sat tirelessly at his bedside telling stories about their children, Philip, Suzy and Gregory, and anecdotes from the war. She also showed him their wedding photographs taken outside a beautiful Catholic church on the Isle of Man. But nothing sparked his memory.

***

"Now you're so much better, I thought you might like a visit from a member of the local synagogue," said Sarah.

"I'm not Jewish," Simon was surprised.

"Mrs Drew put your religion down as *Jewish* on your admittance form."

"That's not possible. My wife showed me pictures of our wedding outside a Catholic church."

"Would you like a visitor from the church?"

"No. I don't follow any religion and I don't want any visitors. Certainly not Jewish or Catholic," Simon replied abruptly.

"Sorry, if I upset you."

"No, I'm sorry," he replied, patting her hand. "I didn't mean to be rude. You're my favourite nurse."

Sarah looked thoughtful before saying,

"I was born Jewish and my husband's Catholic. Isn't that a coincidence?"

He ignored her question.

"Nurse Brady said you still don't remember anything from before the accident," Sarah continued.

"No, but it's strange I'm having exotic dreams in bright colours. It's like I'm in a cinema watching a film. But I still don't recognise my family. It's like they're strangers and it frightens me."

"When you get home, everything will come flooding back. Tell me about your dreams."

"I'm about twenty. And, the strange thing is, everyone, including me, is speaking a foreign language and I *can* understand them! I think it's German. But I can't speak German and I don't think I've been to Germany. How do you explain that?"

"I can't. Ask your wife. She will know if you have any German connections." Sarah replied.

"Do you believe in reincarnation? Do you think it's possible I was German in a previous life?"

"I don't believe in reincarnation." Simon's conversation was now becoming too deep and personal and Sarah didn't want to get further involved. "I must get on. Maybe we can speak later," she replied briskly.

"One last thing,"

"Be quick, I'm behind schedule."

"One person I do remember in my dreams of my previous life is you."

"Now you're being ridiculous."

***

"Nurse Brady told me you're going home tomorrow," said Sarah plumping up Simon's pillows. "Will you come back for physiotherapy?"

"Yes. And the doctor also suggested a few sessions of psychotherapy. What are your thoughts on psychotherapy?"

"I think it can be very helpful to talk over your worries. Don't quote me, I'm very new here, but I believe it can be very therapeutic," Sarah replied.

"Nurse Brady said it should unblock my brain. I still can't remember anything from before the accident."

"In that case, I think it's a very good idea. You've certainly got to unblock something."

Simon laughed. "I've always been scared of shrinks."

"Our therapists are very good."

"I won't worry then. All the staff in the hospital are wonderful."

"It can be a long process for both your body and brain to recover from such trauma."

"You've been a wonderful nurse. Maybe we could have coffee sometime when I come back for treatment," Simon asked boldly.

"We'll see. Once you get home things will look different. I'll be a distant memory. You mustn't worry. Simple things will spark recognition from the past. Things you and Rosie did together. Memories will all come flooding back."

"That's what Nurse Brady said."

"Well, there you are. She knows what she's talking about."

"She's been very understanding and helped me think more clearly. So have you, and I've enjoyed our chats."

"Rosie said to be ready and waiting for her in the common room tomorrow at eleven o'clock."

"Thanks for everything."

***

Simon fell into a deep sleep and continued to dream in bright colours. In tonight's episode, he was lying on a beach of soft white sand, watching the waves gently break on to the shore. The sea was Caribbean turquoise blue. A beautiful woman in a tiny red bikini emerged from the water. The sun shone on the girl's face hiding her identity.

"Julie, is that you?" he called.

"No, this is Nurse Sarah Michaels. You can't have forgotten me. We chatted only this afternoon."

That's impossible. The girl running towards him was clearly Julie, or, was she Nurse Sarah? He couldn't be sure. He was puzzled. He was in no doubt it was Nurse Sarah calling him, but the voice was Julie's. He would never forget her lyrical, mellifluous voice. Why had he called Julie's' name, when clearly it was Nurse Sarah calling him? The girls gradually merged together to become one. Sarah and Julie, Julie and Sarah were co-joined. Like two peas in a pod. But Julie was wearing a 1940s swimsuit whilst Sarah wore a fashionable red bikini of the 1970s. Nevertheless, they were like two identical twins. Julie would soon become Simon Drew's beautiful bride.

But Simon would never marry his beautiful bride, Julie. He was a German refugee living in London during the Blitz and Julie was pregnant with his baby. A week before their planned wedding he was arrested and taken to the Isle of Man internment camp for Germans and enemies of the allies, where he remained for the entire war. Tragically, Simon would have to wait thirty years before he discovered the full truth about what happened to his beautiful fiancée Julie and their baby.

The dream finished abruptly. Lights suddenly flashed on beneath him. He found himself sitting on the edge of a narrow ledge, his legs dangling precariously over a deep precipice. Below was an enormous illuminated carousel. It reminded him of an oversized airport carousel.

Simon peered down over the chasm with fear. To his amazement, he saw a body slowly moving around on the huge 360-degree carousel. He was mortified. This wasn't any body. This was his body going around and around, faster and faster. As the body re-emerged from a blind spot on the furthest side of the circuit, he saw an arm or a leg was missing. Faster, faster and faster on its 360-degree journey. Each time it circled more body parts disappeared, until finally the carousel was empty. There was a second explosion of light. Then all that remained was blackness.

"Nurse Brady, come quickly. I can't find Mr Drew's pulse," called Nurse Sarah Michaels.

Chapter 54

"I think my father's just died." Sarah was having lunch with Sam in the hospital canteen.

"I thought your father died years ago,"

"Not **THAT** father! My real father, my birth father," Sarah replied excitedly.

"Calm down, otherwise I might think you've lost your mind," Sam joked, then placed an affectionate arm around her friend's shoulder.

"I told you about the road traffic accident patient a few weeks back."

"You get lots of road traffic accidents on your ward. I don't remember you mentioning anyone special," Sam replied.

"This man was brought in almost dead about six weeks ago. Well, he just died."

"What's so special about him?"

"I told you. I think he was my real father. He said he remembers me from a previous life."

"He sounds delusional. A consequence from the accident," said Sam.

"No. He really believed it, and I think it could be true."

"Now I do think you've got a screw loose. They've been working you too hard. What on earth are you talking about?"

"No, just listen. Something inside me really believes he is my *genuine* birth father. He lost his memory in the car accident. His wife Rosie signed him in on the hospital admission form as being Jewish, but the family are Catholic. And his name was Simon. Don't you remember in the letter my birth mother wrote, she said my father's name was *Simon*?"

"You need more than that to go on."

"There's more. When he was asleep I heard him rambling in a foreign language, I think it was German.

When he woke up, he said he couldn't speak a single word of German. The whole thing is weird. I said he should ask his wife if he has any connection with Germany. It could also help restore his memory with other things. He never told me whether he'd asked her."

"Did you believe him when he said he couldn't speak German?"

"I think so. One thing he said, which was a bit spooky, is that after the car accident he dreamed in colour and he saw me in his dreams."

"Oh my, in the end, he could just be a dirty old man."

"He wasn't like that. In the letter my birth mother Julie left me, she wrote her boyfriend Simon was German and disappeared before their wedding. She said he could have been arrested by the police because he was German. Don't you remember? That's probably why they never got married."

"It's still a long shot. You haven't got much to go on. I suppose you could speak to his widow, Rosie."

"I can't do that, it's not professional and, to be honest, I never liked her. She sat with him for four long weeks when he was in the coma, and when he regained consciousness, he said didn't know her."

"He couldn't remember his own wife?"

"That's what he said."

"Did he remember his children?"

"I'm not sure. He kept asking me questions. He said he thought he knew me, or someone just like me. I thought at first he was crazy. But nothing explains how he could speak German while he was asleep, but when he woke up he said he knew nothing about Germany, he'd never been there, and couldn't speak a word of the language. Explain that?"

"I can't. It could be he just fancied you."

"It's more than that. I also felt a strong affinity to him. But sadly, I'll never know the truth now."

"Have a quiet chat with his wife."

"I don't want to give her any more pain."

***

"I did what you suggested," said Sarah. "I spoke to Rosie Drew, Simon Drew's widow. She was very nice, and you won't believe what she told me.

"She said Simon Drew was born a Jew in Germany. Somehow he managed to get to London just before the war. He lost all his family in the war. Well, Rosie said, he met this girl in London. I asked her if she could remember the girl's name. Was it Julie? She said she didn't know. Anyway, Simon and his girlfriend were going to get married. She was pregnant, but just before the wedding he was arrested and taken to a prisoner of war camp on the Isle of Man. Rosie told me that during the summer the prisoners were sent to pick fruit on the local farms. That's how she met Simon. He worked on Rosie's parents' farm and they got married after the war."

"That's a story and a half. You could make a film about it," said Sam.

"So you see everything he said was true. He was just confused. And if I *am* Simon's daughter, maybe I look a lot like my mother, his girlfriend! What do you think?"

"Unbelievable," replied Sam.

"That means if Simon Drew is my real father, then their children, Philip, Suzy and Gregory are my half-siblings!"

Chapter 55

It was Paul's turn to supervise the children's baths, put them to bed and read them a story while Sarah and Sandra cleared away after dinner.

"All's quiet on the western front." He popped his head around the kitchen door before settling down on the sofa in the living room to read his medical journal.

"Thanks. I'll go and check on them when we're finished," replied Sarah, then turned her attention back to Sandra.

"We've been wondering about David. It seems ages since we last saw him. I don't want to be nosey, but didn't you see him last night?"

"Yes. He apologised for not coming in. The embassy's short-staffed and he's working all hours. They're having problems filling an important vacancy in the London office and want to extend his contract for another six months."

"That's good news."

"There's more. We had a long talk about our future and his work, and he's decided to settle in London."

"Will he continue working at the embassy?" replied Sarah.

"That depends. If he can't get suitable employment there, he will have to look elsewhere. But either way, he wants to stay in London."

"You never wanted to move to America."

"I'm too old to start a new life, and America's so far away. His rental flat expires in three months and he wants me to start house-hunting."

"How exciting. Where does he want to live?"

"He likes this neighbourhood, and it's easy for him to travel to the embassy from here. He wants us to live close to you, so we can help with the children. You know how much he's grown to love the children."

"Well, I'm blown away."

"So … will you come house-hunting with me?"

"You bet. David's been the best thing that's ever happened to you. You look twenty years younger, or should I say, you now look a million bucks?"

Sandra laughed. "He's a wonderful man. Your father was very different. But there you go … I'm lucky to have a second chance."

"And you, who never even had a passport, and never left England for your summer holidays. What would Dad have said if you'd asked him to take you to America?"

"He would say I was crazy. He always said, 'what's wrong with England?' Anyhow that was then, this is now," Sandra replied.

"How you've changed. I'm so proud of you," said Sarah. Recalling, when her mother was married to her father, she would never question his decisions.

"What about the wedding?"

"We're planning on a spring wedding, next April. How would you feel about spending a holiday in America? David still wants us to get married in Tampa, Florida."

"I'd love it. You know I've always wanted to go to America. I'll have to get my atlas out. I don't even know what Florida looks like. Is Tampa near Miami?" Sarah asked.

"No." Sandra laughed. "Miami's on the Atlantic coast. Tampa's on the Gulf Coast, further north. David wants to book the best hotel in the area. It's called The Don Cesar. Locals call it the *pink palace*. It's on the beach, in St Petersburg, just south of Tampa and a popular place for film stars."

"Film stars, wow." Sarah was fascinated. "Will we see Rock Hudson?"

"It's possible. I think I prefer Cary Grant."

"This is all unbelievable. Could you ever have imagined five years ago us bumping into film stars, in a big posh hotel in America?"

"Not in my wildest dreams," replied Sandra, giggling.

"I must tell Paul."

Sarah ran into the living room where Paul was stretched out on the sofa reading about another hopeful breakthrough in cancer research. She nudged him, "How would you feel about going on holiday to America?" she asked excitedly. "David's going to book the wedding for next April in Florida."

"Can't see why not. As long as I can get a locum to cover," he replied.

***

The following evening David joined the family for dinner.

"Did you know there are alligators and bears roaming the streets of Florida," Emma told him.

"I've seen alligators in Florida, but I don't think you'll find bears there," David laughed.

"I want to see bears. Like my cuddly bear, Boffin, I take to bed with me every night," replied Emma grumpily.

"I promise I'll take you to see real live alligators and dolphins, and ENORMOUS amphibious mammals called manatees, nicknamed sea elephants. These gigantic creatures swim under the sea in shallow water. They breathe in air just like us, so every so often they have to pop their noses above the water to breathe." replied David.

"That sounds funny. I don't like the sound of those animals. I want to see bears."

"We'll have to go to Canada to see bears, and they won't be roaming the streets. They stay in the countryside," added Paul.

"That's not always true," replied David. "There have been frequent reports of bears wandering into townships."

"This all sounds very different from England. Florida will be a real-life geography lesson for all of us. Something Emma will always remember. It's a shame Stephen's still too young to understand," said Sarah, almost in awe of their impending trip.

"His time will come. More people are flying, and it's getting cheaper," David replied.

"Package holidays are responsible for that," added Paul.

"Did you know Florida was originally the home of the red Indians?" said David. "When the white men arrived, they killed off the Indians and took their land. Red Indians also died from white man fever because their bodies couldn't fight off the white men's diseases."

"And because it's so very hot and humid, they have lots of exotic birds and fish we can only see in our zoos," Paul's voice peaked with the excitement of a young boy.

"I can't wait to go," said Emma jumping up and down with excitement.

"I hope you can take an extra week or two off when Mum gets married so we can tour around?" Sarah pleaded.

"I've already told you, as long as I can give the hospital plenty of notice and arrange for a locum, I can't see a problem. I don't want to miss all the fun," Paul replied.

***

In truth, the impending trip was becoming a defining major crisis in their marriage. Currently, Paul was enjoying self-indulgent mid-week stays with Rona. Now Sandra and David's forthcoming marriage, and the family's trip to America, caused him fresh anxiety. Clearly this wasn't the appropriate time to tell Sarah he was leaving her to make a fresh start with her one-time friend Rona.

With the flights and hotels booked, Paul looked forward to spending holiday leisure time with Emma and Stephen. The decision about his future with Sarah would have to wait until after the wedding.

Any mention of Sarah, and Rona exploded with rage. When Paul told her about his planned trip to America, she sulked and refused speak to him for more than a week. She later apologised and confessed she was jealous he would leave her for Sarah. Paul made it crystal clear their marital love life was well and truly dead. He stayed because of the children. Rona then admitted she was envious of the time he spent with Emma and Stephen.

The day before his trip Rona sulked again and wouldn't speak to him. Finally, when the taxi arrived to take Paul to the airport, she locked herself in the bathroom and refused to say goodbye.

Rona was a beautiful, volatile, intelligent and highly sexed woman. In spite of all the aggravation he loved her. Or was he confusing love with lustful sex?

Chapter 56

Florida - The Sunshine State

For centuries Florida was just swampy marshlands, home to tribes of Indians and the only place on earth where crocodiles and alligators existed together. Brutal heat and humidity kept the white man away from the most southerly state of the USA.

This was until the 19th century, when pioneers began to drain the swamps and business men spotted huge money-making schemes by transforming huge chunks of marshlands into valuable money-spinning real estate. Ever since, thousands of square miles of everglades have been developed into towns, whilst vast swathes of swampy wetlands and networks of forests and prairies have disappeared forever, causing irreparable destruction to the fragile ecosystems.

***

"How do I get my marriage back on track?" Sarah asked Tracy Williams, her friend and confidant since returning to work at the hospital. "I sometimes think he's acting out and only coming home for the children."

"Romance him. Have a romantic dinner together. Flirt with him. You still love him, don't you?"

"Yes, in spite of all the other women."

"How do you know there are other women?"

"I've had my suspicions lots of times. I found red lipstick on his scarf once. I don't use red lipstick. He said it happened when he bumped into an old friend of mine. He told me she was in a bad way and cried on his shoulder."

"Do you believe him?"

"I don't know."

"If you're still suspicious, ask him again," replied Tracy.

"I don't want to have a flaming row just before we go away."

"If you really want to keep him, you've got to fight for him. Buy some sexy nightdresses, seduce him. I bet your nightdresses are old and shabby."

"Since the children I've chosen them for comfort. I feel stupid trying to seduce him after all these years."

"For heaven's sake, he's your husband! Speak to him! Especially if you think he's got wandering eyes."

"I just want to relax and enjoy Mum's wedding."

"You won't enjoy the wedding until you've cleared the air with Paul. Kiss him. Give him a cuddle. Relax. Then you'll enjoy the wedding. You said you still love him."

"I do."

"Then for heaven's sake go away and show him you love him … send me a card. Tell me how you're getting on."

Tracy waved and blew a kiss. "Have a fab time. See you in two weeks."

***

The family flew into New York, en route to Miami. David's sister Doreen and husband Drew, met them at the airport and drove them north to Tampa. Paul's first impressions of Florida was the intense sunshine, tropical plants, searing humid heat and massive five lane highways. As Emma said,

"Everything in America is enormous."

Emma couldn't believe her eyes when she saw the length of the cars. She later told school friends in England, "The cars are as long as our street." Sarah loved the shoes and fashion. "So stylish, and half the price I would have to pay in London." And Stephen loved the hotdogs, beef-burgers and milkshakes in the *Steak'n'Shake* Burger bar.

David had booked the family into the Don Cesar Hotel for three nights, the venue for the wedding. The hotel was breath-taking. Truly, a *pink palace*. With several huge marbled atriums, swimming pools and restaurants. Sarah and Paul's large bedroom had a corner bath, a shower and two king-sized beds. Sarah wondered which bed she would be sleeping in tonight. All this, alongside a stunning sugar-white sandy beach.

***

The wedding was a truly memorable affair. Emma was a bridesmaid with Lyla, David's granddaughter. The marriage was solemnised on the beach under a huge wedding canopy smothered in flowers. After the ceremony the wedding party withdrew into a large ballroom to enjoy a sumptuous Caribbean buffet. Finally, back to the beach to dance the night away under the stars to the sounds of an ebullient Caribbean steel band.

Sarah enjoyed the good meal. She remembered Tracy's words of encouragement so she deliberately consumed a little too much wine and champagne, just enough to make herself a little bit tipsy, lose her inhibitions and give her courage to seduce Paul. The balmy perfumed night air aroused her sensitivity. Her body tingled from the tips of her fingers to the soles of her feet as the alcohol coursed around her body and her head began to spin round and around. In truth, she'd drunk too much alcohol and was blind drunk, and she knew it. Sarah could barely control her emotions. The intoxicating liquid was forcing her whole being to want sex with Paul, right there and then, on the beach. But her upbringing and modesty screamed *no*.

Once more she blamed herself for their failed marriage. After her brief affair with George, and Stephen's birth, she guiltily avoided sex. Paul deserved better. He'd been a tower of strength during her breakdown. But as soon as she recovered, they began to drift apart again. She attributed this to his complex work schedule.

Throughout the day she felt sexy in her new pale blue silk figure-hugging evening dress, she could ill-afford, but impetuously bought to attract Paul back. She firmly believed if nothing happened tonight, in this romantic setting, their marriage was as good as dead and buried.

So, whilst Paul was in the bathroom she quickly slipped into her new black organza and lace nightdress and climbed into one of the big king-size beds. She didn't want to appear too bold and nervously waited for Paul to take the initiative. She was relieved when he left the second bed vacant and climbed in beside her and slipped the delicate lace strap over her shoulder.

"You looked stunning today. I watched all the men's envious eyes on you," he whispered in her ear.

She moved to face him.

"You didn't look so bad yourself in your white tuxedo."

"What's gone wrong?" he asked.

"It's my fault ... I'm sorry."

"We've both got things to answer for. I suppose I must be a glutton for punishment, because I still love you."

"I love you too. I thought I'd ruined things between us forever."

"Today I fell in love with you all over again," he replied.

His words left her speechless. He'd now mentioned the word *love* twice, and she thought she'd lost him.

"Wait and see how we feel at the end of the holiday," she replied nibbling on his ear. "I just want to enjoy our holiday."

Time for talk was over. They made love to the sounds of soft waves lapping on the shoreline. A full moon and stars twinkled over a millpond sea enhanced only by the exotic atmosphere.

Paul was warm and gentle, and Sarah responded with hungry enthusiasm. But would one night of bliss be enough to save their marriage? She drifted into a deep luxuriant sleep.

***

The following morning the family relaxed on the soft white sandy beach. Paul was enjoying unlimited time with Emma and Stephen as they worked together constructing an elaborate sandcastle.

"Last night was good," Sarah whispered into his ear. He responded with warm a smile.

"These shells are pretty. Why don't we use them to decorate the sandcastle?" Sarah suggested.

After they finished building the castle Paul began to dig a moat. The children then had the never-ending task of filling the moat with buckets of sea water.

"Daddy, why is the water going down so fast into the sand?" Emma asked.

Sarah left them for her luxury cabana, while the three remained absorbed in their project.

"Don't work too hard," she called.

"I'm letting them do all the work," he smiled.

"Come on Daddy, hurry up, help us fill the moat," said Emma, handing him Stephen's bucket.

Temporarily relieved from his moat digging duties, Paul followed the children to the water's edge, holding Stephen's bucket and splashing his feet in the water searching for more sea shells.

"Why don't we put these big shells on the floor of the moat then the water might not disappear so quickly?" he suggested.

"Let's do it. I'll fill my bucket with shells and you can fill Stephen's with water," replied an excited Emma. "Come on."

Meanwhile, Sarah remained inactive soaking up the sun on her cabana.

"I've been so looking forward to this holiday," she called out.

"So have I. It's not often I have this much time with the children. Come and help us build sandcastles," he replied.

"I've already built my sandcastles in the air!" she answered.

"I thought the phrase was 'building sandcastles in the sky'."

"Does it matter?"

"No. I didn't mean to upset you," he replied. Paul turned to the children.

"Daddy's tired. I'm going to sit with Mummy for a bit. Carry on with the building. I'll watch you. I can be your supervisor." He sat beside Sarah.

"It's wonderful relaxing as a family again. I love watching the children enjoying themselves with you. They miss you during the week," said Sarah.

"I miss them."

"Can we try again," she asked.

I wondered when that would come up."

"Last night you said you loved me, and I'm not responsible for everything that's gone wrong."

"I never said you were. But sometimes, when I look back, I think my parents could have been right. Oil and water don't mix," he replied.

"That's cruel. I thought you were stronger than your parents."

"So did I."

"I love you and don't want to lose you."

"We can't talk now with the children … the question is, can we still live together? Last night was fantastic, but I'm too tired to go back over old chestnuts," replied Paul.

"It's just wonderful the four of us being together again. I want to celebrate Mum and David's wedding, and I want all of us to have a fabulous holiday."

"Believe me, so do I."

After a long pause, Sarah continued, "I think things could change if you weren't away so much."

"It's the good job that keeps you in the lap of luxury."

"We miss you. I promise I'm a different person now. Mum will tell you. I also love my job. It was difficult settling back into work, but I love it now."

"I hate to say this, but my sympathy ran out when you were in the psychiatric hospital. I couldn't leave you then. You always had excuses for your depression. Your mother, the house, you were unbearable. Truthfully, if it hadn't been for the children, I would have walked out ages ago. Can a leopard ever change its spots?"

"Yes, I can," she pleaded. "I was awful then. I'm never going to go back to that. I promise."

He began to dwell on the present and the recent past. Sex with Sarah last night was amazing. During their lovemaking he remembered telling her he loved her. But how was this possible when he was in love with Rona? And Sarah had never said anything to suggest she was suspicious he was being unfaithful.

Paul's thoughts drifted to Rona. He wondered what she was doing this Sunday afternoon in England and whether she was missing him. Was she lonely? He wanted to tell her he was sorry they had argued the day he left for the airport.

Sarah broke into his reverie. "I've grown up a lot."

"How do I know nothing like that will happen again?"

"I've changed. I'm doing well in my job, they like me, and I'm more confident."

"How can I believe a word you say? I know my job hasn't helped, and it's put both of us under a lot of extra pressure."

"Can't you see it's made me stronger? I still love you," she pleaded.

"You haven't shown me much affection over the years."

"It was hard when Mum came to live with us and I always thought Stephen was born too soon. We said we'd wait until Emma went to school before having another baby. You know you were amazing when Stephen went missing."

"It was always about you. You never gave any thought to how upset I was."

"I was horrible. I was too wrapped up in myself."

"You can say that again. I also needed support."

"I know that now. I felt so overloaded with grief that I didn't think about your feelings."

"That's a shocking thing to admit."

"You always seemed to be running off. We never had time to speak honestly together and enjoy the children."

"Do you honestly think we can put all the bad times behind us and start again?"

"Yes. We can't forget the past. But I think remembering, and admitting our mistakes, will make us stronger. We know all the pitfalls," she replied.

"I can't just throw up a good job. The children are growing up and becoming more expensive. I'm pleased you enjoy your job, but my job pays the bills."

"You can see how much Emma and Stephen love us being together as a family," she replied.

Paul returned to the children.

"You're doing a grand job. How about we build a second sandcastle alongside? Let's pretend the king and queen are rich enough to have a sandcastle of their own."

"Can I dig the moat this time?" asked Emma.

"No, me, me," pleaded Stephen.

"Stephen can start digging one side and Emma the other, and we can meet in the middle."

"Good one," said Emma.

Sarah smiled and went back to reading her book.

***

"You'll never guess who I saw in the swimming pool this morning," said Sarah.

"Who?" Emma yelled.

"Tony Curtis and Janet Leigh."

"Who are they?"

"Film stars. He looks every bit as handsome as he does in the films. He was in the pool when I went for my early morning swim. He was with his wife Janet Leigh. Do you remember her in the film *Psycho*, when she gets stabbed in the shower? It's all so exciting, don't you think, seeing all these glamorous film stars in the flesh?"

"Yes, but don't let all this go to your head. Soon we'll be home and you'll be back on the wards."

"How can you be so unromantic?" Sarah proclaimed.

***

"You were restless last night," said Sarah.

"I was thinking about our conversation yesterday."

"What have you decided?" she asked.

"I'm going to move back home full-time and find a new job."

"We will make it work, I promise."

"I just want an easy life from now on."

***

The family took a semi-circular road tour of central Florida. They enjoyed the new must-see *Disney World of Adventures* in Orlando. Paul then drove to the *Kennedy Space Centre* on the east coast. Then continued south, through the swampy wilderness of the Everglades National Park, where they visited a genuine Miccosukee Indian village. For centuries the Everglades was populated by Indian tribes. Culminating with an exciting airboat ride over alligator infested swamps.

Finally, they flew home from Miami Airport. Sarah and Paul agreed it had been a bonding and educational experience for the whole family, one they would remember for years to come.

As they were leaving the aeroplane in London, Emma said, "I think all the ladies in the hotel are film stars because they're all so very beautiful."

Chapter 57

Rona's first words to Paul were, "I'm pregnant."

Stunned, he replied, "How do you know?"

"Don't you think I know my own body?" she responded with indignation.

He swept her off her feet. "Forgive me, I'm sorry. How are you?"

"Feeling rotten and sick."

"Well, now I'm back I can look after you."

"Good trip?"

"The wedding was wonderful and Florida was very hot." He reached into his carry-on case. "I've got something to cheer you up."

She opened the small jewellery box and carefully took out the fragile sparkling ruby pendant, surrounded by tiny diamonds.

"Oh wow, it's beautiful, thank you." She reached up to kiss him.

"My present from Tampa. I remembered we saw one like this and knew immediately this was meant for you."

"This is much prettier and more delicate. Ruby's my birth-stone."

"I know. Compensation for going away."

"You didn't have to."

"I missed you."

"I'm sorry about the row. I've got to stop being jealous. I was out of order and miserable after you left."

"Me too."

"I promise I'll never be jealous again."

"I told you before, you've got no reason to be jealous … and what a wonderful home-coming, we're going to have a baby."

"I thought you'd be angry. It's going to make your life more complicated."

"We'll manage," he replied. But his true thoughts were very different from his passive reassurances. 'How come I keep getting myself deeper and deeper into the shit?' He inwardly sighed.

"Don't worry, we'll sort things out. But remember, I'll always be responsible for Emma and Stephen and I've still got Sarah to think about."

***

The unplanned pregnancy was a disaster from the very beginning. During Rona's second month she was diagnosed with suffering from *hyperemesis gravidarum*. Generally thought to be due to a rise in hormone levels. She vomited relentlessly day and night, even at the very sight of food. She lost weight and spent two months in hospital, her nourishment and medication needs fed intravenously through drips.

With ever-mounting demands, Paul had no time, nor the energy, to search for another job. He employed Mr Mitchell, as a temporary manager, to run Rona's boutique in Chelsea and, in spite of working long hours in the hospital, Paul made time to check the shop once a week. He always reported back to Rona that Mr Mitchell had everything under control. But Rona was uneasy.

There was huge relief when Shelly was born a beautiful, healthy baby. It took Rona several weeks to recuperate, after months of compulsory bed-rest. Life slowly began to return to a modicum of normalcy with the help of Nanny Maureen.

During her difficult pregnancy, and immediately after Shelly's birth, Rona pestered Paul to drive her to the boutique to check on Mr Mitchell. She wasn't sure she could trust Paul's weekly reports. Rona had met Mr Mitchell just once for his interview. That was almost a year ago. At that time, she wrote him copious lists of instructions. As the months passed, she was desperate to meet him again to see for herself whether he was following her instructions.

***

Shelly was just six weeks old when Paul first drove Rona to the boutique. As she had expected, Mr Mitchell's working standards hadn't quite met hers. However, after stipulations and negotiations, Rona agreed to extend his contract for a further six months. It suited her to have a second pair of hands. Everything would change when she returned to work full-time. She just needed a few more weeks to regain her strength.

Rona enjoyed going back to work in the boutique, with one eye on Mr Mitchell. She also had some exciting new ideas. Her first love was fashion design. She planned to concentrate on designing and manufacturing a new line of contemporary ground-breaking clothes for her loyal and savvy customers. However, a month after returning to the boutique, Rona began to struggle with exhaustion. Her doctor told her to take three months rest. Rona was distraught. She employed a new manager and two more staff in the boutique. Now her dreams of creating her own annual exclusive range of innovative designs would have to wait.

***

Rona was restless as a stay-at-home mum. She disliked the hum-drum life of domesticity. She described motherhood as *tiresome*, and began to look for outside interests. Nanny Maureen voiced her worries. In her opinion, Rona still wasn't attempting to bond with Shelly. When Paul gently spoke to Rona, she replied, "I'm not the maternal kind. I find it boring caring for an unresponsive tiny baby."

Meanwhile, one rainy day, when Rona was home alone with Shelly, she baked a cake to pull herself out of the doldrums. To her surprise, she discovered she had a flair for baking and found the process therapeutic. Soon her kitchen was filled with many pies and cakes, far more than they could ever consume. So, she began selling them to neighbours, and they went *like hot cakes.*

By chance she had found a second string to her bow and began to develop her new hobby, through her love of baking, into a worthwhile business. She named her new company, *Simple Delights.* At the same time, she supported Paul's work raising funds for cancer charities by adding a few pennies to each item.

For two years Rona used her kitchen for the bakery. Her reputation for making exceptional pies and cakes grew so fast she had to move into bespoke factory premises, whilst, at the same time, she continued to raise money for cancer research. The company grew beyond her imagination to dizzy heights. As the years rolled by, she opened three new factories and employed over a fifty people.

It was during this time, Paul was promoted to specialist consultant oncologist covering the two hospitals. Now he was established, he rented private consultancy rooms in Harley Street and shared his new-found prosperity with Sarah and their children.

***

Sarah's career also flourished. She studied for a teaching degree, followed by a master's and was eventually promoted to deputy matron. She gained confidence through her academia and promotions, but sadly she still reached for the anti-depressant bottle to get her through stressful times. Stephen's paternity continued to be a major cause for concern. As he grew older, Sarah's anxiety increased, and she had no solution to her problem.

And Paul still continued to divide his week between his wife and children in Edmonton and Rona and Shelly in south London. That was until Stephen's burst appendix and his resultant blood transfusion. The consequences of which would blow Paul's mind, and impact on him emotionally for the next two decades.

Chapter 58

1978

Stephen's burst appendix changed everything.

Two days before the *Junior Babes* under-twelves tennis tournament, Stephen complained of tummy pains. The next evening he vomited, which was uncharacteristic. Stephen normally had a stomach of steel. The second morning he woke up moaning of more tummy pains. Fortunately, Paul was at home and gave an off-the-cuff diagnosis of a grumbling appendix and suggested Sarah should take him to the accident & emergency department at the local hospital.

Stephen didn't want to miss the tournament. He convinced Sarah he was better, and refused to go to the hospital. During the afternoon the pain returned and he was forced to abandon his match. That evening Stephen collapsed at home. Paul was furious Sarah could be so manipulated by their ten-year-old son. He drove Stephen to hospital where a swift diagnosis of a burst appendix was made and he was on the operating table within half an hour.

The area became infected. Stephen developed an allergic reaction to the first antibiotic medication, and for two days he had a raging temperature. The hospital dispensed a new medication and he was responding well. Five days later the consultant telephoned Paul to say Stephen was making a sound recovery and should be on his way home in a couple of days.

It was during Stephen's hospitalisation, Paul discovered something that would fester for the next two decades. He now had serious concerns about his son's paternity.

"How old is Stephen?" Paul shouted.

"Is this a joke," Sarah replied.

"I'll ask you just one more time. If I don't get an honest reply I'm packing my bags, and believe me, you won't see me for dust," he yelled.

"You know Stephen had problems with the blood transfusion," Sarah screamed.

"If it wasn't for the transfusion, I wouldn't be asking the question. How old is Stephen?"

"For heaven's sake, he's ten. Why are you asking me such a silly question when he's still so ill?"

"He could've died because you've been untruthful. If he'd been given the wrong blood, he could have died."

"They always test for blood group first."

"You're right. But wouldn't you think he'd be 'O' Rh positive like us? Did you know he's 'AB'. Can you explain that? What were you doing eleven years ago?" Paul shouted.

"I don't understand. What are you saying?"

"Why doesn't Stephen share our blood group?"

"Must be a throw-back."

"That's not possible. Tell me honestly, is Stephen my child?"

"Of course he is," Sarah replied in floods of tears.

"Then how do you explain his blood group?"

"I don't know."

"You know full well if both parents are blood type 'O' in all probability the child will also be type 'O'. For heaven's sake! You're a nurse, you must know that. If one parent has type 'A' and the other has type 'O' the baby could be 'A' or 'O'. Explain how Stephen is type 'AB'. He's not mine, is he?"

Sarah looked at Paul horrified.

"Speak to me."

Playing for time she replied, "It's a mistake."

"Don't take me for an idiot," he yelled.

"Stop shouting! I just want Stephen to get better. I'm going back to the hospital," she cried angrily, pushing Paul against the front door.

"I will get to the bottom of this. You're lying and you know it!" he yelled back at her.

"Get out of my way! I've got to get back to the hospital," she screamed.

"If you go now without telling me the truth, believe me, as soon as Stephen is better, I'm gone."

Sarah jumped into the car, her nerves in tatters. She carelessly scrunched the gears to reverse the car along the driveway. She lost control and the car sped back too fast and crashed into her neighbour Anne's parked car on the opposite side of the road. In a moment of heightened anxiety, and lack of concentration, she had destroyed two cars. The rear end of Sarah's car had firmly locked into the side of Anne's shiny new one. Sarah's car wouldn't start. It was a distorted mess which now blocked any vehicle free access along the street.

Paul heard the loud crash and couldn't believe his eyes. He ran out of the house.

"Oh, my God, what the hell? Are you okay? Can you get out?" Sarah sat in the car sobbing and shaking. He eased the car door open and pulled her from the wreckage. She flopped lifelessly into his arms.

"What on earth happened? Did your brakes fail?"

"I don't know," she sobbed.

"Listen. I have something good to tell you. The hospital's just phoned and said Stephen can come home."

She stood up limply to her full height. Still sobbing, she replied, "Thank God."

"Go inside. I'll ring the police and get the cars moved. Then I'll make you some tea and go over and speak to Anne."

But Anne was already walking around the cars in shock.

Sarah stood by the window watching Paul and Anne in deep discussion.

"I've told her I'll pay for a rental car and I'll sort everything out on our insurance. She was very upset. I said you would go and talk to her when you felt a bit better."

"Was she very angry?"

"Wouldn't you be? She only bought the car three months ago. But I managed to calm her down. Don't leave it too long before you go over."

"I've destroyed two cars, Anne's friendship and I've ruined our marriage."

"Stop feeling sorry for yourself. Calm down, have a cup of tea then go over and speak to Anne. I'll go with you if you want. Then we can talk rationally."

Chapter 59

"I've been worrying about Stephen for years. I always believed he was yours," stuttered Sarah.

"Now the truth's coming out."

"I hoped nothing like this would happen, and you'd never find out, because I was always sure Stephen's was yours."

"How could you hide something so important as Stephen's paternity?" Paul shouted. "Didn't you ever think Stephen and I had a right to know?"

"Of course. The whole thing's driven me crazy."

"Who did you sleep with?"

"It was very brief and unimportant."

"It wasn't unimportant if it produced a child."

"I always thought Stephen was yours."

"Prove it!"

"I can't. I only slept with him a couple of times. I always thought Stephen was yours."

"Stop repeating yourself. Who's *him*?"

"I had one brief affair. His name was George."

"That accounts for Stephen's rare blood group. When did you have these affairs?"

"I haven't had affairs. I've only slept with one other man. His name was George, and it was only a couple of times," Sarah mumbled. "It was the year we went to Majorca. He went to university in the September and I never saw him again. I promise, I've never been with another man but you."

"You only need to do it once. How can I believe you?"

"Because it's true. That's why I suffered years of depression. It was the most stupid thing I've ever done."

"Tell me about it. I thought you were depressed because you didn't want another baby so soon."

Tears welled up in her eyes.

"It wasn't just that, it was lots of other things. I never meant to deceive you. After Stephen was born, I couldn't find the courage to tell you. And when I saw you with him it got even harder."

"I always thought of us as a team. We looked after each other. It's always been that way. You said lots of other things upset you. Tell me."

"Remember in the early days it was hard living with my mother upstairs. Emma was very demanding and you were working all hours. I was tired and depressed and I've always had a problem with this house. You know I felt guilty taking it away from your parents and falling out with them. They thought I was a gold digger and a burden being so dependent on you," she sobbed.

"You don't know what they thought. They fell out with me, not you. Now you're being ridiculous."

"They never see the children."

"That's their fault. They always made excuses."

"Because of me, they don't see the children," replied Sarah.

"That's not true. I could always take the children to see them."

Sarah sat shredding her handkerchief.

"I can't believe you've kept Stephen's paternity a secret all these years," said Paul.

"I've always believed he is your son. Everyone says how much he looks like you."

"I've always put you first. As for the house, you read Grandfather Cyril's letter. He wanted us to have it. He addressed his letter to you and me. I didn't want to fall out with Mum and Dad, they fell out with us. They were wrong. They assumed they'd inherit for their retirement funds. I wish now I had given them the damned house. It's been nothing but bad luck. Grandfather Cyril wanted a young family to live in his house. Why couldn't we have been happy? Sometimes I think he's somewhere up there looking down and all he sees is misery. All he wanted was his home to be filled with children."

"I feel so stupid and ashamed."

"I don't get it. If we had to pay a mortgage, and I made you go out to work, that wouldn't be right either!"

"I love my work."

"I can't bear any more excuses, otherwise I'll also end up in the looney-bin. I just want to know the truth about Stephen."

"If I had told you years ago that Stephen might not be your son, would you still have loved him?"

"How can I answer that?"

"I've paid a high price for what I did. Remember all those years ago when Stephen went missing from Selfridges you diagnosed postnatal depression. You even said I could have deliberately left him in Selfridges. Even now I'm not sure what happened. After he was born everything seemed unreal. I drove myself mad with worry that maybe he wasn't yours, which in the end led to my breakdown," wailed Sarah.

"I still don't understand how you could leave a baby in a strange store, on the basis you wasn't sure if I was his father? We could have lost him forever. What the hell were you thinking of? What did you expect me to say? I can understand your depression. It's your deceit and lies I can't live with anymore," Paul replied.

It was an extraordinary paradox. Paul was incapable of forgiving Sarah for her indiscretions, yet, he remained oblivious of the times he'd been unfaithful and his adulterous behaviour with Rona, resulting in the birth of Shelley.

"Can you ever forgive me," she sobbed. "I love you. I'm not a bad person. I once did a stupid thing and paid for it a million times over. You're not perfect."

"I don't want to say something now I may later regret. I love Stephen, of course I do, and I want to see him through his illness since you seem incapable. Then I'll decide what to do with you."

Chapter 60

At first glance Sarah thought they'd been burgled. But there was no obvious evidence of a forced entry.

She had always been fastidious with her clothes. Now her wardrobe doors were wide open. Her chest of drawers pulled out and underwear strewn all over the floor. She was horrified to see an exquisite white silk nightdress covered in bright red lipstick. Skirts and dresses were piled high on the bed. She hadn't noticed anything unusual when she arrived home. Sarah rushed downstairs to check again the rooms and windows. Nothing had been touched. The windows remained intact. She ran back upstairs. It was then she noticed Paul's wardrobe and chest of drawers remained untouched. His suits and trousers still hung neatly on his side of the wardrobe.

She slammed her wardrobe door shut. To her horror on the front of the door was a message scrawled in same bright red lipstick used to ruin her expensive white silk nightdress.

I'm gone. Will be back to collect the rest of my stuff. Can't take any more.
Paul.

Her body tensed. She heard the front door open, then footsteps on the stairs.

"Paul, is that you?" Sarah called.

Sandra stood on the landing.

"It's me. I knocked first but you didn't hear. I hope you don't mind I used my key."

"No." Sarah looked distracted.

"Did you forget I was coming? We've got the dinner at the embassy tonight. I've come to get my cocktail dress."

"I hadn't forgotten. It's hanging up in your old room."

Sarah swiftly shut her bedroom door. She didn't want her mother to see the mess and start asking difficult questions.

"Sorry, I've had some difficult patients today. Have you seen Paul?" asked Sarah.

"No. Are you expecting him?"

"I'm not sure. Come downstairs, I'll make a pot of tea before David comes."

"I don't want to hold you up if you're busy. He'll be here in about half-an-hour."

"Come down. There's something I want to tell you," persuaded Sarah.

"You don't look well. Is something wrong?" asked Sandra.

"Paul's moving out. We're having a trial separation," announced Sarah.

"David and I sensed you were having problems. If there's anything we can do ...?"

"No. We've got some sorting out to do. I don't want to talk about it now, it'll take too long and I don't want to spoil your evening. I'll call you tomorrow."

***

After Sandra and David had left, Sarah returned to the bedroom to clear up the mess. She carefully folded and put away her clothes. Her head was spinning. Their marriage began full of high hopes. Now it was in ruins. She still loved Paul and she was concerned how divorce would damage their children.

She pushed Paul's suits and trousers to one side. 'If only she could resolve, beyond all shadow of doubt, that Paul is Stephen's father. This house contained too many ghosts. We should have sold it years ago and bought another,' she thought.

She ran her fingers along the collars of Paul's jackets then opened his sweater drawer and buried her nose in his clothes and imbibed his evocative musky aroma. They had chosen many of his sweaters together. She took out the green fisherman's jumper they bought on a holiday to Fair Isle in Scotland.

Like most married couples, they'd had their arguments, but on the whole, she thought, Paul was content in their marriage. Now looking back, Sarah began to pinpoint the time when their marriage began to fall apart. It was after Emma was born when she devoted herself to motherhood and domesticity, without much thought for Paul's needs. She was exhausted with night feeds and daily chores and lost interest in the physical side of their marriage.

As a result, Paul spent most of his recreational time in the pub and, she suspected, had a few women friends for compensation. The marriage shakily survived. Once Sarah was pregnant with Stephen, and her agony over his questionable paternity, it was inevitable the marriage was on a slippery slope.

"I'll show him," she said out loud.

Sarah went down stairs to the kitchen and selected the sharpest scissors from her sewing basket and returned to the bedroom. She climbed on a chair and pulled down a large suitcase from the top of the wardrobe.

She began with Paul's shirts. One by one she carefully snipped off the sleeves and collars. Then moved to his trousers, hanging neatly in the wardrobe, and cut every pair through the middle of the legs. She continued to work on his treasured jackets, cutting chunks from the front and arms. Then carefully unravelled his woollen sweaters.

When she had finished, she folded up all the tattered clothing and packed them in the suitcase. She dragged it downstairs and left it in the hall, with a short note, where it would be waiting for Paul when he deigned to return.

Dear Paul

I'm sure you will be pleased to see I have saved you the trouble of packing. I've done it all for you. Have a good life.

Sarah

She threw herself on to their bed and sobbed her heart out.

Paul returned the following day for the remainder of his clothes. She handed him the suitcase of shredded debris.

"Thanks."

"Can't we try again?" Sarah pleaded. "We've got so much history and so much going for us."

It was incomprehensible. The following morning, Sarah had no recollection of the night before. How she had destroyed Paul's clothes. She was in denial for weeks. Ever since Stephen's operation, when the hospital discovered the shocking truth about his rare blood group and the humiliation of destroying her neighbour's car. She now survived in a bubble, dream-like, and had lost all sense of reality. Over the weeks her memory slowly recovered. But now, on the day Paul was finally leaving home, she slipped back into an acute state of amnesia.

"I've put up with too much. I want a divorce. I've been living with another woman for years and we're getting married," Paul snapped.

"I don't understand."

"I'm through with all your rubbish and shenanigans. The latest business with Stephen was the last straw. I'm selling the house. I'll give you half the money. Now your mum's gone you can find something smaller. The children can decide who they want to live with. I think my parents were right. The two religions don't mix. We're like oil and water."

"Can't we discuss this like grown-ups?"

"No. I'm exhausted from trying. I've done everything to make our marriage work. I bust a gut every day working for you and the kids. I've nursed you through depression. I've looked after you and your mum. I'm tired. I want a grown-up relationship. Now I've finally got a grown-up relationship, an equal relationship, with a wonderful woman and I want to marry her."

"I don't believe you."

"You've got to believe me."

"How long have you been seeing her?"

"A long time. I don't know what happened to you. You're not the woman I married. If you want to know who I'm marrying, remember our bridesmaid, Rona? Oh, and by the way, we have a little girl called Shelley."

The colour drained from Sarah's face.

"I don't believe you. You're joking."

"Believe me, this is no joking matter."

"Can't we try again?"

"No, no, no," he replied. He stormed out of the room and the house, and slammed the front door with such aggression a glass panel in the door fell out and smashed into tiny pieces.

***

"Sam, I need to see you. Can you come over?" Sarah pleaded.

"How's Stephen?"

"Thank God he's doing fine now, but the shit's hit the fan. Stephen needed a blood transfusion and they discovered he has a rare blood group which doesn't match Paul or me. So you can imagine what happened. He found out I slept with someone else and he hit the roof. He went ballistic. He's moved out and wants a divorce. I'm at my wits end."

"After all these years. I'm so sorry. I can hardly believe it."

"You won't believe this. When he got promotion all those years ago to work in Croydon Hospital he went to stay with Rona. He's been leading a double life with her for eight years and they have a child called Shelly and he wants to marry her."

"He's with Rona. He always said he didn't like her!"

"I think he fancied her all along."

"Calm down. I'll be right over," said Sam.

Chapter 61

56 Sussex Way
Brighton   6th July 1981
Dear Sarah & Paul

Let's commiserate or celebrate our new status together. We're now fully-fledged middle-aged women! This is our special year. The girls from Grosvenor Gardens turn forty!

Come to our 'Fair, Fat & Forties', party on 17th August at the Coconut Grove, Brighton.
Love Jennifer, Carole & Suzy
P.S. We hope you can come to our reunion. It's too long since we saw you. Hope you are both well.

Sarah answered the ringing phone.

"Hi Sarah. It's Jennifer. How are you?"

"Okay. It's so good to hear your voice after so many years. How are you?"

"Fine."

"I'm sorry I haven't replied to your invitation," replied Sarah.

"Are you coming?"

"I'm not sure I can make it."

"That's a shame. I told the girls the invitations went out too late. Will you be on holiday in August?"

"No, it's not that. It's just ... I'm not going anywhere just now. Not since the divorce," replied Sarah.

"You and Paul divorced!" Jennifer was shocked to hear Sarah's news. "No one told me. You were the first to get married. We always thought you were the perfect couple ... please come. It's such a perfect occasion for us all to meet up."

"I'm not good company at the moment," said Sarah.

"Come on, Sarah. We'll all miss you if you don't come."

"How's life treated you?"

"Ups and downs. The last year was terrible. My husband and mother died."

"Oh Jennifer, I'm so sorry. I liked Stanley, and your mum was always good to me. It makes me sound so trivial. It's not that I don't want to see all of you. It's just … I'm not good on social occasions right now since the divorce."

"It'll be good for you. It's a wonderful opportunity for us girls to meet up again. Can you imagine all those years back in Grosvenor Gardens we'd ever reach middle-age like our mums?" replied Jennifer.

"I don't think we'll ever be like our mums. The 1960s generation will still be young at seventy," said Sarah.

"I hope you're right," Jennifer replied with a giggle.

The phone went silent.

"Sarah, are you there?"

"Yes, yes. I'm sorry, I'm being very silly. I'd love to come. I can't wait to find out what you've all been up to."

"Great. In that case, have I got the perfect man for you," Jennifer replied enthusiastically.

"Slowly, slowly."

"I'll introduce you to Adrian. I think you two will get on like a house on fire. You've got lots in common. He's a doctor and very handsome. He's also got two children, twelve-year-old Danny and eight-year-old Lauren. His wife died of cancer three years ago. And oh, he's Jewish. He says he's a secular Jew, whatever that means."

"It means he's not a practising Jew, like me. Sounds like you're already trying to arrange our *shidduch*. But slowly, slowly," Sarah laughed, thinking, 'How wonderful of Jennifer to look after my interests.'

"Have I said something wrong?" replied Jennifer.

"No. *Shidduch* means an arranged marriage in Yiddish. So you're the matchmaker arranging our wedding," Sarah laughed, adding, "I love you, you're such a tonic."

"I didn't mean to sound pushy," Jennifer was contrite. "It's just, I think you'll like him. I know he's been on dates, but he's very sensitive because of his children."

"Thank you for thinking of me," replied Sarah.

"He's a lovely man and just your type."

"I'd love to meet Adrian. Have you seen Rona?" Sarah asked.

"Not for years."

"Is she invited?"

"Carole sent her an invitation, but I don't think she's replied."

"You don't know then?"

"Know what?" asked Jennifer.

"Rona and Paul are married and have a daughter, Shelley."

"You're joking!"

"I don't want to see them. Although Paul and I do speak occasionally regarding the children."

"I understand ... we'll look after you. Look, why don't you stay for the weekend? Lorraine and her husband Tom are coming down. They're living in Yorkshire. August by the sea, when the sun shines, is very restorative and we've got so much catching up to do."

"That sounds wonderful. I'd like that. To hell with Paul and Rona. I've got to force myself out of hibernation sometime."

"Atta girl."

"I'm looking forward to seeing you all again. It's been too long ... and meeting Dr Adrian. And, do you know what? I don't care if Rona and Paul are there, I can deal with them.

***

Sarah spotted Rona seated with Suzy and Sam as soon as she entered the room. Determined to get the difficult part of the evening over first, she took a deep breath and walked resolutely over to Rona.

"Well, how are you, Rona? Life treating you well?" she asked casually, her knees shaking.

"Couldn't be better."

"Is Paul with you?"

"He's working. You still nursing?" Rona asked.

"Yes. It's the best job in the world. And I teach. I hear you're now a successful baker," said Sarah, somewhat disingenuously, deliberately undermining her ex-friend's achievements, knowing full-well Rona was the CEO of the most famous pie and cake making business in the country.

"I don't bake anymore. I've got three factories and a staff of over fifty."

"Well now. That's incredible."

"You haven't changed a bit. How long has it been?" asked Rona.

"At least fifteen years."

Sarah's cheeks burned the colour of beetroot. Her duty complete.

"Excuse me," she said, with as much confidence as she could muster, and walked away. She had no intention to speak to Rona again during the evening.

Rona always had a flare for fashion. Why was it she always made Sarah feel so frumpy and unfashionable? This evening she looked more stunning than ever. As far back as their first year of nurses training, when Rona bought clothes from bargain basements stores, they were always innovative and well-coordinated. She only had to fling a scarf around her neck to look perfect. Tonight was no exception. And now Rona had reached the dizzy heights of successful business woman, she could afford to wear exclusive designer labels.

Paul had lived a double life for years. Sarah still couldn't comprehend how he had managed to keep Rona a secret for so long and cunningly ensure they never met.

***

Jennifer seated Sarah next to Adrian Shapiro a pleasant man in his early forties. He lived in Highgate, London and talked about his two children, twelve-year-old Danny and eight-year-old Lauren and his favourite television programmes. He was relaxed and conversation flowed when they eventually discovered they were both theatre enthusiasts and enjoyed reading the same authors.

During the evening Jennifer came over for casual chats and a confidential whisper in Sarah's ear,

"Don't you think Rona looks ridiculous, with her neckline reaching her waist?"

"I think her assets have shrunk with age," added Sarah, laughing.

Jennifer giggled, "See you later."

"Jennifer was talking about Rona," Sarah told Adrian. "We used to be friends. Now she's married to my ex and runs the very successful pie and cake company called *Simple Delights*."

"So that's the lady. I thought I recognised her from one of the Sunday supplements. Good publicity. I buy her pies. The children love them. I'm not a good cook and they're very good," he replied.

Sarah wanted to reply, 'not what I need to hear,' but held her tongue.

She deliberately avoided a second meeting with Rona. As they were leaving, Adrian asked, "Have you read about the new blockbuster film *Chariots of Fire*? It's about the Jewish athlete Harold Abrahams who competed in the 1924 Olympics."

"Yes, it's been well reviewed."

"Would you like to join me?"

"I'd love to."

***

Sarah and Adrian had been dating for two months. She enjoyed his company and he made no demands on her. Then one day he suggested,

"I'd like our children to meet. Aren't Danny and Stephen close in age?"

Sarah was fond of Adrian, but she wasn't ready to get involved in a serious relationship. She hesitated, then decided there was no reason why the children shouldn't meet.

"Bring them over for tea on Saturday. Emma's a bit of a madam now she's sixteen, and she's always busy with friends. But I'm sure Stephen and Danny will get on well."

"Did Stephen have a bar mitzvah?" Adrian asked.

"No. I never followed the religion, and my ex-husband is Catholic."

"That's a pity. I thought you might help me arrange Danny's bar mitzvah party. He'll be thirteen next year. We were never religious, but Danny always wanted a bar mitzvah and I promised my wife Melanie he would have his day in synagogue and be called up to read his Torah portion."

"I'm sorry Melanie won't be there to see Danny."

"She's been a hard loss."

"She must have been looking forward to Danny's bar mitzvah."

"She was." There was a pause in the conversation before Adrian continued, "Would you take her place and be my hostess?"

"I could never take Melanie's place."

"It would make me happy, and I know Melanie would have liked you. When she was ill she said she didn't want me to stay alone."

Sarah was speechless. 'This is all happening too quickly,' she thought. 'I like him a lot, but do I really want to get involved with his family so soon?' Then to Adrian,

"Have you told your family about me?"

"Yes, and they're looking forward to meeting you."

Sarah wasn't ready for a serious relationship and Emma and Stephen were still hurting from the divorce.

"Melanie was a tragedy. My family want me to get on with my life, and so would Melanie. It will make me very happy and give me peace of mind," he replied.

Are you having a lot of people?"

"Not many. Both our families are small and, of course, Danny's friends. I was wondering if you could recommend a nice hall and a caterer in north London."

"I'll give it some thought ... a nice buffet and a disco would be fun. Let's find out what Danny wants on Saturday."

Chapter 62

Emma and Stephen were now sixteen and fourteen and lived fulltime with Sarah. It was particularly hard for Emma to adjust after the divorce. She didn't like Rona and resented the inflexibility of alternate weekend visits to Paul. Stephen appeared to accept the situation. Sarah's emotions were no longer raw and Paul was just a phone call away to thrash out any problems with the children.

***

Three months after the girls' Fair, Fat & Forties party, Paul made one such call.

"I hear you have a new boyfriend and he came to tea with his children."

"Adrian's good company. It's up to me who comes here. Anyway, it's none of your business," Sarah replied curtly.

"I had Emma crying down the phone, so it is my business."

"Emma didn't stay for that tea. She put her head around the door and said she was off to see her friend. Adrian's the first man I've been out with since you left. You've got no right to question who I have round for tea. If it wasn't for the children, we would have made a clean break years ago. Just don't interfere into my life."

She slammed the phone down.

***

The following week Paul phoned Sarah for a second time. On this occasion his voice was slurred. Clearly, he'd been drinking.

"You know Sarah, I realise now I never loved Rona. It was just pure lust, sex and fear of a long-term responsibility, and, knowing the type of woman she is, I could always walk away."

"Why are you telling me this now? You're drunk?"

"Because it's you I love. I want some comfort. You hurt me hard when I found out Stephen isn't my son."

"Stephen is your son. He's just like you."

"We both messed up. You know I slept with Rona the night I bumped into her in the pub on my way home from seeing you in the hospital?"

"Stop it!"

"I was depressed and needed cheering up."

"I don't want to know."

"That Friday night I was on my way home from Wimbourne, but instead of going home I stayed two nights with Rona," said Paul.

"Do you want me to say 'well done'?"

"No. It's just when you needed me most I behaved like a bloody idiot. I should never have seen Rona again."

"No, you shouldn't." The phone went silent.

"Adrian's asked me to marry him,"

"Will you?"

"Maybe. He would make me a better husband than you any day. I should have met him years ago."

"Would you believe me if I told you that throughout the years, I've never fallen out of love with you? I've been a bloody fool," Paul confessed.

"You're jealous someone else wants me. Stop it! You're driving me mad. Go to bed and sleep off all that bloody alcohol."

***

Adrian proposed marriage. He had lost his wife Melanie to cancer, and now lived with the hope that one day Sarah would agree to marry him. He was an easy-going man and content to be with Sarah, to love and protect her. More than anything, he didn't want to risk losing her. Sarah was fond of Adrian, but she wasn't in love with him. She was still in love with Paul. Even during the hurtful times, when she suspected Paul of sleeping with other women, and throughout his marriage to Rona, Sarah always loved Paul.

Sarah dithered. How can she marry Adrian, when she was still in love with Paul? Her marriage and life with Paul was over long ago. And yet ... just recently he said he loved her. It would be foolish to think they could turn the clock back. Deep down she believed they would simply continue to destroy each other. And she still had to consider what was best for Emma and Stephen. Especially with Stephen's paternity still in question.

Chapter 63

1986

Stephen turned eighteen and Paul's marriage to Rona hit an all-time low. He filed for divorce and gradually inveigled his way back into Sarah's life and home, initially pleading temporary homelessness.

Rona continued to spend most week days travelling to promote her very successful pie and cake business, *Simple Delights*. Shelley was left with neighbours and friends after school and Paul had parental rights on alternate weekends. During the divorce proceedings Rona admitted marriage and motherhood didn't suit her. She was happier living a precarious lifestyle knowing she was enjoying someone else's husband. Paul said she got her thrills *living on the edge*, being the mistress, not the wife.

"Can I stay with you until I get myself straight?" begged Paul as he staggered into Sarah's hallway dropping four suitcases.

"You've got some *chutzpah*! I must be crazy giving you a place to stay after what you've put me through."

Later Sarah confessed, "In spite of everything, I've never stopped loving you. Although I know I'm crazy. I could now be living a quiet life with Adrian with no aggravation."

"You know you've always loved a challenge," Paul replied with a twinkle in his eye.

***

There was no easy way for Sarah and Paul to discuss with Stephen the taboo subject of his questionable paternity. As he approached his eighteenth birthday, they both agreed he had to know the truth.

"Don't be too hard on Mum. Humans are frail and we all make mistakes. It's only a slim possibility," said Paul.

"If you aren't my dad, then who is?" Stephen pointed an accusing finger at Sarah, demanding an answer.

"A student," replied Sarah, with her hands covering her face.

"I'm not a child and I'm not stupid. I know all about the birds and bees. Are you trying to tell me it's not important," Stephen replied.

"Of course not. It's just a slim chance. Remember how many people say you look just like me," replied Paul.

"They also say people grow to look like their dogs! Why didn't you tell me years ago?"

"It first came up when you had a blood transfusion years ago after your burst appendix operation and they discovered your blood group is incompatible with ours," replied Paul.

"Are you saying Mum kept it secret from you all that time? Mum, who's my father?" Stephen shouted.

"I said it's a slim chance. I was just like you at your age. We couldn't be more alike," replied Paul.

"Come on. Whose side are you on? Why are you covering up for her?"

"I'm not. I don't want us to fall out," replied Paul.

"All through my life I took it for granted you were my Father, now you're telling me my father *could* be some little shit of a student. What kind of life have you both lived? How could you lie like that?"

"Life's not always that straightforward," replied Sarah.

"Not if you sleep around," said Stephen.

"I didn't. I slipped up just once," replied Sarah.

"It only takes once."

"Stop it. You've gone too far," replied Paul.

"She's disgusting. She went too far. Other parents manage it," said Stephen pointing a finger.

"You can't speak to your mother like that," Paul replied.

"I'm an adult now. I can say whatever I want. Emma and I had a rotten childhood with Dad always away. Then we found out he's given us a half-sister. What kind of parents are you?"

"We want to make it up to you," said Paul.

"The only way you can make it up to me is if you tell me, without a shadow of doubt, I'm Dad's biological son. And you can't."

"Let's all calm down and talk about it another time," suggested Sarah.

"No, today, tomorrow, next week, it's not going to make a smidgen of difference. All we'll do is talk around the same thing and I'll get more angry. I can't stay in this shitty house with liars and strangers a moment longer."

Stephen packed his bags and left.

He left a note.

> To Mum & Dad???
> **I WILL NEVER, NEVER FORGIVE YOU.**
> SIGNED Stephen Michaels, or am I Stephen Shitty Student???????????

Chapter 64

1996 - Ten years later

Sarah answered the telephone.

"Mum, is that you?"

"I think you've got a wrong number."

"Mum, I'd know your voice anywhere Mum. It's Stephen."

"What!" Sarah screamed, then threw the phone in Paul's direction.

"Stephen is that really you?" he yelled.

"Of course it's really me."

Paul wasn't sure whether to show anger or pleasure. He handed the phone back to Sarah.

"Stephen, where are you? How are you?" She was trembling.

"I'm living in Cardiff. These have been ten terrible years. I'm sorry I ran out like that. I've been wanting to get in touch for years, but just couldn't manage it."

"Are you well. What are you doing?"

"I went through a bad time. Did drugs. Had some counselling. I didn't want you to see me in that state. I'm married now and live in Cardiff. Mum, can we come and see you. I'd like you to meet my wife and children. Can you ever forgive me?"

"Of course."

"Can I speak to Dad?"

"Hello Stephen. We didn't know if our son was alive or dead. But I'm so happy to hear your voice."

"You wouldn't have wanted to know me a few years back. I was living in a squat. Somehow, I got a good social worker. She put me in a flat and I managed to get training. I'm now working in computers and got a lovely wife Debbie and two children. She's been urging me to get in touch for ages. I've been such a wimp and just plucked up the courage to phone."

"I don't know what to say. We're over the moon."

"I've got a new job and we're moving to London in a few weeks. What happened between us, and me running out like that, was awful and I've been too proud to get in touch. Debbie's amazing. She's made me whole again. Can we come and see you?"

"Of course. You caught us just in time. We're also moving next week. Take down our new address," replied Paul. He handed the phone back to Sarah.

"Phone us when you get to London. I can't believe this. It's the best thing that's ever happened."

"Can't wait to see you again," replied Stephen.

"Me too. Bye for now."

"What do you think he wants?" asked Paul.

"Why do you always look for ulterior motives? Aren't you happy he's well and married?"

"Of course. As long as it's not money. I don't intend to write him back into my will."

***

Stephen stood on the threshold. Behind him, almost in single file, was a young woman and two small children.

Sarah looked them up and down. Stephen stood aside.

"This is my wife Debbie, and this is Nikki and Simon. Nikki's five and Simon's two."

Paul stood speechless. There were hugs and kisses all round.

Sarah directed them into the living room.

"You must have come into money. This house must have cost a fortune," said Stephen looking around.

"You should be proud of your father. He's now one of the top oncologists in England," said Sarah.

"I know. I've been following his career in the media," replied Stephen. Then, as if he could read his father's mind, he said, "I haven't come for money."

"Well, that's okay then. Why are you here?" asked Paul.

"I can't believe you said that," said Sarah. "Don't start off with bad feelings. Put the past behind us. We've got a new family and new beginnings. Sit down and I'll make us all some tea. We've got lots of catching up to do."

They all enjoyed tea and small talk, before Stephen brought up the subject close to his heart.

"Debbie's been wanting me to get in touch since before we got married. I'm so happy you've met Debbie and the children. What I want to say is not easy, but look, I'm not going to beat around the bush. I want Dad and me to have DNA tests. Clear the air. I think it's important for the kids to know the truth."

Sarah's face blanched.

"As long as we're both man enough to accept whatever the results throw up," said Paul.

"I agree," replied Stephen.

"I think Stephen's right," said Sarah bravely.

"I've never thought of you as anyone else's child. You'll always be my son," replied Paul.

"You'll always be my dad. I'm sorry for what I said as an eighteen-year-old idiot student. I've missed you all these years and been too proud to get in touch. I should never have run away like I did. Debbie's been a life saver, and whatever the results of the DNA tests I want us to be a family again. You know you'll always be my beloved parents. I said some unforgivable things that I only really understood as an adult. You're the parents who brought me up, cared for me and loved me. I'm sorry you've not been part of my life the last ten years."

Sarah listened in tears. Even Paul fought to squeeze his tears away. More hugs and tears.

"How's Emma?"

"She's doing well. She's a lawyer and married to Richard, also a lawyer. She says they're concentrating on their careers before having a family," replied Paul.

"And Grandma and David?"

"They're doing great. David's retired and they spend much of the year in their Florida villa near David's sister Doreen in America."

"That's wonderful. Send them all my love," Stephen replied.

"You can do that yourself. They're back in England next month."

"I'm so pleased we've broken the ice. You've made me a very happy man."

***

Paul and Stephen took DNA tests which proved beyond doubt they were parent and child.

"Why does Stephen have a rare blood group?" asked Sarah.

"Who knows? After all that grief, I'm just relieved. It's unusual, but Stephen's blood group could be a result of mutation or a genetic throwback from previous generations. You know, I really don't care."

"Well, that's a relief. I can't tell you how happy I am."

"Me too. Our family's now complete again. You know, Sarah, I been thinking, I'm going to write Stephen back into my will. What do you think?" asked Paul.

"That will make me very happy," replied Sarah, smiling.

Paul then knelt down on one knee.

"Sarah Michaels, you've made me the happiest man alive. Will you marry me?"

"I thought you'd never ask," she replied.

Chapter 65

123 Merry Way
Chelsea, London

24th June 2000

Dear Mrs Michaels

This is a very difficult letter for us to write, and we hope it doesn't upset you. Briefly, our mother, Julie Lawrence (neé Shaw) died last year. Amongst her belongings was a letter relating to an adoption. After further investigation, we discovered you saw a counsellor at the Jewish adoption society and was given our mother Julie Shaw's name as being your birth mother. So that makes you our half-sister. We assure you this is no hoax. Please take this letter seriously.

Mum kept you a secret all her life. You can imagine the news of a sister came as a shock to us, but we would love to meet you.

Our best wishes

Harry & Joey Lawrence.

"Read this." Sarah unfolded the letter and handed it to Sam. "It came the other day. What do you think?"

"Oh my God. This is unbelievable," Sam replied.

"Do you think it's genuine?"

"Definitely. Isn't this what you always wanted? To find your family, and now they've found you. They sound really nice."

"What am I going to do?"

"Aren't you going to meet them?"

"I'm not sure," Sarah replied solemnly.

"You've got two brothers and probably lots more relations. How exciting."

"I wonder what they're like."

"You won't know unless you meet them," Sam replied.

"Don't you think it's a bit scary?"

"Emotionally yes, but how exciting. Would you like me to come along?"

"No. I need to do this myself."

"Suggest you meet them in a public place, so you can leave if you feel uncomfortable," Sam advised.

***

Harry and Joey Lawrence agreed to meet Sarah in the Hilton Hotel on Park Lane in central London. So they would recognise each other, she told the brothers she would wear a camel-haired coat with a matching hat. Harry said he would wear a blue tie and Joey a red. As it happened, as soon as Sarah walked into the hotel vestibule, she spotted two men waving and pointing in her direction. Harry and Joey were in their early fifties. Both men looked younger than their age, still with youthful good looks. Sarah was almost a decade older.

"Sarah?" Harry held out a hand.

"Yes. How did you know it was me?" she looked confused.

"I'd know you anywhere." He kissed his half-sister on the cheek.

"How come?" Sarah asked.

"You're a striking Lawrence. A younger Mum," replied Joey.

"I'm not normally stumped for words, but I am now," said Sarah. Tears began to trickle down her cheeks. A waitress approached and directed them to a vacant table.

"Let's have a cream tea and get acquainted," suggested Harry.

"How did you find me?" Sarah asked.

"It's a long story," Joey began. "In a nutshell, as I said in our letter, after mum died we were clearing out her flat and found documents relating to your adoption. We couldn't believe our eyes. So we got in touch with the adoption society. After a long search they told us there was a note on your file that you were seen by a counsellor way back in

1968 and given information about your adoption, but then you decided to take it no further."

"Yes, that's true."

"Why didn't you try to find us then?" Harry asked.

"Because I thought if your mum had kept me a secret, I didn't want to upset the family. And it's true, you never knew about me?"

Harry and Joey looked serious and shook their heads.

"No. The only person alive today who remembers you is our Uncle David, mum's brother. But he couldn't tell us much," replied Harry.

"I saw a counsellor when I was expecting my son Stephen," said Sarah. "He's thirty-two now. Back then I was young and curious and wanted to know about my birth parents. The adoption society gave me my original birth certificate, with Julie Shaw's name on it and some letters. But I decided not to look for her at the time just in case she'd got married and her husband didn't know about me."

"As far as we know she didn't tell Dad. If she had, they both kept you a big secret. I'm so, so sorry," said Harry.

"I can't believe you've found me after all these years," replied Sarah.

The waitress came with a huge tray of sandwiches, pastries, scones, jam, clotted cream and enough tea to satisfy six people.

"Thanks, this tea looks delicious. Shall I be Mum?" Sarah asked timidly. Harry and Joey smiled and nodded.

"Waitress, can we also have a bottle of your best champagne to celebrate meeting our long-lost sister for the first time," asked Harry.

Sarah stood up and extended an arm towards the men and giggled.

"I feel drunk with happiness, and I haven't even had a sip of champagne. Isn't this wonderful? I'm celebrating meeting my long-lost brothers after fifty years." They all laughed and Sarah felt more at ease.

"Yes, sir," the waitress smiled and quickly withdrew.

"Thanks. I love champagne. I need something to calm me down. I was very nervous about meeting you. I nearly didn't come."

"We understand," Joey replied.

"We've also been on an emotional journey after finding out about you," added Harry.

"I can see now how lucky I am to be meeting you. It all feels dream-like," replied Sarah.

"I promise you we're real," added Joey leaning across the table to give Sarah a reassuring pat on her hand.

After dabbing away a tear or two, Sarah continued. "I'd love to know about your mum, our mum, Julie. I've dreamed so much about her, and what she was like, over the years."

"She was a very special person and clever. She was born in 1919. Her parents were Esther and Sid Shavinsky. They changed their name to Shaw after they came to England from Poland early in the century to avoid the pogroms, and lived in the East End of London. They were poor. Mum's a rags to riches story. She began work at fourteen as a seamstress. She was always good at arithmetic, and managed to get herself a job as a bookkeeper and eventually she married the boss." Harry was proud of his mother Julie's achievements, and excited to tell her story.

"She worked in a small dress factory as a bookkeeper, then studied to become an accountant and eventually she became the financial director. Our father was Sir Tom Lawrence," added Joey.

"Wasn't he the owner of the Lorenzo Fashion Group?" Sarah exclaimed.

"Yes. He would have loved you He died years ago. Mum was his second wife and he was almost twenty years older than her. So she did find happiness in the end," sighed Joey.

"I'm glad I didn't ruin her life." added Sarah.

"I'm sad we didn't find you until after she'd died. The world has changed, and it's heart-breaking to think she kept you a secret for all our lives," said Joey soulfully. "But she was part of that generation."

"She was talented, beautiful and they had wealth and fame," Harry continued. "Mum and Dad mixed with the rich and famous. But, at the same time, I often saw a sadness in her eyes. I remember her once saying, 'September's a bad month for me,' which seemed a bit odd to me, then I thought, maybe it's because September's the end of summer."

"I was born in September," replied Sarah.

"That makes sense. I have three children and I don't think a mother would ever forget the day she gave birth to a child," added Harry.

"We'll introduce you to Uncle David, Mum's older brother. He remembers when you were born. It's incredible how they kept you a secret for all these years," Joey repeated with emotion.

"I'd like to meet him. This is all so unreal. You're both so good looking. I can't tell you how strange it is seeing blood relations. It's hard to explain, but when you're adopted you're part of a family, but it's not the same as being part of your biological family. Nobody's ever said to me, you look like someone else in the family," said Sarah.

"I never thought about that," said Joey.

"I can see we missed out on having a lovely big sister. We can't lose you again," replied Harry. He bent down and pulled out a photograph from his briefcase.

"I brought this for you to keep. It was taken a couple of years ago. Mum with her brother, our uncle, David."

"She was very elegant and beautiful. Thank you, I'll treasure it. I've also got something to give you." Sarah fumbled inside her open handbag and handed them a copy of Julie's letter written at the time of Sarah's adoption.

To My Darling Daughter

16th September 1942

I hope one day when you are a grown woman, you will read this letter and understand that everything I did was with your future happiness in mind. I believe your new parents may change your name. But that's unimportant. What is important is that you have a good life. I want you to know how much I love you and will continue to love you even though we will be living apart. I sincerely believe the adoption is in your best interests and you will be loved and cared for by a good family.

Your father, Simon, and I did intend to marry but there is so much confusion at the present time and I don't believe this is now going to happen. Simon came from Germany, a Jewish refugee. He is a good and loving man.

He went missing one night before you were born and we haven't been able to trace him. We believe he was picked up by the police and taken away. The Government is suspicious of all Germans, even Jewish refugees! I never heard from him again.

There's so much stigma attached to being an unmarried mother so I gave birth to you in a mother and baby home. I love you so much I didn't want to give you away. I looked after you for nearly a year but it became clear it would be impossible for me to care for you single-handedly. It was then I decided you deserved a proper mother and father.

You will always be a special person to me, and I know you will grow up to lead a happy and fulfilling life. It was a privilege to be your mother.

With love.

The brothers were stunned into silence. They read the letter through slowly for a second time.

"That's incredible," said Harry.

"It must have been very painful for Mum. So painful she was unable to tell us about you," said Joey.

"In those days there was nothing more shaming for a nice girl than to have a baby out of wedlock. Before I saw this letter, I was angry. Then I forgave her, and now I'm sad because I think she really wanted to keep me," replied Sarah.

"I'm so sorry Mum couldn't have shared you with us. You were lost to us for all those years. We will make it up to you," said Harry.

Subtly changing the subject, Joey asked, "And tell us about your past life, big sister. Were you happy with your adopted family?"

"There was friction, because we were very different. They meant well, but there was always that big question of where I came from. Who were my real parents? Do you understand?"

"Of course," replied Harry.

"They told me I was specially chosen, but it didn't satisfy my curiosity."

"I can understand that," said Joey, adding, "Do you have a family?"

"My husband Paul and I have two children, Emma and Stephen and three grandchildren. Nikki, nine and Simon, six. They're Stephen and Debbie's. And Emma and Richard have Sophie, who's two and expecting their second baby in September."

"It sounds things have worked out well," said Joey.

"Yes, but strange as it may seem, it's been hard for me to accept that my children will never know their biological grandparents. It's like I'm at the top of a family tree with no blood parents above me. But now I have grandchildren, my family tree has three generations of growth and growing. This means a lot to me. And now, of course, they have two new special uncles."

"We've all missed out on so much," replied Joey with a sigh.

"Mum's also missed out," replied Harry, tears welling up in his eyes. "I can't wait to meet Emma and Stephen and their children."

"Well big sister, now we've found you, we're never gonna let you go," said Joey. The brothers simultaneously stood and gave Sarah a big warm hug.

The waitress came with a bottle of champagne in an ice bucket.

"It's champagne time," announced Joey loudly. People seated nearby looked up and smiled. He popped the cork and champagne splashed all over them. "It's time to raise our glasses to our new-found sister, Sarah."

"The toast is to our lovely sister Sarah," said Harry.

"We must never be separated again," added Joey.

"To Sarah. Cheers. L'chaim. To life," the brothers repeated in unison.

The end

I have researched the medical references to the best of my ability. Please accept my apologies for any inaccuracies.

Discussion for book club

1. Do you understand why, when Sarah was pregnant with Stephen, she was reluctant to find her birth mother and father?
2. What do you think principally influences our development? Nature or nurture? If you believe the answer is nature, does this explain why Sarah was so competitive and anxious to have a career, rather than spend her time between school and marriage doing an undemanding job?
3. Thankfully our lives have changed enormously since the 1940s. I think we all agree to remove a baby from his/her birth mother, against her will, to give to a couple the authorities decide is *more deserving*, is abhorrent. I don't believe contemporary generations will ever understand Julie's parents' behaviour. How they could disown their daughter at such a sensitive time. But eighty years on, have we become too easy-going? Should we be more responsible for our actions?
4. When our children use social media inappropriately it can cause distress and has, on occasions, ended in tragedy. How do we educate society and our children to use social media responsibly?
5. In the 1940s it was unacceptable to have children outside marriage. In a bad marriage the husband was frequently dominant. He gave *the wife the housekeeping money.* And woe betide if she overspent! However, as late as the 1960s, Sarah's generation, it was still generally expected the woman was the passive partner in a marriage, the homemaker and the main child carer. Do our under-fives benefit from being in full-time day care?

Linda Ferrer

If you've enjoyed *After Julie*, you may now like to read my first book,

Forever a Stranger.
A story of love, war and family breakdown. It follows the lives of three generations in crisis during the 20th century.

Sid Shavinsky and Esther Kopitch are children when they flee the pogroms of Russia and Poland with their parents early in the century. Both families settle in the East End of London. Sid and Esther marry. Sid enthusiastically enlists to fight for Britain in World War One. He returns home a changed man. An amputee suffering with depression and post-traumatic stress syndrome. The war destroys their marriage and future. Two decades later their daughter Julie is faced with giving birth to an illegitimate child after her fiancé Simon disappears. Simon fled Nazi Germany in 1939.

Forever a Stranger. A selection of Amazon reviews

Reviewed in the United Kingdom on 29 August 2014
Verified Purchase
An enjoyable read, plot was strong and I liked the way it kept your attention all the way through the book. I felt sympathy with the characters and the ending fulfilled my expectations, which is always a bonus!

Victorselwyn Excellent holiday read.
Reviewed in the United Kingdom on 29 September 2014
A most enjoyable book. Kept my attention. Delightful first book.

Amazon Customer
5.0 out of 5 stars Don't miss this new perspective into World War II London!
Reviewed in the United States on 18 August 2014

Verified Purchase
I was amazed! Ms. Ferrer captures the essence of the Jewish experience during and after World War II. At times what she tells is gut wrenching, at times cliff-hanging suspense and at times, just good history. The book has a wonderful plot line and the character development is superb. "Forever a Stranger" is about more than anti-Semitism, it is about the cruelty and life disruption of bigotry in all of its forms. This book is absolutely life changing!

Beech 5.0 out of 5 stars
Reviewed in the United States on 1 September 2014
Verified Purchase
Thoroughly enjoyed this well told story of immigrants to London in the early twentieth century. The plot was well thought out, and the characters well drawn. I wanted it to go on longer. Bravo, Linda Ferrer, for a great first novel.

Linda Altner 4.0 out of 5 stars I enjoyed the book very much
Reviewed in the United States on 29 October 2014
Verified Purchase
Although this book is fiction, the story is one that mirrors events which happened in real life. It is very moving. I enjoyed the book very much.

Nanci Coller 5.0 out of 5 stars Loved this book.
Reviewed in the United States on 21 November 2014
Verified Purchase
This was a well-written book containing both fiction and non-fiction. And, when it ended, I wanted it to continue. The title of the book explains how in many cases adoptive parents and their natural born children view their future. The book flowed smoothly and was very easy to read. It would be wonderful if the author wrote a sequel.

Nancy 5.0 out of 5 stars Five Stars
Reviewed in the United States on 12 February 2015

Verified Purchase
Linda, a lovely book whose characters stay with me.

Judy Curtin   Reviewed in the United States on 6 October 2014
Verified Purchase
Kept my interest and educated me about Jewish trauma and struggles. I hope author writes more books.

Lightning Source UK Ltd.
Milton Keynes UK
UKHW010723260122
397718UK00001B/9

9 781800 310353